The Spirit of Silk

Catherine MacBeth

To Judy!

with love

Published in 2018 by FeedARead.com Publishing

A CIP catalogue record for this title is available from the British Library.

This fictitious story was inspired by
The Jungle is Neutral (F.S.Chapman)
and
the admirable *zishūnŭ* (self-combed women).
Any resemblance of the characters to anyone dead or alive is purely coincidental.

Note:
Instead of *pinyin* Chinese, names of places and words are in the Wades-Giles system (romanised spelling of Chinese words) which is more appropriate as the dialogue of the characters are spoken in Cantonese and not Mandarin.
I took the liberty of bringing forward the invention of the transistor radio by a few years.

Also by Catherine MacBeth

Songs in the Night

The Golden Anklet

www.catherinemacbeth.com

Catherine MacBeth was born and grew up in Malaysia. She came over to England and after obtaining her PhD she worked in clinical research. Writing fiction has always been her passion and dream. She now divides her time between writing, golf and painting.

ACKNOWLEDGEMENT

My very sincere thanks to:

Mr Ron Woods, my friend-in-writing, for reading the text and his insightful suggestions,

Colonel R.G.W. Lamb (Assistant Superintendent, the Malayan Police Force 1948-1956) for revisiting with me and guiding me through the landscape of *Emergency* Malaya,

Mr and Mrs Kang Ah Nee for enlightening me on pre- and post-war town development in Malaya,

Mr Lim Aik Leong for an illuminating tour of the oil palm plantation,

And all the friends who have offered me glimpses in the various facets of life that I would otherwise not have known.

Dedicated to my husband Bob with much love

Part 1

Chapter1

Kwantung, South East China
1928

Her left hand was clasped over the handle of the sword on her left hip. Holding the lance in her right hand she felt a rush of pride flood her being. A sense of thrill and excitement swamped her so she could barely feel the weight of the spectacular armour on her shoulders and the helmet on her head or the boots on her feet. And to top it all she was sitting astride the most beautiful and strong horse which was at one with her and was going to take her across the plains towards the invading enemies charging from the northern borders. It knew what she wanted and expected of it at the slightest tug of the rein. She sensed its anxiousness and felt its pulse racing. She felt lifted by the silent force of the army of men behind her on their horses; the horses were grunting and snorting, raring to go. Stretching before her was flat barren land and, beyond, the enemies were waiting too. The tension in the air was as tight as the drums waiting for her signal. She was ready. She raised her hand. Instantly the sound of bugles soared and drums roared. To battle, to defend the Emperor and country!

Su Yin sighed. The legend of Hua Mu Lan the woman warrior never failed to stir her whenever she played it over in her mind. She had loved it from the time her father told her how the young woman, who was skilled in fighting/combat, disguised herself as a man to take her father's place in the army because he was ill. She went to war to defend the country against the invading enemies, soaring through the ranks for her bravery and skill and ultimately winning the war. Su Yin would do the same, go in her father's stead if he, a mere rice-grower, were called up to fight but was unable to. The Ching dynasty had long fallen. The last of the Manchu emperors had been deposed; there was no emperor now to call up the men to join the army. In the distant north, in the city of Shanghai almost a thousand miles away, thanks to a fellow Cantonese from the same province of Kwantung - Sun Yat Sen – there was a struggle for democracy, for free vote. There had been rumblings and stories of discontent and political unrest. There were rebellions against greedy foreign powers that wanted a slice of the country; according to her father the foreigners were grabbing their country like snatching up segments of a juicy peeled pomelo. But there was no war on the horizon that would warrant her going to fight. In any case she had never ridden a horse before even though she had sat on top of her father's buffalo in the rice field out of sheer curiosity to find out what it felt like while her sisters and brothers laughed as they looked on. She had not seen a real horse before apart from the fiery-looking one in the water-colour painting on a yellowed scroll that hung on the wall in their front room, an old painting that her father had inherited from his father.

Su Yin sighed again and looked down at the wriggling silkworms busy chomping at the mulberry leaves in the tray in front of her. She scattered more leaves from her basket onto the tray making sure all the caterpillars had an easy feast. They were now the size of her fingers, almost white in colour and velvety to touch; they did nothing else but guzzle the leaves. Strange, she suddenly thought, how she had got used to the smell of the room full of silkworms doing nothing but just eating and eating the leaves. She often thought that if the sound of their eating could be amplified it would fill the entire factory and drown everything else. When she was little she had once got close down to the worms to see if she could hear them gnawing away. She smiled at the memory of her then stealing a single worm, when she thought her mother was not looking, putting it in a glass jar so she could see what it developed into. After a few weeks of feeding it, it turned into an oval ball of the finest white thread and eventually into a pale looking butterfly. Then she had felt very sorry that the worms had to be sacrificed when she saw what had to be done to the white balls of thread: they were boiled and so never became butterflies. But if that wasn't done then she, her sisters and their mother, and her mother before her, would never have been able to make a living as well as they had. She had been told that the silk industry had not only been thriving for centuries, according to the superintendent of the factory, this region was recognised as producing most of the world's silk and of the best quality. She was proud to be part of it. Her mother was regarded as the best reeler in the district; she was not only able to unwind the silk filaments from several cocoons at the same time without breaking them but she could do it faster than most people in the factory. For that Su Yin was grateful and always said a little prayer of thanks when the cocoon balls were ready to give up their fine filaments so she and her family could survive. And not just them, but all the women who worked in the factory and their families.

'*Wey!* Su Yin, you are dreaming again!' Su Yin snapped out of her reverie. She looked across the room to see her sister Mei smiling and shaking her head. 'The worms can't fetch the leaves themselves, so hurry up and go and get some more before they die of hunger!'

'As if they would. Look at them. They are so fat, ready to spin their shell,' replied Su Yin. She noticed Mei's pink cheeks; she had been going around with a secret smile that slipped out every so often and Su Yin knew why. She was happy for her older sister, older by ten months, a fact that made their mother blush whenever they were asked their ages. Sixteen years old with the clearest complexion and as smooth as fine Kwantung porcelain, Mei was beaming; her slanted almond-shaped eyes radiated contentment and would melt anyone including Ah Kok the oldest and grumpiest man in the village who would growl at anyone daring to approach him but only smiled whenever Mei went near him. Today she had good reason to be even happier: their parents had approved of the match arranged by the matchmaker. Mei couldn't believe her luck. The man in question was only the man she had known since they were little and had secretly liked. He was now in charge of his father's pig farm which had prospered considerably in the last three years and that made him a very good catch by anyone's reckoning. But Su Yin was pleased for Mei because he was a good man, one of very few according to their mother. Looking at Mei now it was hard to believe that Mei had bound her chest with a band of cloth when her breasts started swelling, screaming that she didn't want them to grow, that she didn't want to change. When her menstruation started she cried in panic and terror. Now she was a picture of womanhood with bosoms that hadn't suffered any damage from the binding and other curves in the right places that she had become proud of but were hidden under the loose beige *samfoo* she was wearing - a blouse with a high collar and pantaloons. Her straight charcoal-black hair was gathered at the nape of her neck into a neat plait that came to her waist. Friends and neighbours had said that the two of them were like twins but Su Yin knew that Mei was by far the better looking. Mei didn't have a small red birthmark about the length and breadth of a cocoon on her left jawline like her, a blemish on her otherwise fair clear skin. She still clearly remembered that as a little girl how hard she rubbed and scrubbed the red patch whenever she washed herself thinking she could scrape it off. But it only became redder. She would rant at her mother: 'Why, Ma, did I get born with this ugly mark? What did I do to deserve it?'

Mei called back. 'Hurry up! I am hungry.'

'Alright, I am coming,' said Su Yin. She too was ready to eat. Their mother had got up early as usual to cook their lunch. At that moment the lunch gong sounded. Su Yin threw down the last of the leaves and with Mei behind her hurried out to the courtyard which was already buzzing with the chatter of the other workers who had gathered with their lunch tiffin-carriers. The fresh air that greeted her was a welcome change to the smell and heavy air inside. She spotted her mother sitting on a bench in the shade of a clump of bamboo trees talking to one of the other women, Mrs Wu, as she loosened the fastener of the tiffin-carrier- a stack of three circular aluminium containers. When she got near her, her mother handed her a container while continuing to talk to Mrs Wu,

'.....yes, I heard. That would be the second son to have gone off to Hong Kong. I heard the first son was doing well, started a restaurant there. I can't imagine him cooking. Doing so well that he sent for his brother to help out.'

'Who are you talking about, Ma?' Su Yin asked.

'Nobody you know,' her mother waved her to be quiet. 'Eat your lunch. Here Mei, this is yours.'

'*Aiyahh,* Su Yin,' said Mrs Wu in her usual loud voice, ' you had better grab yourself a husband quickly. The men are leaving like there is a gold rush on. Look at your sister.' She turned and pointed to Mei, 'She has done well. A fine match.' Her face burst into a wide grin showing a big gap in her top row of teeth, a sight that normally made Su Yin want to giggle but now she stumbled for words. Mei came to her rescue.

'I heard that the European missionaries have opened another school just outside Canton,' she said as if she had not heard Mrs Wu.

Su Yin leapt in. 'Pity it is not nearer in Seundak. I would like to learn to read and write English.'

'What use is that?' asked Mrs Wu. 'Although I suppose it is always good to know another language but I was thinking that it's of no use here working in the factory, is it? Especially when I can't even read or write Chinese!' She gave a short laugh.

'Who knows, Mrs Wu? We might one day have an Englishman here wanting to do business with us.' said Su Yin. 'Then it would be useful to speak their language.' Secretly Su Yin wondered at the possibility of that ever happening. Although she loved the village nothing exciting ever happened apart from the usual festival celebrations, not to mention the occasional noisy funeral with the accompanying drums thundering during the procession. The area as far as the eye could see, criss-crossed with canals like the one behind the factory, was lush green with rice fields as it was now waiting to turn into gold later and groves of mulberry trees. There was a six-sided temple with its six points of the roof curling up like the petals of a lotus flower and its entrance flanked by red and gold pillars. Set in the middle of a lake, this was where the villagers went to pray. The other magnificent building was the Han family's ancestral hall to commemorate the deceased male ancestors whose names were inscribed in gold on black tablets and where her father had sometimes been invited for some functions. She and her younger brothers could only peek through the windows to stare at and admire the beautiful carvings of animals and plants on the ceiling and the hanging scrolls with beautiful calligraphy in the unfurnished hall, and wonder why no one actually lived in the house. It was surrounded by magnolia trees and bamboo fences with a pond alive with carp and lotus flowers. The rest of the houses in the village were either stone or wooden ones like the one she and her family lived in.

'Well I suppose so,' said Mrs Wu, her mouth full of food. Turning to Su Yin's mother she asked, 'Mrs Wong, where did you find this bright daughter of yours?' and hurriedly tucked into her lunch container.

Su Yin's mother shook her head as if she was embarrassed. 'Better eat before your lunch gets cold.' She handed chopsticks and spoons to the sisters who each took their container which was neatly packed with rice, fried pomfret and beans.

Su Yin and Mei sat down on the bench next to their mother and dived into their food. With Mei between her and their mother who was engrossed in conversation with Mrs Wu, Su Yin whispered, 'I can't imagine not being able to read and write. What would we miss out on.' Then a louder voice she turned to her mother, 'Ma, this fish is delicious.' Her mother nodded.

Mei looked in front of her as she chewed. They were facing the circular entrance of the brick wall where there were two large gatherings of mulberry trees that were now mostly stripped of their fruit. 'We are lucky Pa bothered to teach us,' she said still staring ahead. Su Yin followed her stare and spotted a couple of bamboo partridges scuttling across beyond the entrance then she turned to look at Mei with a mock frown.

'You are thinking of your future husband, aren't you? Don't pretend.'

Two patches of red appeared on Mei's cheeks. 'So what if I am?'

Su Yin said nothing. 'You are lucky. I would only marry someone I loved very much. Can't imagine marrying someone you don't know.' She screwed up her nose. She knew that in the factory alone, of the hundred-strong female workers, those who were married had their marriages arranged with strangers. Her own future in that department would soon be on her mother's agenda. But why did she have to marry? After all, she had a job and it afforded her a good wage. If she married her money would go to her husband and his family. The unfairness of it always stirred up angry feelings inside her, like spraying kerosene on glowing cinder. Curiosity got the better of her. 'How does it feel to love someone? Tell me.' She studied Mei's face which now looked as if she was lost in another place. Su Yin prodded her.

'You know that is the way it's always been done and, yes, I'm very lucky. How does it feel to love? I think about him all the time. As soon as I wake he is there in my head. I want to see him, be near him. And .. and I have this funny feeling when I think of him. But why do you want to know about love?' Mei poked a finger at Su Yin's side in return. 'It's that young man in the butcher's shop, that young helper, isn't it? I saw him eyeing you very closely and I think you like him too!'

'What man?'

'Don't pretend.' Mei gave Su Yin a nudge. 'You know exactly who I mean.'

Su Yin didn't know many young men and of the ones she knew in the village she didn't think much of them. None grabbed her interest or curiosity but she felt her cheeks warming as her mind flew back to the time she saw the man that Mei was referring to when they went to the market. There was a brazen air about him which the older women customers didn't seem to mind. She watched the women waiting at the stall as the middle-aged butcher deftly cut and sliced from the slabs of pork on the wooden board. The young man was standing between the butcher on his left and a pig carcass on his right hanging from the crossbeam of the stall. His short black fringe of hair peeped from under a brown cloth hat. The small apron over his brown jacket was stained with blood, he was telling stories which made the women laugh and when the butcher handed him the prepared cut of meat he'd wrap them up in newspaper and neatly tied the package with straw string. As Su Yin got nearer the stall she heard one of the women say he was cheeky and then walked off with a smile carrying her package. And then when he looked up their eyes locked momentarily but long enough for Su Yin to see his eyes sparkle, lighting up his grinning face. It had made her heart jump.

The sound of her name burst her dream bubble. Annoyed, she turned to see Lan Yee her closest friend hurrying towards them. 'Have you eaten yet?' she asked.

"Yes, and you? Ready for a walk?' asked Lan Yee.

'Yes I am.' Su Yin passed her lunch container to Mei then linked her arm through Lan Yee's and together they dashed out of the courtyard.

'So what have you got to report today?' asked Su Yin when they were out on the path separating the factory from a forest of mulberry trees fronted by bamboo trees. A breeze whistled through the bamboo trees as the leaves danced.

Lan Yee's head jerked left then right, her two plaits of hair swinging as she did. Satisfied that no one was within earshot she started in a conspiratorial tone. 'Mr Man has been in a grumpy mood. He scolded one of the girls because she broke a filament when she was uncoiling it from the cocoons saying we could not afford to waste good silk. You should have seen her. She was nearly in tears!'

'Which girl is it? My mother would be mortified. She taught most of us how to reel as you know,' said Su Yin wondering what her mother would say to the incident.

'There's more,' Lan Yee paused for effect, 'I overheard him saying to the supervisor that it was such a nuisance so-and-so was going off soon to have her baby. He was *cross* that he was soft and didn't stick to his father's policy of giving first preference to unmarried girls. At least they won't run off to have babies, that was his reason.'

'Is that so?' Su Yin almost sneered. 'He should be more careful what he says. See what will happen if we girls all down tools. The factory will collapse! My grandmother told me that was what they did once when they were refused a reasonable lunch break, they had to gobble their lunch and run back to work. They even had to get permission to go to the toilet!'

Lan Yee nodded vigorously. '*Hmmm*..down tools! That should be an experience.'

'What I don't understand is this,' said Su Yin as her brow slowly furrowed, 'we girls marry because of men and we don't marry because of them as well. Some women even bind their feet because men find them attractive. I have seen a woman with feet so tiny that they were like a doll's feet..in..in pretty embroidered shoes with tiny heels which I had never ever seen before. Saw her in the city when my father took me there. She looked so odd, she couldn't really balance herself. Why?' She threw open her hands. 'Why should we have to go to such lengths to please them? What is attractive about the small feet apart from the agony the women had to go through? And now they are saying that they prefer to employ women who are not married!' She shuddered at the thought of the bones being crushed to prevent them growing while the girls were growing up.

'At least we can choose not to marry,' said Lan Yee.

'You are right,' said Su Yin.

'I've been thinking. I've been talking to my spinster aunt.' Lan Yee paused and looked thoughtful.

Su Yin peered at Lan Yee's face. She knew her aunt who mostly worked in the reeling department, another expert in teasing out and uncoiling the silk filaments from the cocoons. 'What have you been thinking about?'

'You know we can afford *not* to marry,' replied Lan Yee. 'As my aunt always said, the money we earn is ours and ours alone. If we marry the money goes straight to the husband and his family. I don't want that. I want to be able to do what I want with my money. Work hard enough for it. Besides, my own family needs my help.'

Su Yin nodded. 'I agree.'

'So I have been thinking... '

'Yes?' Su Yin wished Lan Yee would hurry and spill what was on her mind.

'I think I am going to do what my aunt and her friends have done - to make a vow not to marry. Join the sisterhood.'

Su Yin's jaw dropped. She felt as if a string of firecrackers had just exploded in her face. She stared at Lan Yee and knew from the set lips that had curled into a soft smile that she had made up her mind. It meant she had been thinking about it for some time and there was no budging from that decision. She knew Lan Yee like herself could be as immovable as her father's buffalo when it had decided it didn't want to go anywhere after it had done a day's work in the rice fields. They had talked about the sisterhood many times before and had admired the women who had chosen that path. It was a custom that had prevailed for a very long time. A good proportion of the workers in the factory had taken up the vow not to marry; their reason was that they refused to be subsumed by men. They didn't need a husband to support them although ironically very possibly it could turn out the other way round where they would have to support the husband's family. But worse than that, and more horrifying, they would have no status in the husband's family; they would be at the bottom of the pile, servants to their in-laws' needs and demands. The women who didn't marry including Lan Yee's aunt seemed very happy. Su Yin concurred with their views passionately but she had no inkling that Lan Yee had considered this path for herself. For a few seconds she could not find her voice. Then, 'So you are sure that's really what you want to do?'

'Definitely. I have thought long and hard about it. That is what I have decided to do.' Lan Yee's face broke into a full smile as if she was relieved and pleased that she had let out the secret.

'Do your parents know?'

'Not yet.'

'Will they, especially your father, approve?' asked Su Yin.

'I don't know but I know they have been talking about finding a match for me.' The look of determination returned to etch Lan Yee's face.

Without thinking Su Yin reached out and stroke Lan Yee's long plaits on her back. She whispered, 'So you are going to comb your own hair.'

Before Lan Yee could respond, the gong sounded for them to return to their tasks.

Chapter 2

Su Yin took the large bowl of melon soup her mother handed her and placed it in the middle of the round table where her six younger brothers and their grandfather were sitting. The boys had already filled bowls with rice as they normally did and now waited for their parents to sit down. Her father sat down next to his father, whom the children called Ah Kong, whose hair was white and whose happy open face was still as bright as a man half his age although he had become noticeably quieter since his wife died. Hong, the youngest brother, was licking his lips and eyeing the plate of steamed pomfret and ginger. Mei came to the table carrying a big plate of fried chicken in soya sauce which brought cheers from the boys. As their mother sat down next to their father the boys turned to face their father waiting for a signal from him to begin eating. A faint smile appeared on his face and then he nodded at which the boys shouted in unison, 'Ah Kong eat, Papa eat, Ma eat,' picked up their chopsticks and dived into the food before them.

Su Yin sat down between Hong and the oldest of her brothers Keng. As she picked up her bowl of rice and chopsticks she looked at each of the deeply tanned faces of her brothers squashed round the table. Keng at fourteen was gangly; he had shot up in the last year and stood taller than Su Yin. The two boys after him would catch up with him soon. She looked at her father and thought how lucky she was to have such a father. He was thin and tall which accentuated the slight stoop of his shoulders. His face, neck and hands were bronzed from working in the fields. Su Yin had noticed a few strands of white in his otherwise black hair which she had never seen ruffled. She realised how fortunate she and Mei were that he believed that his daughters should also learn to read and write. He would teach them whenever he came in from the fields so that reading a book was as natural as learning to walk and writing with a brush and ink was part of play when they were growing up. She remembered clearly the first time he taught her to write. They were sitting at the same table that they were sitting at now. He put down the pipe he had been puffing at and picked up the brush that was resting on the inkwell. 'This is your surname – Wong,' as he held his brush upright and then proceeded to write. Before her eyes, with a few elegant strokes on the paper before her he produced the beautiful character of their family name. As little girls she and Mei went to school in the mornings and then directly to the factory to work after school then all that had to stop when her brothers came along. Her grandmother had been caring for them; now not only did her mother need more help at home - to cook, wash, clean and care for the baby brothers - the two sisters had to put in more hours at the factory. But it didn't stop her reading whatever material she could lay her hands on such as her brothers' school books and old newspapers that were recycled as wrappers in the market. The news that there was going to be a new school run by missionaries had piqued her curiosity. If the foreigners could speak Cantonese, why shouldn't she learn their language?

For a while, under the warm glow of the paraffin lamp, no one spoke and all that was audible was the sound of slurping of soup. Then Mr Wong asked in a soft voice, 'Keng, you have made sure the chicken are all safely in their pen?' Apart from the time he let rip when Keng skipped a class at school to practise rowing, Su Yin had never heard him raise his voice at any one of them. And he didn't say much unlike her mother who had more fire and more to say.

'Yes, Papa, I've repaired the gap in the fence that you told me about and I have also filled the troughs with water,' replied Keng with his mouth full and wiping a grain of rice off his chin.

'I fed the pigs and made sure they are alright,' said Peng, the second son who would rather bury his head in his books besides examining the parts of his father's pig's anatomy.

'And I have done my homework, Papa,' Hong piped up, his small eyes smiling, looking very pleased with himself.

Mr Wong nodded his approval. 'So what did you learn today?'

'New characters and how to write them, so I have been practising that and done four pages,' answered Hong.

'That's very good,' said Mr Wong. Looking at his fourth son, 'And what about you, Fung?'

Fung, aged seven, put his bowl down on the table and continued chewing as he held his father's gaze. For a few moments he looked puzzled then he said, 'We did sums today but they were so easy. I finished them before anyone else!'

'But did you get them all correct?' asked Mr Wong.

'Yes, of course,' replied Fung, his eyes shining. Mr Wong merely smiled.

'You are a show-off!' Peng said through his mouthful of food.

'And you are a sweet potato head!' retorted Fung which brought on a round of sniggers.

'In that case you are a bigger potato head than me!' said Peng with a smirk. More sniggers which the boys hoped would detract their father from scolding them for the mess they had made when they were kicking around pretending to be *Kung fu* fighters in the backyard.

'Papa,' said Su Yin, 'I heard that there is a new school which the missionaries have built outside Canton. It would be so good to learn to speak another language, don't you think?'

Mr Wong didn't answer right away. He looked at Su Yin. 'It is a bit far, too far for us to attend even if we could afford to.' It pained him to have to say that but the fees for the boys were eating into their savings. The last crop of rice had not been as much as he had hoped thanks to the unexpected rain during harvest ruining a great chunk of the crop.

Su Yin kept quiet not wishing to upset her father. She decided it was best to drop the subject when she saw that her mother's eyes had said as much. She wasn't really jealous of her brothers going to school; she accepted that boys were given the preferential treatment in any family and she would want her own brothers to do well. Now and again though she did feel a stab of envy, she would admit; she just wished she was going with them. Suddenly all the brothers started talking at once.

Her mind went back to what Lan Yee had said after lunch. Since she heard of Lan Yee's decision to take up the vow she had felt unsettled. It was a huge step Lan Yee was taking; it was not like giving up eating rice for the rest of her life. Together they had rebelled against the idea of marrying someone they hadn't met until the day of the wedding; it went against their grain. Together they had been horrified at the thought of marrying an old or ugly man at which they had both shuddered and screamed. A worse fate would be marrying a man who turned out to be violent and cruel to them. What sort of future would that lead to? The prospects always made her shiver. She looked at her mother. In her opinion her mother was lucky because the man she was married to was a kind man; her contentment was evident. Even when she was busy and rushing around she would sometimes hum or sing as if she didn't have a care in the world. Su Yin felt she could not tell her mother yet what Lan Yee had decided to do. She wasn't sure how she would react but something told her she would not be shocked. But she wasn't sure about Lan Yee's parents.

Su Yin felt a leap of respect and admiration for Lan Yee for her courage and determination in making such a life-changing choice. Her situation was in sharp contrast to Mei's. Mei was happy to marry and was going to marry someone she liked. A streak of annoyance crept in; she was cross with herself that she hadn't suspected that Lan Yee would contemplate making a vow to confirm her choice. Should she be thinking like her friend? Should she do as Lan Yee had chosen to do instead of thinking of learning a foreign language? With the questions swirling around in her head she looked at her brothers chattering away happily. She looked at Hong sitting beside her happily chewing away. She reached out to the plate of pomfret at the centre of the table, picked up a juicy bit of fish and put it in Hong's bowl. She wondered if the brothers would ever have to decide whether to marry or not.

After carefully removing the soiled leaves from among the guzzling silkworms and adding more fresh leaves to the trays, Su Yin left Mei and hurried along the high-ceiling corridor towards the far end of the factory. Although the sun had not long risen and the cockerels had ceased crowing the whole building was alive with the busy chatter of the women workers as if it had not gone to sleep at all. As she moved along the corridor the grassy smell of the mulberry leaves faded; she was walking past the section which she called the

Changing Room where the silkworms were silently spinning their threads around themselves to prepare for a dramatic change when they had finished building their white cocoon. Here various stages of the spinning were evident as judged by the size of the pods embedded in the vertical meshes of twigs and straws. Then as she approached the reeling section the smell was quickly replaced by what she always thought reminded her of a combination of her mother's boiled medicinal herbs and rotting meat. Although she had got accustomed to the stench, she still didn't like it. It had percolated from the huge steamy room where three long neat rows of large woks of cocoons were boiling on wood fire stoves. There Lan Yee and dozens of women were reeling, uncoiling the silk filament from the off-white balls in the hot water. The steamy room was not her favourite place but all the workers had to rotate through the different sections so that anyone could step into any role that was required of them. A few of the women including Lan Yee turned in her direction as she walked in. They smiled in acknowledgement. '*Wey,* how are you?' they called out to her. Su Yin smiled back.

'What are you doing here?' asked Lan Yee. 'Aren't you supposed to be feeding the worms?' she continued winding the silk thread with her fingers over the wooden bobbins above the steaming pot of cocoons. Like her own Lan Yee's finger tips were hardened by the years of dipping into the near- boiling water to fish out the cocoons and then searching for the beginnings of the silk threads like scratching for the start of a ball of wool.

Su Yin stood beside her and started gently stirring the cocoons with a ladle in case the manager came in and caught her doing nothing. 'I want to know if you have told your parents about what you told me yesterday.' She lowered her voice, 'And are you really sure you want to join the sisterhood?'

'I haven't yet. There hasn't been a good time….but I will very soon. Maybe even tonight.' There was no hint of concern in her voice. Su Yin looked at her friend's heart-shaped face, her dark brown eyes focussed on the threads she was handling. There was always a look of mischief and curiosity that matched her reputation of being the font of gossip. But this morning Su Yin thought she looked different; she looked sombre with a hint of grey. She wondered if it was the weight of her new commitment that had caused the change. Perhaps it was the worry of facing her parents and telling them about it. To her surprise, Lan Yee turned round to her and asked, 'Is it something you might want to do too?'

Su Yin was stumped; she felt as if she had been knocked off her stool. She had not considered taking the vow of celibacy as an option for herself, certainly not yet. What was wrong with her? Would she take the vow? She felt as if she had betrayed Lan Yee. 'Don't know..I...I'm not sure, haven't thought about it. Shall we go and treat ourselves to *dim sum* at Mrs Chong's restaurant tomorrow? We can talk more then. I have to go back to my wriggly friends before Mr Man catches me here.'

Chapter 3

For a long time Lan Yee had been burdened with the question of marriage. Since she'd made her choice she had felt at peace. Last in the line of four sisters and five brothers her parents had been especially concerned about making sure she was married off. With all her sisters married off successfully they regarded her as their last challenge. Although she rarely saw her sisters – the last sister was married a year ago and she had not returned home to visit them yet – she sensed that married life was not necessarily a happy place. She recalled her First Sister once saying that marriage was like a prison where women willingly walked into with their eyes wide open. She hadn't understood then but she had not forgotten it. Since then her eyes and ears had been tuned to spot tell-tale signs of marriages that she knew of, particularly of friends', not that she knew what to look out for. But she was eager to know what her sister meant and she had not been able to ask her to elucidate. Yet she knew she didn't have to look very far to get some hint of what she'd meant; it was right under her nose in her family's home. Her two older brothers were married and lived with their wives in the same house. According to the unwritten law, the sisters -in-law assumed the lowest rung on the family ladder. On the day the eldest brother and his wife were married Lan Yee greeted her new sister-in-law as she would an elder as she was a couple of years older. To Lan Yee's surprise her sister-in-law bowed to her. Her sister-in-law was called *Dai So* which meant Big Sister-in-law and therefore in the order of things she should be above Lan Yee. But *Dai So* automatically assumed a servant's role. Since then she had been almost servile which both embarrassed and irritated

Lan Yee. She felt sorry for her and could see that *Dai So* had to keep on the good side of her mother whose fiery temper could be easily unleashed. She had witnessed her mother scolding *Dai So* for the smallest of reasons. And for someone who was small and bird-like she had a voice that could pierce the roof. The thought of having a mother-in-law in that mould somehow terrified her. In contrast to *Dai So,* her Second Sister appeared to be blossoming and was ballooning the few times she returned home for a visit, each time with one more child than the time before.

What Lan Yee had observed so far had not convinced her of the benefits or virtues of marriage. She had looked to her spinster paternal aunt for enlightenment, a model of quiet contentment and self-sufficiency. Lan Yee wanted to be free of the cobweb of family arguments and strife. Besides, she was quite sure she didn't want children.

Given the track record where her sisters were concerned she suspected her mother would have enlisted the help of a matchmaker very likely even before she hit puberty. But she couldn't be certain what she had been up to and the prospect of facing her and her father frightened her. She knew she had to declare her intention and the sooner the better. She had to choose the right moment.

Her heart was pounding mercilessly. Her eyes fixed on her mother's stony face. Lan Yee eventually found her voice. The words came rushing out of her mouth. 'Papa, Ma, I have decided to join the sisterhood. I don't want to get married. I want to be like aunty.'

Mother's face gradually turned into a storm. 'What do you mean?' she shrieked.

'I don't want to get married,' Lan Yee's voice had shrivelled.

'No! You can't do that!' Her mother turned to her father who looked shocked but lost for words. 'She can't do that, can she? Tell her!'

'*Aiyahh*, child, your mother has already fixed a match for you...'

'You can't, Ma!' Lan Yee's heart was pounding even harder now.

'What do you mean I can't? I am your mother and you do as your father and I say.' Her mother's eyes were hard and her cheeks had turned red. She took a deep breath and continued, 'In fact we were going to tell you all about it - the man that Mrs Ling has found for you is a very nice man...'

'But Ma, I don't need a nice man to look after me,' Lan Yee grabbed her mother's hand.

'It's not just you that needs looking after.' Her mother struggled to keep her voice calm as she patted Lan Yee's hand. 'Your father and I too need looking after. The man is wealthy,' she gave a small smile, 'and he has offered a very generous dowry.'

Lan Yee pulled her hand away. 'I am not an animal you sell.'

Father now raised his voice. 'You are a selfish child. You will do as we say. The match is agreed and there is no going back. We cannot renege on it. You will not make us a laughing stock.' he stood up and stormed out of the house.

Tears ran down Lan Yee's cheeks. 'Ma, please, please don't make me.'

'Your father has spoken and what he says goes. You should be ashamed of yourself disobeying your parents. I never thought my own daughter would turn out like this. Besides it is not natural, not wanting to marry,' she walked away to catch up with her husband.

Lan Yee felt as if her heart would rip.

Mrs Chong's restaurant was already buzzing when Su Yin arrived - customers chatting, waiters shouting orders. In front of the restaurant more tables had been set up on the wide path to accommodate more hungry customers. Su Yin was one of them and most of the tables were already taken. In spite of the awning the heat of the afternoon sun penetrated into the eating area but it did little to dampen Su Yin's appetite. Instead the smell of the wonton soup emanating from the steaming urn in the open restaurant reminded her that she had skipped her breakfast and heightened her anticipation of the treat that was to come. She was glad she had managed to get a table. The waiters, towels slung over their shoulders, were shouting orders to Mrs Chong in the kitchen who was churning out bowls of delicious noodles and wonton. From where she was sitting she could look into the restaurant to see old Pang the noodle-maker at his worktop bent over, meticulously slicing the concertina folds of noodle pastry to produce thin strings of noodles. Then he stopped cutting, straightened up and took a handful of the strings and shaped them into a nest of noodles. As ever Su Yin was mesmerised by the deft movements of his hands as Pang conjured up a row of noodle nests ready for the cook. From further inside the kitchen she could just hear the sound of rhythmic chopping and although she couldn't see she knew it was Mrs Chong's son mincing pork with a cleaver in each hand.

She didn't hear Lan Yee approach the table but something made her turn to see Lan Yee pulling out the stool from under the table and then she sat down across from her. Su Yin suppressed a gasp. Lan Yee had been crying; her eyelids were swollen and the sparkle in her eyes had vanished. She reminded Su Yin of an injured bird she once found on the way to the factory. Her hair which was always neatly plaited looked like she had not bothered to comb and re-plait it when she got up that morning. She was wearing the same *samfoo* she had worn the day before. 'What happened?' Su Yin asked as she reached out to take her hands that were clasped together on the table.

Lan Yee simply shook her head. Her eyes started brimming with tears, her lips quivered.

Su Yin looked around and seeing that more and more customers were streaming into the forecourt of the restaurant she said quickly, 'Let's go for a walk instead, let's go to our place.' She ignored the rumblings of her stomach.

Lan Yee let herself be guided by Su Yin and as they walked away Su Yin shouted to the waiter approaching them that they would return later.

A cyclist overtook them as they walked along the dry mud path past a small temple in front of which fat joss sticks in a large urn were smoking and throwing out a heady scent. A screen of bamboo trees separated the temple from a row of shops and a cluster of houses on the left. To the right was a canal where a group of giggling children watched a boy jump into the water. Further downstream where the water was still, a man wearing a wide-brimmed straw hat was fishing from his sampan. They then came to an old gazebo which had been newly painted, its pillars now a magnificent red ready for the forthcoming boat race festival. The round granite table and stools had also been scrubbed clean. Oleander bushes with pink and white flowers surrounded the gazebo. As soon as they sat down Lan Yee told Su Yin what had happened the night before.

'...My aunt said I could go and live in the hall with the other sisters if necessary, if my parents throw me out of the house.' Su Yin knew the hall she was referring to; it was a large building which was paid for and owned by the sisterhood. It was for women who had retired or those in their old age with no one to look after them.

'Would you do that?'

'But I don't want to do that.'

'So what will you do? Do you know who the man is, this man that your parents want you to marry?'

'No. They don't say he is young which makes me think he is old. He's probably old and decrepit and desperate to have a wife. I don't want to be his wife and servant. I keep telling my parents I don't need a man to look after me as long as I can work.' She clenched her fists and pounded her lap, her voice turning into a squeal, 'I *don't* want to marry. Why can't my mother understand? She is a woman and should know how I feel. Instead she says it is unnatural not to marry, to have children and all the rest. Why can't she understand? Why can't I do what I want?'

'Can't your aunt speak for you?'

'What? No! My father doesn't get on with her. He has forgotten that when their mother died when he was very young, she, his own sister, slogged hard in the factory so that she could help to put food on the table. He just thinks it was her duty. He is selfish. All he thinks of is making money; he thinks I am one of his animals and how much he can get for me.' Lan Yee burst into tears again.

Su Yin was lost for words. What could she say? She couldn't dissuade Lan Yee to give up her choice; it had now dawned on her that Lan Yee was very serious. She had half expected that Lan Yee would change her mind. They had been through phases together when they were quite sure they were committed to a plan only to falter and do a U-turn like the time they decided to become vegetarian, imitating the nuns who resided in the temple they had just walked past.

They secretly made a pledge. which didn't last long; a week later when faced with Su Yin's mother's special dish of braised pig trotters in wine and soya sauce, their will-power crumbled.

Su Yin had never faced a problem of this proportion before and she didn't know what she should say or do. Talking about matchmaking and marriage was one thing – that was easy. But to be actually confronted with parents who had completely different plans for their daughters and were adamant that their wish was adhered to was a totally different matter. Seeing Lan Yee sobbing broke her heart; she felt utterly helpless.

'Surely your father wouldn't throw you out of the house if you disobeyed him?'

'You don't know my father. The grumpy side you have seen is the nice side,' Lan Yee replied. She paused as she looked ahead of her, her face tensed. When she spoke again her voice was throbbing with anger. 'There was the time when he tied my brother Ah Tong to the tree in the yard and whipped him with his cane.' Tears started to well up again in her eyes. 'Ah Tong was only six and all he had done was refuse to eat the mushroom because it had made him sick. None of us was allowed to help him. No one dared. I kept shouting to Father to stop. Ah Tong screamed and cried but Father wouldn't stop. He was like a mad man.' Lan Yee shook her head. 'That is the kind of man he is.'

The picture of the little boy tied to a tree screaming and crying turned Su Yin cold. She shuddered. She had always been a little intimidated by Lan Yee's father whose face reminded her of her father's goat's with his ears sticking up and his pointed chin and always seemed to be set in a permanent scowl. And whenever she greeted him he would only grunt. But she never suspected he could do what he did to Ah Tong. 'How was Ah Tong afterwards?' she asked.

'He seemed to bounce back but I think that there was a big corner of fear in his heart, fear of Father,' said Lan Yee. She wiped her tears with the back of her hand then let out a short laugh, 'I noticed Mother didn't cook mushrooms after that. So you see what I am up against? How can I appeal to him? He is an unreasonable man.'

They sat in silence, each lost in their own thoughts. Then Su Yin asked, 'What will you do?'

Lan Yee took a deep breath then replied, 'I don't know.'

On her way home Su Yin was like someone on an opium trip; her thoughts were scattered and fuzzy but one thought that refused to go away was that she couldn't understand how Lan Yee's father could be so horrible to his own sister who gave up marrying in order to support the family including him. In fact as far as Su Yin knew the villagers respected these spinsters who contributed as well as the men, so she couldn’t understand the reason for his meanness towards his own sister or towards his daughter's wish to remain a spinster. Su Yin was oblivious to the trees and birds as she walked back home. A couple of women had called out and waved frantically at her but she didn't see or hear them and continued on the path home. As she approached the front of the house she suddenly heard screams coming from the back of the house. Panicking she ran in through the house and when she got to the back door she saw what had happened: her father had fallen off a ladder and was now lying on his back on top of a stack of hay. His face was white with shock and pain.

Chapter 4

As Su Yin gently stirred the chopped shallots frying in the wok, strains of flute music drifted into the kitchen. It lifted her heart - her father was definitely on the mend after hurting his back. It was good to see that he was back to his usual self after the weeks of worry when he was laid up after the fall. During dinner he had been talking animatedly. He had been incensed by the fact that the country up north was being ransacked by the Japanese. Then he railed at the Europeans taking chunks of the country like peeling a pomelo and snatching segments of the fruit. How could he accept the religion of a people who could barge into another country and take over as if they had every right? He hated their audacity in trying to convert them to their religion. Then when her mother interjected saying that she was going to make dumplings once again he repeated the story of the origin of the rice dumplings. It was for the benefit of the younger brothers lest they forgot the reason for commemorating the fifth day of the fifth lunar month. So once again Su Yin and Mei had to listen to the story of the patriotic statesman and poet Chu Yuan who died during the period of the Warring States between 475 and 221BC. Chu Yuan loved his country, the Chu State; he believed and advocated that talents from all social levels should be nurtured in order to enrich society and build up the military forces. This, however, was contrary to the interests of the aristocracy who accused him of conspiracy against the sovereign resulting in his exile. When the Chu state was overrun by the Chin army he was so devastated that he jumped into the river to kill himself. Legend had it that fishermen went out in their boats to look for his body and threw food into the river to distract the fish from eating him. Since then every year on that same day the making and eating of dumplings had been carried out in memory of the hero. A dragon boat race was also part of the celebration and this was Su Yin's brother Keng's cue to announce that he had been selected to row with the team he had been training with. He was bubbling with excitement; the race was going to be even bigger than previous years with many teams from other districts.

Once the shallots started to brown Su Yin added garlic and then the ready-mixed five spices and soya sauce. Mrs Wong came to her side and looked at the frying mixture in the wok as it sizzled throwing up the distinct aroma of the anise, cloves, cinnamon, fennel and ginger and filling the whole kitchen. 'Yes, you can add the rice now.' Su Yin scooped up the glutinous rice which had been soaked overnight in a ceramic urn and added it to the spices. Mrs Wong then busied herself with sorting the soaked bamboo leaves picking out the perfect ones for her purpose and then laid them next to the bowls of cooked pork, chestnuts and mushrooms on the wooden work top. 'Su Yin, make sure you taste the rice, see if it is seasoned enough.' Su Yin nodded.

'Ma, the water is heating up,' said Mei walking from a big pan of water over a roaring wood fire in a stove on the floor.

Mrs Wong positioned herself on a low stool in front of a bunch of twine hanging from a hook from the crossbeam of the ceiling to the side of the worktop where all her ingredients were. She picked up two leaves and folded them to form a cone in her left palm and proceeded to fill it with a spoonful of the glutinous rice and pieces of pork, chestnuts and mushroom. Then she packed it with some more rice. Su Yin watched carefully for despite the practice she'd had she could not emulate the perfect geometric shape that her mother effortlessly produced after folding back the leaf ends over the rice mix and then tying it with a piece of twine. Mei had no trouble doing the same.

'I am going to try and make one just like yours,' said Su Yin admiring the sticky rice dumpling with its four equal sides and perfect points. She did exactly as her mother did and it was only at the third attempt that she managed to produce one that looked as good as her mother's which made her squeal with delight.

After an hour and some sixty dumplings were made Mei started to place bunches of tens into the boiling water to cook while Mrs Wong and Su Yin cleared away the utensils and washed up. Once done Mrs Wong went to her bedroom and returned carrying a large cotton bag. She checked that the table was clean and dry before putting it down on the table. She called out to Mei and Su Yin, 'Come, I have something to show you.' Mei and Su Yin rushed to the table as Mrs Wong pulled out a folded piece of glimmering cherry-red silk. The sisters gasped and simultaneously let out a soft '*Wah*!' Gently they slid their palms across the fabric savouring its softness.

'This is beautiful. What is it for?' asked Mei.

'So this is what you have been doing in the weaving room,' said Su Yin had noticed her working at the loom in the weaving room at the end of her shift for a few weeks. Looking at the beautiful shiny fabric Su Yin knew it would have cost her a lot of money, possibly six months' wages, if she had bought it ready made. The richness of the fabric meant that it was made with only the finest silk threads and not the waste filaments which would normally be turned into an inferior fabric. A garment made with such luxurious quality silk was almost out of their reach.

Mrs Wong nodded. 'Mei, I am going to make an outfit for you.'

'But, Ma, I don't deserve this,' Mei said quickly.

'It is for your wedding dress, silly,' replied Mrs Wong.

'*Wah,* Mei, I know what you should have!' Su Yin's face lit up; she became excited. 'I have seen the latest fashion in Shanghai. It is the rave. It is called a *cheongsam.* It is just like the *samfoo* from the waist up,' she gestured at the top she was wearing, 'but it is one piece and more fitting and here,' she pointed to the sides of her thighs, 'here there are slits. Ma, it would look so lovely on Mei.'

'That is a bit daring showing off your legs like that,' Mei looked doubtful, watching her mother's face for signs of disapproval. But Mrs Wong's face was unreadable.

'I don't think so,' said Su Yin. 'It is quite modest. It is like how the old costumes used to be; you need the slits so you can walk otherwise your legs are bound together and you won't be able to walk. It is for your special day so you should have something different, something spectacular.'

Both Su Yin and Mrs Wong looked at Mei and waited for her response.'I don't know.. I don't know what people will say,' said Mei.

'Who cares what people will say! I say you should have a *cheongsam,'* said Su Yin. 'Don't you agree, Ma? Especially as you have gone to so much trouble weaving this silk yourself. You'd want to show it off the best you can.' Su Yin grabbed the silk and wrapped it round Mei's torso.

Mrs Wong said nothing as she looked on. After a while she addressed Mei, 'Would you like this..this *cheongsam* then?' Mei's eyes widened, a smile broke out. Then she nodded her head vigorously holding up the silk wrap against her body. Mrs Wong turned to Su Yin who looked pleased with herself. 'Su Yin, yours will have to wait until I have time to weave another piece.'

'Me?' Surprise spread across Su Yin's face. 'But I thought this was for Mei's wedding outfit only.'

'We have to make one for you as well,' answered Mrs Wong. Sensing a change in Su Yin she asked, 'What's on your mind?'

Su Yin looked thoughtful. She hesitated then she pulled out a stool from under the table. Patting the seat she said, 'Ma, you'd better sit down.'

Mrs Wong sat down without taking her eyes off Su Yin. Mei put the silk down on the table and sat down as well. 'So what is the matter?' asked Mrs Wong.

Su Yin started to bite her bottom lip as she wrung her hands. She thought her mother looked a little worn out, her short black hair with a side parting framed her dainty features. Although there were fine lines around her eyes they did not detract from the twinkle that she sometimes glimpsed when they sat facing each other at the table in the kitchen peeling sweet potatoes or stringing beans. And when she frowned when Su Yin told her the pranks that the boys got up to, she could see that beyond the furrowed brow there was a gentleness in her eyes that told how much she loved them. Suddenly she wondered if this was a good time to tell her. 'I don't know how to begin.'

'Just say what is on your mind,' urged Mei. 'Ma will understand.'

'Understand what?' asked Mrs Wong, her brow started to gather.

Su Yin could feel her heart racing, she turned to look in the direction of where her father was as if she was afraid he would hear her and then the words rushed out, 'I am not sure that I want to get married.'

She waited for them to land. She was afraid that her mother might say that she had already arranged a match for her. Mrs Wong's face revealed nothing while Mei looked nervous with her eyes fixed on Su Yin. It seemed a long time before their mother spoke; her voice was soft when she eventually did.

'Have you thought this through carefully?' she asked. 'And why do you think you don't want to marry?'

Su Yin felt a gush of relief. She had expected a tirade. 'Yes, yes, I have. At least I don't want to rush into it.' Since her father's accident, she had felt even more strongly about wanting to be there for him, if necessary, to stand up and take his place to look after her mother and brothers. The boys were bright and eager to learn and her father had said that he hoped they would become more than what he was. She had accepted that if she couldn't be educated then it was imperative her brothers could. And if they were to continue in their education someone needed to work to put food on the table. Her mother alone could not do that if her father was in some way incapacitated. She wouldn't mind if she had to look after and support her brothers; it would be *her* choice if she had to make sacrifices. To her mind that would be far better than being an unpaid slave in somebody else's household or even more unthinkable, a concubine. But she couldn't tell her mother that; her mother had been very worried about her father and it was only after he'd started walking about that her anxiety lifted. 'I don't want to marry someone I don't know. What if they turn out to be monsters? What guarantee is there that they won't change once they've got you after the wedding?'

'I didn't know your father when I married him,' Mrs Wong said softly.

'I know but it has worked out well for you. And Mei is lucky she knows the man she wants to marry.' Su Yin was eager to press her point. 'Besides, why would I want to leave my family and join some other family that might not even like me or treat me well? I don't need to marry. I have a good job; I can look after myself. I don't want to depend on my husband. I have you and Papa even if my sister and all my brothers marry. And I would rather give my earnings to you than to some man and his family.'

Mrs Wong knew she was lucky, very lucky that her husband had turned out to be such a good man. She had been terrified when her mother told her she was to marry a young gangly farmer. It had seemed like the normal thing to do. She didn't rebel; it didn't occur to her to do anything different. After all her four sisters before her had married. At the age of fifteen, just like Su Yin was now, she was married to a man who was kind and considerate. It was like picking an oyster out of a basket of oysters then opening it to find a pearl inside. She had heard too many stories of unhappy matches amongst her friends. 'Marriage is a gamble,' she said, 'there is no doubt about it. It could turn out very well for you.'

'It is a gamble that I am not sure I want to take,' Su Yin responded.

'What about you, Mei? Do you have any doubts?'

Mei merely shook her head.

Su Yin rushed in. 'That is my point: we should do what we feel is right for us, not what others think we should do or stick to traditions. Look at our precious imperial dynasties that have ruled us for all these millions of years. They have gone. A new different government has taken over. It is what the people want.' Su Yin paused to take a breath. 'Whether it is good for us or not we will see.'

Mei spoke, 'Ma, I agree with her. After all that is what you have always taught us to do – to stand up for ourselves. I am not ashamed that I want to marry just like Su Yin doesn't want to.'

Mrs Wong said nothing as the two sisters waited. Then looking straight into Su Yin's eyes. She asked, 'So are you thinking of joining the sisterhood?'

'I...I don't know,' replied Su Yin.

'Lan Yee wants to do just that,' Mei chipped in.

Mrs Wong's eyes shot across to Mei and then to Su Yin. 'Is that right? And do her parents know?'

Su Yin sighed. 'They do now.' She wasn't sure whether she should divulge the fact that they had other plans for Lan Yee fearing that it would affect her mother's view. Besides sooner or later she was bound to hear from Lan Yee's mother, aunt or one of the women in the factory. Since that conversation with Lan Yee at the gazebo by the canal she had not only been worried about her but had also found herself searching her own heart.

'You are not influenced by her, are you?' asked Mrs Wong.

'No, of course not. I have a mind of my own.' Su Yin pouted.

'It is a big decision, not one that you want to rush into. I know lots of women who have opted for this path are happy enough. I can't help thinking it will be lonely later on when you are older. Living with the other sisters is not the same as having your own family. Don't you want children?'

Su Yin hesitated. Then she said, 'I don't think so.' She liked children but she could not understand the logic of having so many children. More hands meant being able to earn more as a family but there were more mouths to feed. What of posterity, of passing on the family name? She heard her father talk about passing on the family name. Was it that important? She wasn’t sure. They were big questions to which she had no answers or at least not her own answers. It was the done thing: every family had at least eight in the family. So many mouths to feed. The thought of physically giving birth to so many children also terrified her especially when she recalled hearing her mother scream when her brothers were being born. 'Ma, you don't have to worry about grandchildren. You will have plenty of them from Mei and the boys. Besides, I want to be independent and free. I want to be able to do what I want and not be a slave to some man whom I might not like or respect.'

No one spoke for a moment. Then Mrs Wong said, 'You might change your mind.'

Su Yin shook her head. 'Ma, you don't object, do you?'

'As long as you know what you are doing.' Mrs Wong studied Su Yin's face. Her own face softened into a hint of a smile, then her eyes glistened with tears. 'Somehow I am not surprised. You've always been strong-willed and no doubt you know what you want.' She stood up and gathered the red silk from the table. 'I will make the dress for you Mei and I will see about yours later.'

'You are not angry or disappointed, are you?' asked Su Yin searching her mother's face for signs.

'What is there to be disappointed about? As you've said, it is your life, your choice. I can only hope for the best for you. We will need to see what your father thinks.'

'Will you speak for me, Ma?'

Mrs Wong didn't answer as she headed towards her bedroom clutching her silk. Neither of the sisters saw the tears that rolled down her cheeks.

Chapter 5

The riverbank was mobbed. People had poured in from the village and nearby villages to watch the annual boat race. The weather conditions were perfect: dry with a clear blue sky and a comfortable temperature for both rowers and spectators. Along the street running parallel to the river, bright yellow and red bunting hanging from the tops of bamboo trees were swaying in the breeze. Restaurants were crowded serving breakfast or early lunch. Dotted in front of the restaurants were stalls selling yet more food - fried noodles, steam buns and glutinous rice dumplings. Little children dressed in their best clothes were clearly excited as they gawped at the hordes of people, pointing here and there at things that caught their attention. Babies bobbed along strapped to their mothers' backs while toddlers sat astride their fathers' shoulders either oblivious to the event or curious at the noise and bustle.

On the water some thirty long wooden boats representing the different districts and towns including Canton waited at the starting line. They came in different colours and designs; some had dragon heads at the bow while others had their names painted on the side. Each was manned by twenty or so young men in pairs with their oars over the side poised to row, their eyes focussed on their coxswain who in turn was holding his arms up ready to hit the drum at the signal. Suddenly they were off. The sound of pounding drums erupted and filled the air. Loud cheers went up as the onlookers and supporters shouted encouragement. Like clockwork churning at a furious speed the rowers pulled at the water in a synchronised way to the rhythmic pacing of the drums. More cheers as the boats propelled smoothly forward, each vying for the lead position. Now they were overtaking the others and then they were being overtaken.

As the boats almost came alongside where Su Yin and Lan Yee were standing they craned their necks to see Keng's boat. They shouted and cheered adding to the deafening sound of the drums. Then Su Yin spotted him. His eyes were fixed ahead. Like his teammates he looked as if he was entranced; wearing headbands to soak their sweat, their faces were taut with tension and red as they puffed and puffed.

'Can you see him?' shouted Lan Yee. She raised her hand to shade her eyes as she peered across the water. 'I can't.'

'Just about,' Su Yin shouted back. 'He's wearing a yellow headband. See? Look at him. He is rowing like a crazed person,' She waved vigorously at Keng as the boats zoomed past them carrying the thunder of the drums with them. Cheers rose in the distance as the boats approached while the crowd around Su Yin and Lan Yee quietened and started to disperse moving in the direction of the finishing line. The two friends automatically moved with the flow. Su Yin was glad that Lan Yee had finally decided to join her. They had attended the event together for the last five years and it was one of the highlights of their year. And as per tradition they had come dressed in their best *samfoo*s – Su Yin in a pink floral cotton one with her hair plaited to one side while Lan Yee wore a plain mauve one with her hair bunched up in a ponytail. Both of them were in high spirits especially after Su Yin told Lan Yee that she had spoken to her mother about not marrying. The fact that Su Yin didn't know what her father's response was - assuming her mother had already told him - didn't matter. What mattered was that she had declared her intention and it hadn't stirred up a typhoon of fury. The two friends felt even closer, bound by a shared aim in life. But lately Lan Yee had appeared withdrawn at times. Her parents had been adamant about sticking to their plans for her and forbade her to ever speak of not complying with their wishes. Seeing her enjoying herself again and her delight when she was handed a bunch of rice dumplings had cheered Su Yin.

'It is so good to see Keng racing like that. I hope he and his team win. Did you see the way they flew past?' said Su Yin.

'Do you know who are in the team?' asked Lan Yee.

'No. I just know that they worked very hard. I know Keng went almost every other day to train. Such dedication.'

'If we hurry we might get to meet them at the finishing line. I am sure Keng would like that. I would,' said Lan Yee grabbing Su Yin's hand and then weaving her way through the crowd. The cheers crescendo-ed as they neared the finishing line. Su Yin felt as if she was racing as well, her heart pounding in rhythm with the thumping of the drums that was becoming louder again. The throng of people had thickened even more; some jumping up and down, others waving frantically, they were shouting the names of the teams they supported willing them on at the final lap. Su Yin and Lan Yee joined in shouting Keng's name even though they couldn't see who was leading the race. Then the name of the winning team was called out but Su yin couldn't make out what it was.

'So who has won?' she shouted to Lan Yee. 'Who's won?' Then she heard the man beside her call out,

'It's the Red Tiger!'

"The Red Tiger?' said Su Yin. '*Ahh,* that is Keng's team! Lan Yee, that's Keng's team. They've won!' She threw her arms around Lan Yee and they jumped up and down screaming with joy.

The area for receiving the competitors by the finishing line was cordoned off. Su Yin and Lan Yee just managed to squeeze their way to the edge to wait for the rowers to appear. Suddenly the cheers grew louder when the rowers appeared in full view of the crowd. Each and every one of their faces was soaked with sweat and beaming. Su Yin's eyes strained to see Keng's and then she saw him. His smile spread right across his face, there was a look of bewilderment and disbelief in his eyes. He saw Su Yin, waved and then turned to motion to the man behind him. It was when the man pulled off his headband that Su Yin realised that it was the butcher's help, the man with the sunny eyes who had got her curious and made her blush when he smiled at her. They were walking towards her and Lan Yee. She reached out and grabbed Keng's hands.

'Did you really win?' she asked.

'Yes!' replied Keng still breathless. 'We did. It is amazing. I don't believe it. Where are Ma and Papa?'

'They are around somewhere. Well done!'

'Yes, well done!' said Lan Yee. 'All that training. Congratulations.'

'Thank you, thank you.' Keng paused to take a big breath and then turned to Su Yin. 'Second Sister, this is my team mate, Liew.'

Su Yin felt self-conscious again just like she did before; her left hand had involuntarily reached up to hide her mark on her face. Liew standing before her smiled the same smile that she'd remembered although this time his face was glistening with sweat. Without taking his eyes off her he bowed. 'I am very happy to meet you,' he said.

Su Yin quickly pulled Lan Yee forward. ‘This is my friend Lan Yee.' Before Lan Yee could say a word to him the two men were whisked off by the organisers for the prize presentation.

'He is a bit forward, isn't he?' said Lan Yee with a mischievous glint in her eyes.

'You think so?' Su Yin replied.

'Not bad looking though,' added Lan Yee. 'Did you see the muscles on their arms?'

'Yes, I did.'

'*Hmm.*' Lan Yee smiled at Su Yin.

'*Hmm.*. what?' asked Su Yin.

After feeding the silkworms Su Yin made her way to the reeling room. It was already humming with activity and the air was warming up as the water in the rows of woks started to boil. Su Yin hurried to Lan Yee's place but there was no sign of her and the wok of water was empty of cocoons while all the others were steaming as the women stood by waiting to pour the cocoons in.

'Aunty Ling where is Lan Yee?' The woman in the place next to Lan Yee's turned to look at her.

' Haven't seen her yet. Not like her to be late,' said Aunty Ling.

'Maybe she is held up at home,' said the woman next to her. ‘Better not be too late. Mr Man is about to do his round.’

Feeling deflated Su Yin walked to her own place in the next row. Her wok of water was beginning to steam. She picked up the empty basket from the floor and headed for The Changing Room to collect the cocoons. It was not like Lan Yee to be late.

Chapter 6

A year later

The first thing Su Yin did was to ask Lan Yee's mother where Lan Yee was.

'How am I to know?' shouted Lan Yee's mother, her face screwed into a scowl. Su Yin wondered how anyone could be so miserable at such an early time in the morning. 'She should be at her place working like the rest of us. The stupid girl has been acting strange. Who knows what she is up to now? She'd better get to her post before she loses her job. Heaven give me patience.'

Not wishing to hear anymore and annoyed at Lan Yee's mother's reaction Su Yin decided that the best option was to wait and see without making any more fuss. Lunchtime seemed a long time away and when Mr Man the manager became hysterical about Lan Yee's absence she decided she would go and look for her.

'Mr Man, maybe she is sick,' Su Yin appealed to her manager. 'If it is alright with you I will go and look for her and I will make up my time and her time if necessary. May I go?'

Mr Man's face was as black as a brewing storm. He glared at Su Yin then said, 'Go, go see what that woman is playing at!' He then muttered something as he marched off.

Su Yin didn't need another invitation; she charged out of the factory onto the street and ran as fast as she could to where Lan Yee lived. Although she knew Lan Yee was in a lot of trouble for being late, something niggled at her and it was not the worry of what Lan Yee would have to face when she got back to work. She was breathless when she arrived at the front door of the house. There was no sign of Lan Yee in the yard and she didn't expect to see anyone else as the rest of the family would be away at work. When no one opened the door she peered through the window grille. She couldn't see Lan Yee and decided that she would walk round to the back of the house. At the side of the house empty buckets and baskets were strewn amidst bushes. She weaved her way past them heading towards the back. Lan Yee was still not to be seen or heard. She banged on the back door as she looked around. On seeing the large wooden outhouse where Lan Yee's father stored his timber and tools she decided to walk over to look inside. The door was ajar. She called out Lan Yee's name a couple of times and when she got no answer she pushed the door wide open. Then she heard herself scream; Lan Yee's limp body was hanging from the beam.

The silvery full moon was partially hidden by a thin veil of cloud; a cool breeze blew in through the open window. Su Yin continued gazing at the moon. Something about its silvery-ness was comforting, as if Lan Yee was looking down at her. She suppressed her tears and heaved a big sigh as she pushed away the memory of that awful morning. How she missed her friend, how she wished that she was there to share and take the next step with her. And yet she couldn't help feeling angry with her, angry because she left her and left without saying goodbye or telling her why. At the same time, she felt she had let Lan Yee down. Why didn't she even suspect that Lan Yee was desperate enough to take her own life? Could she have stopped her? It didn't help that there were precedents; when the news got around that Lan Yee had committed suicide some of the older women in the factory started recounting similar instances in the past as if they were talking about someone changing jobs.

And she was angry with Lan Yee's parents too. She had avoided seeing them altogether, turning away from Lan Yee's mother whenever she spotted her in the market or in the shops. The first time Su Yin saw her in the market after the tragedy she wanted to run up to her and tell her it was all her fault. She wanted to call her a murderer and say she'd killed her daughter. But she didn't; she swung round and walked in the opposite direction, her heart thumping with fury. In her worst moments she wished that both parents would be so heartbroken and remorseful that they too would die; but when the anger had subsided she knew that that was too easy a way out. Her own heart was broken, shredded and at times she felt she couldn't cope with the loss and grief. *Why did Lan Yee have to kill herself? Was the alternative her parents wanted for her so unbearable?* The questions kept coming but she had no answers. Suddenly Mei's soft voice pulled her back from the blackness of her thoughts and she became aware of Mei's hand on her shoulder.

'Are you sure you still want to do this?' Mei asked, her voice was tender as if she was afraid that Su Yin would crack.

'Yes,' said Su Yin. As she nodded tears trickled down her cheeks. She quickly wiped them away with the back of her free hand, the other wrapped tightly round a gold clasp. She turned to look into the mirror in front of where she was sitting. She noticed the wallpaper on the wall behind her; she remembered her father telling her that it was very expensive when his father bought it but now not only had the pink peonies on it turned brown but the paper had started to peel and curl in parts.

As was the pre-wedding custom, Su Yin's long black hair had been washed earlier in water that had been infused with pomegranate leaves. It now hung loose around her shoulders and down her back to her waist. Mei picked up the ivory comb next to the paraffin lamp on the table by her side and started to comb Su Yin's hair. Mei had insisted on combing her hair for her. Su Yin could see that Mei was fighting back her tears. She couldn't believe that Mei had now been married for more than three months. On her wedding day she wore the stunning red silk cheongsam that their mother had made and she had looked amazing in it. She was truly happy. There had been so much fuss and elaborate preparations for the wedding including the exchange of presents between them and the groom's family. Family and friends had gathered to celebrate. But tonight, the whole affair was subdued – no drums or music, no presents and no red lanterns hanging over the front door and no serving of tea to the parents-in-law. The hair-combing ritual was the same as before a wedding ceremony; her cousins, aunts and the women including her friends from the factory- confirmed spinsters and others- were there to support her. She could hear them talking in the kitchen. Outside the house her father, brothers and grandfather were sitting with their cups of tea, simply chatting or smoking. In the morning the women would attend the temple of Kwan Yin - goddess of mercy - to offer prayers. There were four other girls taking the vow with her so she didn't feel too alone. Su Yin's exquisite red cheongsam was already laid out on the bed. She felt a sense of being on the brink of achieving her ambition, of being there for her father and mother now she was the eldest of her siblings still living with their parents. She knew that the next step she was going to take was life-changing.

Mei looked up at the mirror; their eyes met. Su Yin smiled at her. 'Don't be sad for me,' she tried to inject lightness into her voice. 'I am very happy just like you were on your wedding day. Tomorrow morning I am going to be confirmed as a spinster. It's not as if I am dying.'

'I know but I can't help feeling sad. It is such a huge step,' said Mei.

'So is marrying,' replied Su Yin. Since marrying Seng, Mei had been back to visit twice. 'Are you happy in your new family?'

Mei smiled and then nodded. 'I am happy enough. Seng has been kind to me. As for the rest of the family, they seem reasonable and considerate. My mother-in-law doesn't say very much, At least she doesn't scold me, not that I give her reason to. By the way she did say she admired you for doing what you are doing.'

'What is there to admire? It is what I want to do and so it can't be difficult,' said Su Yin.

'That may be so. I can't believe that this is the last time I can comb your hair,' Mei gently pulled the comb through the length of Su Yin's perfumed hair.

'Yes. From tomorrow onwards I comb it myself,' said Su Yin knowing the full weight of the symbolism.

The door to their room opened and their mother walked in. Her face was serious but when she saw the two sisters looking at her she turned on a smile. Mei took one more stroke at Su Yin's hair and handed Mrs Wong the comb. Both sisters could tell that their mother too had been crying from the redness of her nose.

'No more tears now,' Mrs Wong said quietly. 'This is supposed to be a happy occasion.' She stroked Su Yin's hair. 'Your father and I are proud of you. But you must know this. He can't bring himself to tell you this: this was not what he wanted you to do. He had hoped that you would get the education you deserved, you and Mei. Then you could have had more options, get a better job, see more of the world. Above all, be independent.'

'Yes, I know but Papa mustn't feel he has failed. Look, I can read and write. I will be independent, Ma. Please tell him I will be fine,' said Su Yin. She remembered the evening she and her father finally got to talk about her intention. They were sitting on the veranda sipping tea while he smoked his pipe in-between sips. She had always been able to talk to him about anything and it was a special privilege. Although he had not said that he disapproved or tried to dissuade her she saw the disappointment in his eyes. The disappointment, she instinctively knew, was not with her but with himself. But nothing she said could erase that and all he said at the end was 'You have my blessing. Whatever you do I know you will give your utmost.' He nodded thoughtfully, 'For that, I am grateful.' Since that day she thought there was a change in her young brothers' attitude. It was as though they were in awe of her but would not tell her what or why and they had been more biddable than ever which had puzzled her. When she asked her mother all she said was that the boys understood the significance what she was doing and respected her for it.

Mrs Wong spoke again. 'Su Yin, I will ask you once more: are you absolutely sure this is what you want to do? It is not too late to change your mind.'

'Yes, Ma. I am sure,' said Su Yin. She opened her palm and seeing the clasp again sent a shooting pain through her heart. It was the only thing she had of Lan Yee's. Lan Yee's mother had handed it to her. At first Su Yin had refused to see her, afraid that she would berate her and accuse her of killing her daughter. She later relented and agreed to see her. To her surprise Lan Yee's mother's attitude had softened. She had looked like something inside her had crumbled when she approached Su Yin, holding out to her a small package wrapped in paper. On it was Su Yin's name; it had been carefully written in Lan Yee's handwriting. Lan Yee's mother said nothing; she merely nodded and then walked away after handing Su Yin the package. The clasp was simple in design – a gold stem of a flower with a round green jade at the centre of the flower. They had bought it together when they were shopping for the New Year. Su Yin raised her palm to her mother. 'Ma, will you put this in my hair?'

Mrs Wong nodded as she took the clasp from her and started to comb Su Yin's hair feeling her hair as if she was caressing her baby's face. She inhaled deeply. She took slow and deliberate long strokes as she combed Su Yin's hair. Then with each stroke she chanted,

'First comb for luck...
second comb for longevity...
third comb for contentment....
fourth comb for safety...
fifth comb for freedom...
sixth comb for courage...
seventh comb for self-belief and finally
eighth comb for health.'

When she had finished she gathered up the hair and twisted it into a bun. She pinned it so it sat at the nape of Su Yin's neck, just like how married women wore their hair. Then she carefully inserted the gold clasp on the side of Su Yin's head.

Part 2

Chapter 7

Kuala Lumpur, Malaya
1951

The very first time Su Yin set eyes on James MacAlpine she was serving dinner to a group of six men seated around the wooden table in the kitchen of her employer Mr Lok's house. They were the Chinese guerrillas who had been camping in the jungle and fighting the Japanese close to the house and the rubber plantation which Mr Lok owned. They had sneaked out for supplies before they moved on further into the jungle. Mr Lok had supplied them several times before – waterproofs, shoes, enamel mugs, toothbrushes, soap, rice, salt, salted fish and sugar. Su Yin had already packed several bags of food earlier and now had cooked a big pot of pork stew for the men before they headed back into the jungle. Su Yin had noticed that the half-starved men looking like they had been dragged through mud were lean and brown, worn out, with parts of their clothes ripped. They were indistinguishable from one another but she kept her eyes down on the floor when she was serving them until she came to and handed James his bowl of rice.

'Thank you,' he said as he looked up at Su Yin. It'd jolted her. He sounded different even though he had said it in Cantonese; the voice that came out of a mass of matted brown beard was deep but more than that, there was a warmth in it which carried heart-felt gratitude. It made her look into his eyes, eyes that were set deep. *This is the 'red-haired devil' that everyone had been talking about,* she thought, *the one that the village men spoke of with admiration*. She was stunned by the blueness which was like that of a clear midday sky after the rain had gone. Then she noticed his yellow hair peeping out from under his straw hat. There had been talk of a red-haired man amongst the jungle-fighters but she had not expected to come face to face with him. Although James's skin was as brown as the other men's and he could hide his blonde hair under a hat, it was his six-foot frame which presented a problem when they came out of the jungle; moving amongst the locals he could easily be spotted by those working with the Japanese. He had to walk hunched in order not to stick out from the group.

Su Yin was instantly filled with admiration for James, firstly for fighting the Japanese especially after what they had done to her people back in China and secondly for his ability to speak her language. That he took the trouble to learn to communicate with the Cantonese people impressed her. Later after he and the other men had gobbled down their food and left she heard Mr Lok say to his sons what a good man James was to fight alongside the Chinese. James who was then twenty-six had come to Malaya in search of adventure after working as an engineer in London. He had been charmed and swayed by the stories of Malaya and the Far East told by his uncle who had travelled far and wide. He got more than he bargained for; little did he know that he would be plunged into a war against the Japanese invaders. The tropical rain forest fascinated him; the blue green swathes of virgin jungle that covered the main mountain range which formed the spine of the Malayan peninsula seduced him. Armed with a compass and a backpack of tinned and dried food he ventured north of Kuala Lumpur towards Fraser's Hill to explore and test his orienteering skills and his ability to survive in the wild. By the time the Japanese attacked Malaya he had fallen in love with the country. When the Chinese retreated into the jungle to fight he volunteered to join them as he knew the jungle. From the tone of Mr Lok's voice Su Yin gathered that he also respected the younger man.

It didn't take Su Yin long to recognise James when he and Mr Lok walked through the front door of the Lok's residence three years later, two years after the Japanese Occupation had ended on 15th August 1945. His face had filled out - the sunken cheeks and rough beard had disappeared revealing a strong jawline and lips that looked like the right side was permanently lifted into a crooked smile. His matted overgrown blonde hair was now smooth and cropped short. His eyes, clear and brighter than before, retained the warmth that had been imprinted on Su Yin's memory. He had fattened up, no longer the frail bundle of skin-and-bone of a man who looked like he would rattle when he walked. His crisp white shirt-sleeves and khaki trousers showed off his trim and toned body. He walked with a slight limp which he didn't have before when she first met him. When he said hello to her on seeing her - as if he'd remembered her – it had made her feel as though she was being re-united with a younger brother whom she hadn't seen for a long time, something she had yearned to do with her own brothers. James's return to Malaya and then to the village to seek out Mr Lok had touched Mr Lok and the villagers and he had been hailed as a hero and a comrade-in-arms coming home. At the same time she was sad that some of the disillusioned younger men who had rushed into the jungle to escape being massacred by the Japanese and fought alongside James had returned to the jungle; only this time, their fight now was against him and his kind.

When James told Mr Lok that he was settling in Kuala Lumpur to work, Mr Lok was delighted. James had decided against joining the Police Force but he wanted to use his knowledge of the jungle to help fight the communists so he volunteered to work at the Jungle Warfare School situated in Kota Tinggi in Johore. Then when James told him he was looking for a domestic helper Mr Lok quickly insisted he would release Su Yin to look after James, his wife and baby. Mr Lok justified his move by reminding James that it was a small gesture on his part for James's support and courage in the fight against the Japanese and added that Su Yin had trained another *amah* so well that she was ready to take over from Su Yin in running his household.

Su Yin was aghast at the idea. She was both dubious and apprehensive. 'But I can't speak his language,' she had reasoned with Mr Lok.

'Don't worry,' James interjected in Cantonese, 'I teach you English and you teach me Cantonese.'

Su Yin was astounded by his command of her language; she had never heard him speak it before. There was no discernible foreign accent, in fact she thought he spoke like a local. When she had heard him and Mr Lok talk they spoke either in English or Malay. Suddenly realising the golden opportunity presented to her she grabbed it. She was not just happy but eager to serve him and his young family. Cameron was just a few months old then. Her best friends Cheng and Joo, who were also *amahs* but working for Chinese families, were horrified at first. Their eyes bulging with curiosity they'd asked, 'Do they insist that you bring your own utensils to cook your own food?'

'No,' Su Yin had replied. 'They don't.'

'That is surprising,' said Joo. 'Many of them think that we are inferior to them or that our eating from the same pots would contaminate their food. You know that sister who works on the other side of the city, well, she has to use her own utensils.' She screwed her face.

'There you go,' said Su Yin, 'it says a lot about this couple I am going to work for.'

'You won't have to cook their kind of food, do you?' asked Cheng. 'Which might mean you eating it and then you would definitely have to cook your own food. I heard that their cuisine is boring. Easy to cook but nothing like ours. Then again it would make life a lot easier for you.'

Before Su Yin could answer Joo leapt in, 'Aren't you scared that those communist jungle fighters would come and set fire to the house or something? I've heard so many stories of violence against the Europeans. They might even attack you just because you work for them!'

'Ironic, isn't it,' replied Su Yin, 'that the people this man fought alongside in the jungle during the Japanese Occupation are now waging war against him and his kind to get rid of them?' Su Yin shook her head. 'But don't worry, it is not as if the house is in the jungle or on a plantation,' she continued. 'That would be dangerous. We are well out of reach. Besides the boss knows the jungle well and he will be careful not to attract their attention. He works in some department in the city, something to do with town planning. It has to do with sanitation and building of houses. Couldn't be safer.'

'It is a magnificent looking house from what I have seen from the street,' said Cheng. 'I know the sister who used to look after the Chinese family that lived there before, years ago.'

Joo shaking her head said, 'You like to live dangerously. I wish you would reconsider the job.'

'I don't think I can. Mr Lok has already released me and we can't go back on our agreement,' said Su Yin. 'Besides there aren't many jobs around.'

Cheng chuckled, 'Maybe you can tell us if these foreigners smell different.'

Su Yin couldn't wait to start working for the English-speaking foreigners.

Chapter 8

Of all the houses that Su Yin had worked and lived in, the MacAlpine's residence was definitely the one she liked most. Located at the edge of city and far enough away from the jungle, the eight-bedroomed one-storey house was raised off the ground on stilts in the traditional Malay style. The stilts allowed circulation of air under and around the building to keep it cool which was one of the pleasing features, as she sometimes found the heat and humidity quite oppressive. The white-painted wooden walls with shutters and the polished teak floor throughout the house imparted a feel of coolness especially when walking barefoot on it. The brown teak floor extended to the wide veranda which ran along the sides and the front with bamboo blinds to keep out the sun. Halfway at the front, a set of concrete steps led down from the main entrance of the house to the drive that swept up from the gate in an arc around a neat lawn, punctuated by oases of red and orange canna lilies, palm trees and bamboos. Fortunately for Su Yin, a Malay woman came once a week to help clean the house.

The kitchen was Su Yin's domain. Located in the right wing of the house, it was a large space with all the modern conveniences she'd never dreamt were possible. She was looking out of the large window in front of the large enamel sink with a wooden draining board. It faced the east which offered her a few moments of the pleasure of watching the sun rise before the day's chores swamped her. To the right of the window were shelves of her sparkling pots, pans and woks that she was fussy about and meticulously scrubbed after use, bamboo steamers and a round wooden chopping board. Hanging on the wall were her trusted cleaver, various ladles and bamboo colanders. And beside them a Chinese lunar calendar that the grocery shop gave away at Chinese New Year which was useful because of its listed festivals. A fridge and cupboards lined the wall to the left and facing it on the opposite wall were clean, almost new-looking electric cookers and the new *G.E.C.* oven that had only recently come on the market. Mr MacAlpine had bought it specially for Mrs MacAlpine because she loved baking and had taught Su Yin how to make bread because she complained that the local bread tasted different - 'too sweet and airy, like eating cotton wool'. Standing in the middle of the kitchen was a large square wooden table where she, and sometimes the children, ate.

The signs were for another warm day, a clear blue sky sparsely dotted with cotton wool balls of clouds. Su Yin was grateful for the breeze blowing through the house as she looked out at the washing on the bamboo poles flapping against the lush verdant lawn edged with a parade of fan-shaped palm trees and a majestic old frangipani tree along a wire fence; in the horizon were the blue-green mountains of the Main Range. In the shade of the frangipani tree sat Muthusamy the Tamil gardener, his glistening ebony-coloured face just visible above a low shrub of bougainvillea, taking a well-earned break. He had cut the grass long before the sun got hotter making sure there were no stagnant pools of water for mosquitoes to breed and that was before James MacAlpine left for work in the blue Vauxhall driven by the loquacious Ah Hock. She could hear old Hassan the peon sweeping the concrete floor in the right wing of the house beneath the wooden floor in the kitchen. She walked from the window to the humming fridge.

The fridge was one of the wonders of modern times to her. Since it had been installed, life had become so much easier. No more melting butter at breakfast. And no more sour milk after it had been bought from Cold Storage, the only shop in town that stocked chilled dairy products for European consumption. Although he never complained before Mr MacAlpine could now enjoy his breakfast of toast with butter and jam washed down with a cup of tea with fresh milk instead of evaporated or powdered milk. Starvation during the Japanese Occupation while isolated in the jungle had inculcated a distinct appreciation and gratitude for food and while he had assimilated many of the local customs and ways, breaking fast with sticky congee or stuffed paratha and dal curry was not one of them. 'I'd devour a curry anytime but not at breakfast,' he had said to Helen after he had come home from a breakfast meeting with his Indian colleagues at a curry house. Helen, on the other hand, turned her nose up on congee for breakfast to which James had laughingly pointed out: 'Darling, the congee is not much different from the porridge you like back home; it just has more bits in it like dried prawns and chopped spring onions.'

Because of the heat, the four children, Cameron, Lexie, Ellie and Thomas, loved their chilled squashes in spite of Su Yin constantly advocating drinking boiled water. Her own old flask of hot water stood on the table by the fridge for her own consumption. Having the fridge also saved time by not having to go to the market every day. Today was one of those days she didn't have to go shopping. And as it was Friday she would have the afternoon soap opera *Forever Yours* on the transistor radio to look forward to. She couldn't wait to find out what secret the woman in the story had been harbouring.

Su Yin opened the fridge and took out a bowl of mutton that she had already cut into pieces to cook a curry. The other ingredients – garlic, onions, curry leaves that Muthusamy had picked for her from his bush in the garden and the spices wrapped in coconut leaf – were out on the table. When she first learnt to cook curry it had surprised her how easy it was especially as the spices had been specially prepared by the Indian seller in the market, a black-skinned man with his head wobbling like it was on a pivot. Just the right amount of chilli for Mr MacAlpine's taste; just enough to 'set off fireworks in his mouth' as he put it. Thankfully the rest of the family also enjoyed a curry even though the youngest, Thomas, was unsure. She had heard many stories from other domestic servants of how fussy some of their charges could be, demanding a different meal which meant they then had to spend more time cooking something more to the children's taste. Su Yin reckoned she had a good deal working for the MacAlpine family who were the third family she had worked for since coming to Malaya. Unlike some of the other domestics who had categorically refused to work for Europeans although they paid better she had had no qualms, armed with just a cluster of English words. She had often wondered if her father might have reservations because of his anti-foreigners' feelings following the invasion of China and its humiliation at the hands of the various European powers. She had been philosophical as she'd hoped her father would be: she needed to work in order to be independent and to send money home to him for all the family. Both Mr and Mrs MacAlpine were good and considerate to her. She couldn't complain. When she started working for them there were only Mr and Mrs MacAlpine and baby Cameron or Cammy as he was often called. Now with four children she sometimes grumbled that there was too much washing and ironing to do even though the bedlinen went to the dhobi. The children thought nothing of throwing off the sweat-soaked clothes for dry ones, which could be twice a day.

She was just about to start on the preparation for the curry when she heard small footsteps hurrying along the corridor heading towards the kitchen. She turned to see Ellie's smiling face framed by shoulder-length blonde hair. Ellie holding up a hairbrush called out to Su Yin, 'Good morning, Amah!'

Su Yin had long grown used to her new name of Amah. Two features distinguished her and her fellow workers from Kwangtung. The first was their uniform - black silk pantaloons and white cotton mandarin-collared top, hence their being referred to as the black-and-white brigade. The second was their name of *amah.* She didn't mind the name for whilst it set them apart as servants it rang of respect as it was what Cantonese children would call their mothers.

'Good morning,' Su Yin said proud of the sound of her own response. None of the other domestics she knew could speak English. 'Good morning' were among the first English words Helen MacAlpine taught her when she joined the family. Helen, a teacher of music in Edinburgh before she arrived in Malaya realised that Su Yin's invaluable help could be enhanced by a common language so she offered to teach her. Su Yin leapt at the chance to learn. Until then communication had been through James MacAlpine who spoke Cantonese and Malay almost flawlessly while Su Yin offered up a few words which she had surreptitiously picked up from the Chinese children of one of her previous employers when they were doing their English homework. The first lessons had started like this:

Su Yin, in a monotonous voice: 'I no want to go.'

Helen, in a melodic voice a couple of octaves higher than Su Yin's: 'It is "I *don't* want to go".'

Su Yin: 'Okay, I *know*.'

Mrs MacAlpine: 'No, it is I *don't* want to go.'

Su Yin exasperated: 'I know. I *don* want to go.'

They'd burst out giggling and Su Yin quickly overcame her initial embarrassment at her difficulty of curling her tongue round some of the words; her childhood dream was being fulfilled. Since she moved in with the family her command of the language had improved with help from the children who quickly accepted her unique way.

Su Yin looked down and smiled at Ellie's impish face now close to her waist, her round eyes were blue like her father's, her nose slightly snub like her mother's and there was a missing top tooth when she smiled. The sight of the little innocent face lightly speckled with freckles always warmed her heart. Ellie, who had only just celebrated her fourth birthday, was wearing the white short-sleeved blouse and polka dot shorts that Su Yin had put out for her. Su Yin asked, 'Now what you want?' She asked although she knew exactly what Ellie wanted; it was a game they played every morning while getting ready to go to kindergarten. Ellie held the brush up to her.

'Please, can you comb my hair?' Ellie said.

'Okay,' said Su Yin as she took the brush from Ellie, 'we go into *udder loom*.' They walked past the large table in the middle of the kitchen which had already been set for breakfast. 'Lexie sleeping?' Su Yin asked. Ellie nodded. Ushered out of the kitchen, Ellie started to skip, her footsteps echoing softly along the long corridor which separated the games and dining rooms on the left on the front half of the house and three bedrooms on the right before the large atrium which was the main reception or living room. Beyond it to the left of the corridor were the study and master bedroom, while to the right were more bedrooms.

They walked past the first door on the right which was the door to Su Yin's room. The location of her room was significant and meant a lot to Su Yin as servants and domestic help were usually housed in the annex at the back of the house, near the kitchen. But Helen MacAlpine was different; she wanted Su Yin to be near the children. When Ellie and Su Yin got to the second door which was ajar they entered the room to find Lexie stirring in her bed under the mosquito net on the far side of the room. Su Yin walked over to the windows and opened the window shutters. She caught a hint of jasmine perfume from the bushes under the windows. '*Aiyahh,* sleepy head, wake up,' said Su Yin. 'You late for *blekfast.*'

Lexie who was a taller double of Ellie for the one-year difference in age stretched her arms and yawned. 'Good morning Amah,' she called out brightly.

'Good, good, good. Better if you get up, or late for school' said Su Yin with a hint of laughter in her voice. 'Quick before *Mamee* come.'

'Quick, I can hear Mummy!' Ellie pretended as she leapt on to her own bed and then swung her legs to the side facing Lexie who had sat up and was rubbing her eyes.

'Come, I comb your hair Ellie,' Su Yin sat down beside Ellie. She started to brush her hair. As she held the silky blonde hair in her hand she was, for the briefest moment, transported back to the silk factory back home in China. Six years ago when she first touched baby Cammy's straw-coloured hair the feeling of its silkiness immediately reminded her of the silk threads she used to handle. She had cried for it'd brought back memories of her youth and intensified her longing to see her family again. Since then the pain and sadness associated with brushing the children's hair had been muted; there were more children to look after and more work to do. No time for day dreams, no time for sentiments.

'I really hear Mummy coming,' Ellie strained her neck towards the door. At the same time, they heard the sound of a car coming up the drive. Lexie had dived into the adjoining toilet. Then Thomas came running into the bedroom, his face beaming as he shouted, 'Mah, Mah!' and charged into Su Yin's open arms. Su Yin lifted him up and gave him a big hug.

Helen MacAlpine walked in. 'So this is where you've been hiding. Good morning, Amah,' she said smiling. Before Su Yin met Helen she had expected a tall big-boned woman, horse-faced, like the European women she had seen from a distance years ago. But Helen was nothing like what she had imagined: she was slim and dainty even though she was taller than Su Yin. Her face was heart-shaped with a small snub nose and brown eyes. Until then Su Yin had thought that all Europeans had blue eyes like James MacAlpine. It was that hint of mischief in her eyes that warmed Su Yin to her. Her skin was fair and pink, her hair was chestnut- brown and long. Her skin was now as brown as the natives' and her hair was short and newly-permed accentuating the heart shape of her tanned face. Su Yin approved of the fact that it was not painted heavily with make-up like some of her European counterparts. Despite four pregnancies she had managed to hold on to her slim figure. She looked cool in a white broderie anglaise dress gathered at the waist with a red patent leather belt.

'Good morning, Mrs Makapeen,' said Su Yin. Although at the start Helen MacAlpine had insisted on her calling her Helen, Su Yin had obstinately stood her ground. 'No,' she had said softly but firmly, 'You boss lady. I servant.' And so it had been Mrs Makapeen ever since.

'Did I hear Ah Hock coming?' asked Helen.

'Yes. I better go get Cammy for school. Don't want to be late,' Su Yin put Thomas down on the floor, finished brushing Ellie's hair and tied it into a ponytail.

'We'd better move, children. Come on Lexie!' said Helen as Su Yin went off to get Cammy who to her surprise was already up and dressed in his school uniform - white short-sleeved shirt and navy-blue shorts with white socks and lace-up plimsolls. At six Cammy was taller than all the children in his class and often mistaken to be older. At first he'd hated going to school where he stood out not only because of his height but because of his appearance. When he first entered the classroom, the sea of faces of various shades of brown - Chinese, Malay and Indian - with open mouths had stared at him. Then the boys sniggered as they pointed at his blonde hair and fair skin. But very quickly he realised that once the initial curiosity wore off the children simply accepted him as one of their own. Now he couldn't wait to go to school. He was packing in his satchel the new catapult that Muthusamy the gardener had taught him how to make from a choice tembusu branch.

'*Wah,* you up! Good. Come eat *blekfast,*' said Su Yin. Cammy held a special place in Su Yin's heart. When she first held him in her arms she was fascinated by the fairness of his skin; his cute little face melted her heart right away especially when he smiled at her. Before Cammy she had brought up other babies, Chinese ones, but none grabbed her as Cammy did. It was the way he accepted her even though she was different from him and his parents. He'd stroked the red birthmark on her left jawline when he started to notice it and then he asked what it was just as the other children before him did. 'I *deen* wash myself *ploperly*, that's why,' she would say. 'So you must wash yourself *ploperly*,' – a warning that worked when the children were little. Because Cammy's parents entertained and socialised frequently in the early years, he was more or less left in her sole care thus strengthening the bond between servant and charge. What made Cammy stand out was that he had an even temperament coupled with a strong sense of fairness and respect for elders which endeared him to Su Yin.

The window shutters were open. Cammy's toy cars, boxes of games and storybooks were carefully arranged on the selves of the book case standing in front of the large window. The mosquito net over his bed had already been neatly gathered and tied into a knot like Cammy had always seen Su Yin do.

'Hello 'Mah, we are going to have a competition today,' said Cammy.

'*Competition*? What means?' asked Su Yin.

Cammy pulled out his catapult from his satchel and pulled at the rubber band of the catapult. 'Play with friends. See who wins.'

'*Aaww,*' Su Yin nodded, delighted that she could add another word to her expanding vocabulary. 'I understand. *Kom.pa..tee..sion*,' she repeated. 'Come, eat *blekfast*. Ah Hock here now, waiting to go to school.'

Su Yin heard James come into the house. She was pleased. His work as an engineer in the Municipal Council responsible for the Town and Planning took him everywhere where his priority was the sanitation and the building of houses. Usually he was able to come home for lunch but hadn't done so for two weeks. So when Helen told her he was coming home she cooked his favourite curry for him. She walked into the corridor to see him bending down to give Helen a kiss. Unlike the first time when she felt her face go hot and didn't know where to look, the sight of their affectionate greeting no longer embarrassed her after all these years. When James saw Su Yin he called out in Cantonese, 'Hello, Amah! I am ready for lunch!'

Su Yin looked at the couple. She thought Helen looked pleased. As for James his tanned face which contrasted with his blonde hair was relaxed and cheerful. He was wearing a white short-sleeved shirt and beige linen trousers with his pistol tucked in at his waist. Since the Emergency was declared in 1948, and the attacks on the mining and estate personnel had mounted James started carrying a pistol. 'That's good. It is ready,' Su Yin said, pointing to the dining room where the table had been set and went back into the kitchen to dish out the curry and rice.

After Su Yin had put the food down on the table and started to walk away she heard Helen say, 'You know I worry when you are away for any length of time.'

'You mustn't worry, love, 'said James as he spooned some curry onto his plate. 'It is just scaremongering on the part of the guerrillas. None of the others in the office is particularly worried. We've just got to be careful that's all. Not go outside town or too near the jungle. I'll be careful.' He took her hand and kissed it.

'But that's just it. You go out of town. You drive to K.T. As far as I am concerned it is at the other end of the world,' said Helen her voice started to tremble. K.T. (for Kota Tinggi town) was two hundred miles away in the state of Johore at the southernmost tip of the peninsula where communist activities were rife. The Jungle Warfare School there was where he taught survival skills in the jungle to the new recruits, soldiers directly from Britain who had never seen a jungle let alone been in it.

'You mustn't worry. I never travel there alone as you know.'

Su Yin eyed the little alarm clock on the top of the fridge again; it was four minutes to two. She hurriedly switched on the transistor in the laundry room adjoining the kitchen where she started to sort out a mountain of washed clothes. Next to it was a rectangular table which was laid out with a folded blanket topped with a cotton layer ready for her to do the ironing on. The electric iron - another of the modern inventions she was grateful for – was plugged in and waiting. No more the old-fashioned iron which had to be filled with smouldering charcoal and then care taken not to smudge the clothes with the ashes. On the dot at two o'clock, the sound of the opening bars of Tchaikovsky's Piano Concerto Number One filled the air; she felt as if she was being lifted away. The music signalled the opening of the afternoon Cantonese soap opera that she had been looking forward to. Hers ears pricked up and soon she was lost in the drama as it unfolded.

About halfway into the story she was startled by loud voices from the dining room. She frowned. She turned down the volume of the transistor and strained to hear, but the talking had stopped. She shook her head and turned up the volume again, pleased that she had not lost track of the saga.

When the opera finally ended half an hour later, Su Yin turned off the radio. It was her cue to clear up after lunch. She couldn't help wondering what the heated discussion over lunch was about but she was sure that any differences between Mr and Mrs MacAlpine would be smoothed over and a line drawn under it with a kiss. She went into the dining room and just as she'd expected, the couple had finished eating and gone into the living room to sit under the fan for a while before James went out again back to work. After clearing up she returned to her ironing and then before long she was cooking again.

As she was stringing the long beans at the table, her mind wandering as usual, the raised voices she'd heard earlier popped up. She was baffled. In all the time she had been with the family, she had rarely heard the couple arguing. But she knew that wasn't because they didn't argue like other married couples did. They were simply more discreet and she liked and respected that. She wondered if it was about the children or if Mrs MacAlpine was trying to impress on Mr MacAlpine how concerned she was about the news she had read of the guerrillas now vociferously targeting Europeans. Su Yin herself was concerned. There was no way she would find out the real reason for the row and, looking at the clock, she realised she had to hurry if she was to finish cooking in time to help wash the children when they came in from school, serve dinner, then clean up the kitchen. There was a mountain of laundry to wash and some sewing to do before she had a shower. All the chores had to be cleared before she could meet Cheng and Joo. More than anything else she hoped that there would be a letter from her parents waiting for her.

Chapter 9

The one perk that the MacAlpines offered Su Yin was a day off a week. It was much more than any domestic could hope for. The norm was one or two days a month so she knew she was better off than most of her sisters in the same role. On the first Saturday of the month she would meet up with Cheng and Joo. As usual, James MacAlpine's chauffer Ah Hock would drive her to meet them in the city. The meeting place was twenty minutes' walk away at a brisk pace and she could easily manage it but James had insisted on Ah Hock driving her; he was concerned about her going out and definitely about coming home late as the curfew was in place for fear of terrorist attacks. The three friends had been meeting in the same coffee shop for years where they could sit and catch up on the latest news as they watched the rest of the world saunter by. But first they would meet at the *coolie fong* or workers' room where she would pick up her letters from her parents.

Su Yin had changed out of her black and white uniform into a pale floral-print *samfoo*, still wearing her hair in a bun and was sitting in the passenger seat beside Ah Hock, carrying the cloth patchwork bag that her sister Mei had made for her. Ah Hock whose youthful looks belied his fifty-five years had looked approvingly at Su Yin when she got into the car. He appreciated Su Yin not wanting to sit at the back because, she said, she was not his boss but an employee like him. She on the other hand was very grateful that he would drive her saving her precious time. They spoke in Cantonese which Ah Hock had mastered although his mother tongue was the Hokkien dialect. As a second generation Chinese in Malaya – his parents were from the Province of Fukien in South-East China - he spoke several dialects and Malay. His only primary school education afforded him sufficient command of English so that he was able to work for Europeans. He started working for James MacAlpine a year or so after Su Yin took charge of James' household. Slender and tall with a straight back, Ah Hock always wore white short-sleeved shirts and khaki trousers whenever he turned up for work clutching his neatly folded newspaper the *Nanyang* Daily News which he would always leave for her when he had finished with it. His shiny black hair sparsely streaked with silver was neatly pasted down with *Brylcreem* the scent of which Su Yin had come to like. He was always punctual and kept his boss's pale blue Vauxhall sparkling clean. Although he didn't talk much about it he once told Su Yin that his younger brother was killed by the Japanese. His brother who was mentally slow did not bow immediately when the Japanese soldiers ordered him and the friends he was with to kowtow. Taking his hesitation to mean defiance, one of the soldiers rammed his bayonet into his chest. When Ah Hock found out that James had fought the Japanese he was immediately won over by him.

When they first met Su Yin immediately noticed Ah Hock's left hand had an extra digit hanging limply at the side of his little finger and then was embarrassed when he held up the hand and said with a smile, 'When I was a child my mother always said to me that I was special to have this extra finger although I couldn't fathom why I was special!' To Su Yin he was special because he was a kind and gentle man which put him above most people she had come across.

As they pulled out of the drive they heard the sound of a siren. From the right a jeep sped past them carrying half a dozen Malay policemen looking very solemn and lethargic, hunched over the butts of their rifles.

'What is it now I wonder?' Ah Hock asked as he carefully turned left towards the city. 'Another arrest was made yesterday. A rubber tapper, a woman, who was caught carrying a bag of rice under her blouse pretending she was pregnant!'

'The punishment is severe, isn't it?' asked Su Yin.

'Yes, it can be death by hanging depending on the circumstances,' answered Ah Hock. 'I don't know what those communists are playing at. They may be hurting the British army but they are also making it difficult for us. It makes the Malays and British suspicious of us Chinese. The war is long over and we should get on with our life.'

'These informers and the ones who supply the terrorists, they must believe in their cause to risk their lives like that,' said Su Yin.

'That's just it,' said Ah Hock, 'ideology doesn't come into it. They are intimidated and terrified by the communists who don't think twice about killing the suppliers' innocent relatives if they don't comply.'

'Back home in China,' said Su Yin, 'communism has swamped the people. All the average person wants is a reasonable life and not worry about whether there would be a bowl of rice on the table. If the new regime could deliver that people would happily go about their work.'

After a short silence Ah Hock asked, 'You are expecting a letter from your family today?'

Su Yin turned to look at his profile and realised that she was no longer drawn to his left hand which was resting lightly on the wheel. 'Yes, I want to know how my mother is doing. She has not been well.'

'I hope she is better. It must be so worrying…' Ah Hock stopped abruptly on realising he wasn't helping matters. 'Now to the coolie room,' he said brightly. After a while as they were cruising along he said, 'It is good that you have your friends.'

'They are very good friends, more like sisters. I don't know where I would be without them,' said Su Yin. She and her two friends Joo and Cheng had indeed grown very close. Their friendship - born of the need for family - was forged on the first day they met in the coolie room, thrown together in an alien country where they knew no one. It was built on solidarity of an army of women – the sisterhood – in search of employment and bound by the tie of shared values. The friendship provided solace when homesickness mercilessly struck. They had comforted each other when back in China various members of their families were killed by the Japanese. Cheng was the youngest of them all by a year and the tallest. Her formless black and white uniform did not detract from her pretty slim face or her gracefulness when she moved – her dark brown eyes were rounder than the average almond shape, her cheek bones prominent and her nose narrow and more pointed than the typical Chinese nose. In Joo and Su Yin's estimation her seductive and alluring smile belied her shy nature which she had gradually overcome. With her good looks she could have been married several times over and her father, a local wine merchant, had wanted to marry her off to one of his friends. But Cheng had insisted on being independent; she had seen how her older sisters had been married off and kept silent about their misery. She put up a hard fight and with support from her mother who was her father's second wife he backed down. In the end, she went to work in a silk factory just like Su Yin had.

Joo and Su Yin were born two months apart in the spring of the same year. As the eldest of four boys and four girls Joo was left to help bring her siblings up when her mother died in childbirth and work in a silk factory to supplement her father's meagre income as a vegetable gardener. Of the three friends Joo was the shortest and slight giving the impression of being frail but Su Yin and Cheng knew that she was by far stronger than either of them; they had seen her carry two buckets of water, one at each end of a pole over her shoulder during the time of water rationing after a season of drought. She had a plain face which was oval-shaped and her mouth curled down at the corners giving her a stern look. But when she smiled her eyes twinkled and when she spoke her voice was warm and inviting unlike many of the loud bellows that came out of many mouths of the women they encountered. Her voice matched her kindness and compassion making her a valued friend.

Su Yin turned to Ah Hock. 'How is your wife?' she asked. 'Is she feeling better now?'

'Yes, yes, she has got over the cold. She complains about this heat and humidity, not good for health,' Ah Hock replied.

'I agree. You can feel not just the heat from the sun but also the heat rising from the ground.'

'Yes, that is bad. Causes so much sickness.'

They drove along a wide recently macadamised road bounded by shops on both sides. Su Yin always looked forward to going into the city. Shops reminiscent of those in China were already bustling with shoppers. At the shop entrances, on the five-foot way, rolls of bright-coloured fabric, gunnysacks of dried produce of mushrooms, salted fish and prawns, alongside stacks of handwoven baskets. Through the open window of the car she could smell the air infused with a mixture of spices and new textiles. A goldsmith's shop glittered with its shiny glass cases of gold and precious stone jewellery. In another, shoes filled every inch of space and overflowed onto the five-foot way. Restaurants were heaving with impatient and hungry customers. The bicycle repair shop was open and two young men could be seen busy working on a couple of bicycles. Next door was the bank - the Overseas Chinese Bank – with a Malay guard in uniform cradling a rifle standing on duty at its entrance. Keeping out of the hot sun shoppers and non-shoppers alike were scuttling along the five-foot way. What never ceased to amaze Su Yin was seeing the mix of different races on the streets with their distinctive flamboyant and colourful clothes. She noticed particularly the women. Malay women - their heads covered with headscarves - wore loose tunics over multi-coloured batik-prints sarongs. They were dark-skinned and had pretty delicate features and a ready smile. A group of half a dozen or so Tamil women in their sarees – vibrant purple, gold, red and yellow - were probably out in town on their precious one free day off work from the rubber plantations like herself and her friends. Pink-skinned European women – their colour depending on how long they had been in the country - flounced in short dresses showing off more flesh than the local women. Peppered amongst the shoppers and workers were the ubiquitous police - Malay and Sikh policemen in khaki uniform, the Sikh ones distinguished by their greater stature, their turbans and beards. In between was the strident presence of the British government Officers, plantation owners and light-suited owners of big businesses going about their day's work. Dozens of trishaws were racing through the street carrying passengers and their morning's shopping while motorcars weaved slowly between them.

On the opposite side of the road, halfway down the row of shops was interrupted by a tract of rubble where three shops used to stand – one of the few remaining reminders of the Japanese attack on the city. Ten families were killed in that bombing. Now a scraggy-looking hibiscus shrub stood proudly in the middle of the arid mess where half a dozen or so children were playing. The clearing and rebuilding of the city was the job of James MacAlpine's department. The latest news was that infestation of rats in deserted bombsites had reduced and the building of new and the clearing of existing monsoon drains had averted flooding in some areas much to the relief of shop owners. Su Yin noticed two Malay policemen with rifles slung over their shoulders. She had learnt that they were called *mata-mata* in Malay, noting that it might be a useful word to know should she need to call for police assistance. Apart from that the few words she needed to know were culinary ones like *assam* for tamarind, *ayam* for chicken and *pedas* for hot when she had to buy her spices at the Indian stall in the market.

She had come to know the city area quite well but she had not been elsewhere except for that one time she visited the Cameron Highlands north of the city. She had gone with Mr Lok and family to their family holiday home there where it was much cooler, fresh and clean. The atmosphere was more relaxed and sedate. The tea plantations with their neat rows of lush green bushes on the hillslopes had reminded her of home, of the hills and the mulberry bushes. One thing she missed was the waterways and rivers which crisscrossed her village. She had made a mental note to go to the Klang riverside one day which was not far from the city.

As they approached the crossroad, without looking Su Yin became aware of the pawnshop to her right. It irritated her that each time she came this way she was reminded. She didn't need reminding that something that belonged to her was there somewhere in the shop waiting for her to redeem it. After the crossroad, they passed the site where the blackened half of the old town hall building had stood with its other half, partially collapsed, covered in lush creepers out of which sprung a tall tree. The land had been cleared and there was talk that the Merchants' Association was going to build their headquarters there.

When they arrived at a block of two-storey shop-houses at the end of the busy area, Ah Hock stopped the car. Opposite the block was a primary school - single storey building in the middle of a large grassy compound where a Malay man was busy cutting the grass while another wearing a handkerchief over his nose and mouth was spraying DDT insecticide at the thick undergrowth along the edge of the grounds as part of the campaign to wipe out mosquitoes. At the entrance to the stairs that led to the coolie room a wiry old man and a dark-skinned grey-bearded man wearing a white turban were deep in conversation as a lean stray dog covered in fleas hovered around sniffing for food.

Chapter 10

No one knew exactly who owned the coolies' room on the top floor of the shophouse but it had always been there for the use of new female immigrants while they waited for a job to turn up, a stop-gap. It was said that the owner was himself from China and had done well, so well that he wanted to help those who came after him. Apart from the occupants who came and went, the room hadn't changed much in the twenty years that Su Yin and her friends had been meeting there except that it was dingier than it used to be. It didn't matter, for the room was vital to them. It was their lifeline because this was where new arrivals could make friends and, more importantly, receive news from their families back home. A tin box nailed to the wall by the door was where all the letters were held. The only item in the room that had been changed was the Chinese calendar on the wooden wall with a new cross added marking another day gone and hopefully another day nearer to getting work, if not, it served as a reminder of how long they had been away from home. Next to it was a square mirror; there was nothing else, not even a picture to brighten the place. Every inch of space was utilised in the large rectangular room; there were five bunkbeds without mattresses. Instead straw mats were laid over the wooden slats. On each bed a neatly folded quilted blanket sat on a pillow and beside it a small pile of folded clothes belonging to the occupant of the bed. The less lucky ones would sleep on the floor. By one of the windows was a small square table with four wooden stools.

As Su Yin, Cheng and Joo entered the coolie room the first thing that greeted them was the same smell of incense from the burning of joss sticks that went with offerings of ardent prayers from the room's occupants to the goddess Kwan Yin. Prayers for their loved ones left behind in China and prayers for speedy employment for themselves. The second thing was the animated chatter amongst four young women who were sitting at the table by the window. As soon as they saw Su Yin, Cheng and Joo they stopped talking and greeted them. There was a look of relief on their faces. The youngest one of them quickly stood up; she was wearing a plain blue *samfoo* and her hair tied up in a ponytail unlike the other three whose hair was in a bun. She held out the letter she had been holding close to her.

'Big Sister, please will you read this for me?' she asked, her voice trembling.

Su Yin recognised her pretty face; although she had not read for her before she remembered that she'd arrived over a month ago and was from a village just outside Canton. Meeting someone from near her home had the effect of bringing home closer to her. They had talked about where they came from. 'Of course, I will,' Su Yin replied taking the letter from her. There was a perceptible sigh of relief from the younger woman as she moved to let Su Yin sit on the stool she had been sitting on. Su Yin sat down while Cheng and Joo went directly to the mailbox. She was dying to find out if there was a letter for her but it would have to wait. She could feel the anxiety and eagerness of the woman and she recalled how she herself had been anxious like her when she first arrived. She set her bag on the table and read out the name on the envelope, 'Tong Ah Mui?'

Tong Ah Mui nodded furiously. 'Yes, that is me,' she said breathlessly, 'I can read and write my name.'

Su Yin opened the letter and started to read slowly:

Mui,

we pray and hope you are safe and well. Both your mother and I are in good health. The weather has been kind so we have been able to grow vegetables to sell in the market. Your brothers have started going to school. They need books. Your sister is now working in an electrical factory. Your grandmother says to keep safe and look after yourself.
Your father

Su Yin looked up at Mui to see tears running down her cheeks. She felt a twinge in her heart recalling her own misery all those years ago when she left home and set sail for a new life but she had no idea what or where she was going to – *Malaya* was only a name to her – and no assurance that she would ever see her family again. She had been very frightened. It was worse than stepping off the edge of a cliff. She reached out and patted Mui's arm. 'At least they are in good health. You will get a job soon,' Su Yin tried to sound optimistic. 'Don't worry. Waiting is part of the game.' She couldn't tell her that she was given a job two weeks after arriving but the wait had been agonising and had seem interminable. 'Do you want to reply to your father's letter?'

Mui wiped her tears away then a look of embarrassment crossed her face. 'Big Sister, I haven't got much money to pay you.'

'No, no,' Su Yin waved her hand, 'you don't need to pay me. Come, let us write to your father and tell him all your news.' She pulled out a writing pad and a ballpoint pen from her bag and waited for Mui to compose her response.

When Su Yin finished writing she looked up at Mui's sad face. Clenching both fists in front of her she said,

'Hang on to all your memories of your family and home, they will comfort you when you are low.'

Before long, Su Yin had read the letters and written their replies for the other three women who had been waiting patiently.

'Ladies,' in his usual hearty voice, Mr Teng the middle-aged Cantonese proprietor with a pot-belly bowed as he greeted Su Yin, Cheng and Joo. 'There's your table.' He pointed to the table in the corner at the far end of the coffee shop which was heaving with customers tucking into their food.

'Thank you, Boss. How are you?' said Cheng.

'Can't complain as long as I can make a living,' Mr Teng said with a big smile.

'And how is your good wife?'

'As usual. She nags at me all the time,' the proprietor answered with a laugh.

'Well, at least she looks after you well,' responded Cheng nodding at his pot-belly. He laughed some more.

'Here are your letters,' Su Yin sat down at the table and handed each a letter. They ordered a cup of coffee from a young Chinese waiter who'd quickly appeared at their table and after making sure that the table was dry all three of them carefully placed their letters on it and proceeded to open them. Su Yin read hers, slowly taking in every word in the letter written by her father. Her eyes glistened and then a tear rolled down her cheek. Joo and Cheng waited nervously. Then Joo reached out and touched Su Yin's hand.

'Is everything alright or not?' she asked softly. Su Yin could only nod as she suppressed a sob.

'That's good,' Joo and Cheng said in unison.

'Is your mother better?' asked Cheng.

'Yes, she is,' Su Yin sniffed and then smiled. 'She is back on her feet again. She can walk about now. Thank Heaven.'

'Will you read mine?' asked Cheng tentatively holding out to Su Yin her letter that she had already opened.

Su Yin took it and read it out to Cheng who listened intently, swallowing every word that Su Yin read. When she had finished, Cheng let out a sigh. 'Good, all is well,' she nodded beaming.

When Su Yin started on Joo's letter and came to the part that said her niece had secured a place at university Joo burst into tears. Then the biggest smile covered her face. 'I have been waiting for this ever since I knew she was interested in studying,' Joo said. 'And I don't even know what she is going to study.'

'Economics,' said Su Yin.

'It sounds clever. Whatever it is I am sure she will do better than me and all my sisters and brothers put together,' said Joo with pride in her voice.

'Well done you,' said Su Yin.

'On that happy note, shall we have something to eat?' said Joo, 'I am hungry and the smell of the satay out there is too tempting.' Out on the five-foot way in the shade of the awning was the same Malay man who had been there grilling skewers of spiced chicken and beef ever since the three friends started coming to the coffee shop. It was here that they were introduced to the Malay style dish and to the spiciness of Malay cuisine. The man looked the same as he had always done, always in a brown shirt with sleeves rolled up, a check sarong wrapped over dark brown trousers and his traditional headgear, a black velvet *songkok*.

'This is a change from your usual! Are you sure you want to spend your money?' Cheng asked. Joo merely smiled.

'I am tempted...' Su Yin started. Her first instinct was to hold back like she had been doing for the last few outings. She wanted to put aside a bit more of her wages towards her fare home to see her family. It wasn't as if she thought she would have enough soon to afford the fare. Recently she had been sending home more than half her wages and in the last few months particularly she'd had to send even more to pay for her mother's operation and to buy a bike for one of the nephews so he could cycle to work. Working for the MacAlpines had improved her financial position by leaps and bounds. Of the eight dollars she was paid each month - which was nearly twice what she used to earn - she had sent at least five dollars to her parents. She had been able to save some of what she kept for her own upkeep which was modest; she didn't need much for herself apart from the three meals and the roof over her head. There was another more pressing reason for her to save; she had had to pawn her silk dress to pay for her mother's operation and now she was just a dollar and fifty cents short of what she needed to redeem it. But today she felt like throwing caution to the four corners of the earth. She was pleased with what she had been able to do so far for her family and for the first time in a long while felt that she now deserved a treat. She would enjoy a bit of her hard-earned cash; she could afford the two cents that the satay lunch would cost, she told herself. 'Yes, I will have some too. Let us celebrate. We work so hard, we deserve to enjoy a little. You agree?'

'Most definitely!' Cheng said.

'You are so right,' said Joo.

They each ordered a portion of chicken from the Malay satay-man and a glass of freshly squeezed sugar juice each from the Chinese man who was busy pushing the sugar canes through the mangle at his stall. As they were savouring their chargrilled chicken with spicy peanut sauce, Joo spoke, looking at Su Yin. 'That first young woman you read for, she is very pretty. If she is as good at working as she is pretty she will be snapped up quickly.'

Su Yin nodded as she continued chewing. 'We all remember how hard it was – the waiting, wondering if we would ever be called to work. I can't forget the despair at times. And worst, missing my family.'

'Yes, that was the worst bit. I also thought at one time: what if I died here? There would be no one from my family to bury me!' said Cheng. 'And would they know?'

Joo nodded; her face turned serious. 'I know we have no regrets about the choice we made…'

'You mean joining the sisterhood?' asked Cheng.

'Yes,' answered Joo, 'somehow I can't help feeling sorry for these young women.'

'Why? Sorry for what?' asked Cheng. She looked puzzled.

Joo didn't answer right away. She picked up another stick of chicken. 'What if they have made the wrong choice?'

'You don't feel that you have made the wrong choice, do you?' asked Cheng.

'No, but look at them. So young, but do they know what is ahead of them?'

'Does anybody?' said Cheng.

'I mean..'

'I think I know what Joo means,' said Su Yin. 'It is so final; once we are set on this path there is no altering the course. Now having come so far, we can look back and think that maybe a different course would have been better. But don't forget why we chose this option in the first place.'

'You are right,' said Cheng.

'We were so young then,' Joo said. 'I mean, seriously did you ever secretly regret? I know we never talked about it but did it ever cross your mind, maybe when you were drifting off to sleep, that maybe we took the wrong course?'

'Don't forget,' said Cheng, 'we had to declare our intention *not* to marry so we could be sure of our jobs, so we could shake off the dreaded match-makers, so we could be independent and not be slaves to men.'

'No, I haven't forgotten. How could I? I am just saying that we were so young then..'

'Yes, but not too young to have had half a dozen children if our parents and the men had their way!' a note of irritation had crept into Cheng's voice. For a few seconds no one spoke. Then Su Yin piped up,

'I remember worrying about the money running out before I got a job. What would I do when it did?' It was that particular worry that steeled her to cope with the frequent hunger. She remembered vividly wearing her purse tied to her waist, feeling it constantly, afraid to lose it and her bag which held all her worldly belongings. She remembered how she had worried and cried together with Joo and Cheng.

'Yes, me too. I hope the young women get a job soon,' said Joo. She then turned to the food on her plate. 'This peanut sauce is delicious.'

Just at that moment the restaurant turned dark as if someone had pulled a giant awning over it, as if someone had switched the daylight off. Outside, the morning's blue sky with brazen white clouds was now a surly grey like a canvas with grey paint splashed across it, waiting to vent on earth. A cold breeze swept into the restaurant. There was a great commotion as stall-keepers rushed to gather up their wares and cover their stalls. The three friends looked out of the coffee shop and saw the angry sky. It spelt thunderstorm. Suddenly there was a large crack of lightening quickly followed by a deafening roar of thunder like an avalanche of rocks across the sky. The three friends looked at the clock on the wall. Although it was not time to return to their employers' homes they knew that the rain would delay their return immeasurably. They hadn't expected this change in the weather. Their lightweight umbrellas which were more for protecting against the sun would be useless in the downpour that was to come. They looked at each other wondering what their next move should be when Joo lowered her voice and pointed towards the entrance of the coffee shop,

'*Ayy!* Look, it is your boss's chauffer. He's heading this way, Su Yin. Look!' Su Yin and Cheng swung round to look. 'He is earlier than usual, isn't he?'

Su Yin gasped. Ah Hock was weaving his way between the tables and coming towards them. Before she could speak he was standing a step away from her. 'Ah Hock, what are you doing here?' she spluttered.

'The sky is about to open so the boss asked me to fetch you and also take your friends home,' said Ah Hock with a smile. He handed Su Yin one of the two oil-papered umbrellas he was carrying. 'I will wait in the car until you are ready.' Without waiting for an answer he walked back the way he came.

'That man is so kind!' said Joo her eyes still trained on Ah Hock as he walked away slowly through the noisy restaurant.

'Are you talking about my boss or Ah Hock?' asked Su Yin.

'Both!' said Joo. 'You are so very lucky.' There was a tinge of envy in her voice.

'Yes, I know,' said Su Yin.

Chapter 11

Cammy, Lexie, Ellie and Thomas had shouted with joy when they saw Su Yin whom they had not expected to see back so soon. 'Oh good, Amah, you can put me to bed!' said Ellie holding Su Yin tightly round her waist. The family had been fed. The wok, pots and pans were scrubbed and dried, dishes were washed, dried and put away. The children were in bed and James and Helen had retreated to the living room for their quiet time together. The day was almost done for Su Yin.

Back in her room, she opened the window which faced the back garden and looked up at the full moon shining, a silver ball surrounded by stars like sparkling sequins. In the distance the silhouette of the leaves of the coconut trees danced with abandon. The air felt it had been washed and cleaned of its stickiness after the rain. She caught a hint of the sweet fragrance of the frangipani flowers and inhaled deeply. The wooden floor felt cool under her bare feet as she turned to walk to her chest of drawers by her bedside. On top of it stood two framed photographs, a round mirror and a jar of *Hazeline* face cream. She picked up the jar of cream and applied a tiny dot of the silvery cream on her face, a treat that she had only recently allowed herself. After gently rubbing the cream in she looked at the black and white photographs and picked up the larger of the two. It was a group photograph of the entire family that had multiplied since she left, three generations now arranged in two long rows for her benefit. Seated in the back row, in front of their house, were her parents and her brothers and their wives. Her grandfather's absence was starkly conspicuous; he died not long after celebrating his eighty-first birthday. Her father looked like her grandfather; he had grown a goatee like how his father had and now wore spectacles. Her mother looked weather-beaten, tiredness etched on her face despite the smile; her hair was still short and straight.

Her little brothers were now the young men in the photograph except that there were three instead of four of them. The missing brother was Peng who was killed when he joined the army to fight against the Japanese in 1937 at the age of nineteen. The bookworm of the family he could have done so much better than anyone else in the family. In her opinion he was the brightest of them all and she was determined to help him on the path to greater things by way of a good education. He had told her that he promised to make her proud of him. On the day before she left home he'd said to her, 'Second Sister, don't you worry, I will study hard. I want to become a vet one day. I want to look after animals like Papa's animals.' He had said it with such confidence, such certainty. And she didn't doubt that he could become a vet or anyone he wanted to be and it had made her all the more determined when she got a job to send as much money home as possible. She'd dreamt of the day he would achieve his ambition as she kept a close eye on his progress in school.

So how did he get caught up in this nationalistic passion? She could understand his passion remembering her own childish fantasy of going to battle in the footsteps of Hua Mu Lan to fight the invaders. She too had felt angry about her country being cut and diced to feed the greed of the British, French and Russian raiders. Her father had said Peng could not stop berating the foreigners. *Red-haired devils and thieves*, he'd called them. She couldn't imagine

Peng shaking his fist at the aggressors. By the time the second imperialistic threat loomed, Peng was already fired by a deep sense of nationalism along with many of his friends at university. He wanted to defend his country against the Japanese invasion and she had worried about him as she listened feverishly every day for news of the war in China. She waited for news from her father; he had kept her informed of the young men rallying to the Chinese leader Chiang Kai-Shek's call to fight the invaders. She had wished she could have been there to do something but she couldn't. She also knew she wouldn't have been able to stop him for she remembered him as a young boy who could be very stubborn and tenacious. Once he'd embarked on something - whether it be a small chore he had to do for their father or a project of his own - he would stick to it until he achieved his goal, which was why she knew he would succeed in becoming a vet. He rushed off to Nanking to face the advancing Japanese. Nothing prepared her for his sudden death along with the thousands of Chinese slaughtered in the war. When she read of the fall of Nanking in the newspaper she remembered thinking that she didn't know there were so many people in the city.

The news of Peng's death catapulted her to a very dark place for a very long time. Her little brother whose life was snuffed out before he had the chance to blossom. She felt for her parents; she knew that their sorrow was far greater than hers. Her own pain and grief were heightened by the distance between them. She had nothing to hold on to except her memories. She still missed him; she could still see him with his head buried in his book completely oblivious to the rest of the world. Her tears had dried up but the pain and void remained. *Was his death in vain now that the country was taken by the communists?*

Her father and eldest brother Keng showed their patriotism differently. Keng turned communist believing that Mao Tze Tung would shake the shackles off the country and make it stand tall again. Their father was persuaded to back the communist because of the land-to-the-tiller reform which the communist party had promised, hoping that he would keep his land. He had managed to work on his rice fields even under Japanese control when he could only stand by and watch the Japanese take their cut of his rice to send to Japan while he and his family had to pull their belts tight and drink water to stave off hunger cramps. Su Yin wondered if Peng had been alive whether the differences in their political views would divide the family. She had no idea what they thought of the communists' guerrilla warfare in Malaya and her working for a *red-haired devil.* She couldn't let what they thought bother her and if they had any sense they would keep their thoughts to themselves, she decided. They could not be choosers.

The youngest two brothers, Fung and Hong, were more reticent about their political views. Fung, now thirty years old and married with three children, was a journalist with an interest in photography. Su Yin sent him a camera which she thought would help him. Besides he could take photographs of the growing family to send to her like the one she was looking at. Since that photograph the camera had been confiscated by the government because they thought he could be a spy in view of his late brother Peng's connection with Kuomintang. Hong was also married with two children and he seemed content with his life as a school teacher and was more interested in teaching Mathematics.

She thought of her sister Mei. She was still happy with married life and her lot. She had put on a bit of weight; her figure had filled out. In the photograph she had sent of herself and her family she was still as pretty as she had always been. Her eyes were still the smiling eyes that Su Yin remembered. Her husband's pig farm had seen changes and although not as prosperous as before they were able to make a reasonable living. That together with the five children who were good to them were reason enough for her contentment. Their oldest son now twenty-one years old and working at one of the electrical factories was making good use of the bike Su Yin had bought for him.

In the front row were the new generation of her seventeen nieces and nephews squatting or sitting on the ground, aged between six and twenty-one. They were all strangers to Su Yin – she had not had the pleasure of holding them in her arms when they were born or watch them grow up - and yet she couldn't help feeling close to them especially when looking at their smiling faces even if they were only smiling for the camera. She knew them, each and every one of them by their names.

Su Yin set the picture down and picked up the other one. It was a faded portrait but clearly showed the happy faces of herself and Lan Yee. They had their arms around each other and were beaming at the camera. Su Yin remembered vividly the day it was taken; it was on the first day of the Lunar New Year when they were dressed in their best clothes and were on their way to visit friends. She caressed Lan Yee's face and then put the picture back in its place.

Su Yin took off the gold hairpin that Lan Yee gave her, pulled the pins that held the bun of her hair at the nape and then slowly unwound the thick rope of hair which came down to her waist. She shook her head to loosen it and then began brushing it. Her hair, the colour of a moonless midnight sky, was the one part of her she liked. As she brushed it the discussion that had taken place earlier in the day between her, Cheng and Joo came back to her. She asked herself again: why ever did Joo raise the question of whether the choice they had made all those years ago was right? Thinking about Lan Yee giving up her life to make a stand for her right not to marry, somehow Joo's questioning whether they had made the right choice or not seemed wrong, almost disrespectful. Su Yin felt she was betraying Lan Yee. But why should Joo now question it? Suddenly Su Yin felt annoyed. Then she tried to convince herself that it was harmless curiosity. Besides, Joo was honest and had the right to ask. Just as she herself often wondered how things would have turned out if Lan Yee had been alive.

After Lan Yee died, work at the silk factory had continued as before. For a long time, it was as if the life and soul of the place had been torn out because she was not there anymore. No more fun and laughter mixed with gossip. For a long while Su Yin would forget and rush off at lunch break thinking she was meeting Lan Yee only to be heartbroken when she realised she had gone. Sometimes she felt numb, other times she felt as though part of her had died too. At times she would withdraw into a quiet mood. In those moods Su Yin would go and sit in the gazebo by the canal where she and Lan Yee shared happy times exchanging secrets and thoughts. Su Yin was still angry that Lan Yee did not tell her her biggest and worst secret of all. Why she didn't want her to know that she wanted to commit suicide Su Yin would never know. She had to accept it and live with it. All she understood was that it was a measure of how strongly Lan Yee objected to marrying against her will. Or was it the terror of marrying some stranger? Or both? But what parents would force their daughter into such a horrible existence? Why couldn't they allow her the freedom to choose?

Although Su Yin had been brought up to obey and respect her parent wishes, a part of her couldn't help asking: what right did they have to force their demand on the children? Whatever it was, it was typical of Lan Yee: she was stubborn if nothing else. But why did she have to kill herself to make the point?

It was only after she died that it became clear to Su Yin why Lan Yee had been insistent on buying her the hairpin. 'So you won't ever forget me,' Lan Yee had said with a smile and told her she would give it to her for Chinese New Year. But she never got round to it. Su Yin cursed that she had been so blind and missed the signs. But would she have been able to stop her taking the ultimate step?

Her mind turned to home. Lush verdant mosaic of rice fields stretching to the blue-green mountains in the horizon, canals criss-crossing the land with sampans drifting lazily along, mulberry trees and wriggling silkworms. She could still hear the rustling of the bamboo leaves, the thundering of the drums on the canal during the boat races and most of all her father's wistful flute music. And she could still smell the putrid air of boiling cocoons which reminded her of her mother's herbal brew. That was her home; that was where her heart was firmly fixed.

There was no tangible difference to her life after her commitment to celibacy. In her favour, her new status as a confirmed spinster meant that the manager regarded her a reliable worker, not likely to run off to have a baby. Hence her job was secure. Work was no different although she became very competent at reeling under her mother's careful instructions. Her fellow workers treated her the same as before. Only her brothers especially the oldest one Keng regarded her differently. She overheard him telling the younger ones one day:

'Second Sister has made that vow so she can continue to work, so that we can afford to go to school. So you all have to work hard, do you understand?' His voice was firm. She could see in her mind's eye the small faces of her younger brothers with furrowed brows looking at Keng.

'But why does she have to do that?'

'Because Father and Mother can't earn enough money for all of us.'

'She loves us.'

'I don't want her to marry and leave us. I want her to live with us all the time.'

'She doesn't like men.'

'She doesn't want babies?'

'She is a good sister.'

'She wants to be the best reeler like Mother. That takes a lot of practice so she can't marry because she would then have to look after her husband and she won't have time to practise.'

Listening to the little brothers throwing in their reasons in their serious voices had made her smile. She didn't want to interrupt them. A few days later Keng approached her.

'I understand why you did what you did,' he said looking half bashful and half apologetic and started cracking his knuckles, something he did when he was unsure of himself.

'Do you?' replied Su Yin. She was surprised that he had taken her action to heart and was curious to hear what he had to say.

'I am ashamed,' Keng hung his head. 'I am the oldest son and so should shoulder the responsibility of looking after our parents, not you. Besides I am only a year younger than you; I am old enough to look after them.'

'Of course you are,' replied Su Yin, 'but the way you can do the right thing for them is to study and get a good job, one better than working in the field for pittance. That is what Father wants. *That* is what I want and then you can look after them.'

Keng was thoughtful for a while. Then with sincerity shining in his eyes and his voice he said, 'And I will look after you too.'

The factory continued to thrive and as long as it did Su Yin's income was safe. No one foresaw that the silk world would turn upside down. The Wall Street Crash happened in 1929. Like the ripples set off by a tsunami the effects of the stock market collapse reached her village; the sale of silk plummeted. Production of silk was cut back; half the jobs disappeared and slowly but conspicuously in the reeling room the water in the woks for boiling the cocoons ceased boiling and then the woks became empty. The room became quieter and felt as if it was in mourning. The population of the silkworms was reduced to occupy a tiny corner of the room. Su Yin's mother lost her job. Her own job was uncertain at first and then the chop came and her job was taken from her. Her father was barely managing on the rice field; it became imperative for her to look elsewhere to find work along with the other girls who had also lost their jobs.

Su Yin had dreamt of travelling one day, of visiting new places and opening her mind. It would be when she had saved enough money, at the time of her choice, to the places she wanted to see. Little did she imagine that she would join the exodus of women to Malaya to work as a domestic servant at the age of eighteen, almost twenty years ago. The memory of her journey by boat, packed like pigs for the market, was still clear.

'First comb for luck...
second comb for longevity...
third comb for contentment…
fourth comb for safety...
fifth comb for freedom...
sixth comb for courage...
seventh comb for self-belief and finally
eighth comb for health.'

Su Yin stopped brushing her hair then put her brush down on top of the chest of drawers. She took out a small wooden box from the top drawer to put her hairpin next to a dried ball of a silken cocoon in a covered glass jar and her purse. She resisted counting again the money in the purse. Instead she picked up the glass jar and looked at the cocoon. The ball of silk had aged – the years had darkened it so it was now a beige colour; it was light but it was still tough, protecting the desiccated silkworm inside. She put the jar back and then retrieved her father's letter from her bag and climbed into her bed under the mosquito net. She made herself comfortable. She thought of Cheng and Joo and how they would want to hear her read their letters again to them at their next meeting. They had already imprinted the contents of previous letters on their minds. Su Yin sighed; she was very lucky. She opened the letter from her father to read it again.

Chapter 12

Cars lined all the way on one side of the drive with several spilling over on to the lawn of the MacAlpines' residence. Earlier Ah Hock had worked hard directing in-coming traffic and made sure that the drivers parked on the same side of the driveway which was lit with red and yellow lanterns. Muthusamy the gardener had gone round early in the afternoon hanging the lanterns from the bamboo trees while Hassan the peon had meticulously swept and tidied all around the house. Inside, the house was buzzing like a glass jar full of wasps. The ceiling fans were whirring overtime as it had been an extremely warm day with no sign of the temperature dropping even though the sun had set. Strains of *Moonlight Serenade* drifted from the turntable in the sitting room. There were over fifty guests to celebrate James' thirty-fifth birthday, including many European expatriates who were either friends or colleagues.

Su Yin could not understand why the children were banished from the parents' celebration. She was brought up to join in, to be part of any celebration in the family. Instead she accepted it was the Europeans' way and hers was not to question but to do as her bosses wished. So Cammy, Ellie, Lexie and Thomas were ushered off into their rooms after their early dinner although not before they were allowed, under the watchful eyes of Ah Hock, to run around in the garden to admire the colourful lanterns that were like glow worms in the dark. The upside was that Su Yin didn't have to worry about them getting under her feet and distracting her while she was serving and waiting on their parents' guests.

Another thing she didn't understand was the fuss that the Europeans made over their birthdays. The only big birthday celebration she recalled was that of her paternal great grandmother's on her eightieth birthday. To her then six-year-old mind, her great grandmother deserved to be honoured and celebrated for she was old. Her back was so hunched that when she walked about she looked as if she was stooping to pick something up off the floor. Her son who lived with her on their farm in a faraway village had slaughtered the fattest pig and roasted it over a charcoal fire out on the lawn. It seemed to her then that all the villagers had come to the party. Su Yin's distinct memory of the grand old lady was of her dressed in her new silk *samfoo*, her thinning grey hair tied into a bun at the nape with a gold pin in it and walking about with her hands behind her back bent like a figure of seven as she surveyed the crowd of well-wishers. She would smile at the children running around playing and laughing and then she would instruct her son on the roasting of the pig. Nearby was a table laden with food especially mountains of noodles for longevity, dumplings and buns and a large steamed whole chicken with its head intact sitting on a plate like a naked lady basking in the sun. Her great grandmother's hunched back had always intrigued her as a little girl. Su Yin didn't see much of her – it was a solid five hours' walk to her village - but when she did her curiosity would take over. She'd once asked her mother, 'Why is great grandma's back so crooked?'

'So many questions!' her mother had replied and that was the end of her asking although it didn't stop her wondering how her great grandmother's back became like that. Did she become bent by carrying the weight of her age on her back? How did she lie on her bed when she went to sleep? But the deformed back didn't stop her doing things;

Su Yin once saw her standing on a wooden platform across a pond of water which was used for everything on the farm and to her amazement she saw her throw a bucket tied to a rope into the water and pull up a filled bucket without any problem. At her funeral, she overheard an aunt saying to another aunt that not long after she'd died her back miraculously straightened so that she lay flat on her bed. 'It became as straight as a plank!' said her bewildered aunt.

Helen MacAlpine had been planning the birthday party for a long time. She had worked on the menu with Su Yin, altering it as the weeks went by. Now after two days of shopping, preparation and cooking, the menu had materialised on the large damask-covered table in the dining room. There was little else Helen could do about it apart from admiring the spread and allowing herself a bit of pride in the help she gave Su Yin. She was pleased that she could show off her latest collection of red Pyrex bowls that she had recently acquired. There were a large platter of sliced leg of lamb alongside a bowl of mustard and mint sauce that Helen's mother had shipped from Scotland, boiled potatoes, beef *rendang*, ladies' finger curry, steamed seabass, roast duck done the Cantonese way Su Yin had always done, deep fried king prawns, stir-fried vegetables, noodles and steamed pork dumplings in baskets. For dessert Helen had made two Victoria sponge cakes, a large sherry trifle and a bowl of mango, watermelon and papaya salad. A late addition was a big tureen of chicken curry which one of the guests, Mrs Indran, had brought. Her husband, the manager of a huge oil palm plantation owned by some English family, had earlier stood at the table eulogising, to anyone who cared to listen, the dishes before him and then in a loud voice went on to say,

'As for this curry that my good wife has cooked, it is an old recipe of my dear mother's. She was the best cook ever.' Rubbing his fingers and thumb in front of his nose as if he was smelling the spices, he continued, 'She could tell from the aroma of the frying spices what was missing and should be added. That was how good she was.' He finished with both his hands in the air as if waiting for applause. His pretty wife in her vibrant red and gold sari stood by looking embarrassed. Helen quickly thanked him once again for his generosity. Su Yin was glad she didn't cook chicken curry, she was sure Mr Indran would have said she had adulterated the dish.

Among the other guests who were regular visitors to the house were husband and wife Anthony and Penny Pendle from Surrey, England. Anthony - thirty-five years old, bald with dark-rimmed spectacles and always wearing his panama hat – was as friendly as his laugh was big. Seldom without his pipe he also kept a pistol, a fact he didn't bother to conceal, claiming that he would not go out without it. He was in the rubber plantation business which he inherited from his uncle who was one of many who came to the country when the price of rubber boomed with the advent of the motorcar. Su Yin liked him – he didn't make her feel small unlike his wife Penny who was always aloof towards her which annoyed her. Bronze, broad-shouldered and athletic-looking with short wavy brown hair and a stern-looking face, she cut an intimidating figure. The couple was childless; Helen had often alluded to how unfortunate it was that Penny didn't have children as she would make a good mother. Like many of Helen's friends she was a lady of leisure of no fixed occupation apart from playing bridge every Thursday afternoon with each of the group taking turns to host. Anthony Pendle was laughing his big laugh with a few of the guests while Penny who had looked miserable earlier was now smiling and talking to Helen.

Su Yin regarded it her job to be attentive as she discreetly glided amongst the guests making sure that they had drinks. She had noticed a woman who had arrived on her own. She was Chinese. It was the red tight-fitting dress and high-heels that had shouted to Su Yin. The woman was young and pretty with long black hair that bounced as she walked. Something about her prickled Su Yin. When she heard her speak to another guest she thought the woman sounded haughty like some of the others. Then she saw Helen walking towards her.

'Hello, I am Helen MacAlpine,' Helen said politely but stiffly, Su Yin thought, although there was a smile on her face. 'You must be Winnie.'

'Yes, thank you for inviting me,' replied Winnie showing off her white teeth.

'Ah, here is James,' Helen pointed to James. 'Please make yourself at home.' With that Helen walked away while James came towards Winnie and shook her outstretched hand.

Su Yin watched Helen; like the perfect host her face remained smiling. She made a mental note of the woman's name. When she took her a drink she thought Winnie was polite but could not shake off the thought that she was a tiger on the prowl. *Shameless*, Su Yin thought. *Was there something going on between her and James MacAlpine,* she wondered with a sinking feeling. Was James capable of that? Mentally she shook her head; no, he wasn't. She was about to check on the two young helpers that Helen had hired to assist her in the kitchen when she noticed her former employer Mr Lok walking towards her. He was carrying a bottle of Remy Martin. She stopped, waited and when he was near enough she said in Cantonese, 'Good evening Mr Lok.'

Mr Lok smiled. 'Good evening, Amah. How are you?'

'I am very well. I hope you and your family are too.'

'Yes, yes. Ming is around somewhere.' He looked around. 'She will be very pleased to see you no doubt.'

'That is good. I will look out for her.'

'Is your family well?'

'Yes, thank you for asking.'

'Good.' He nodded. 'Ah, there is Eddie. I need to talk to him about some drains.' He pointed to a slim tall bespectacled man with dark features and wavy hair. Su Yin recognised Eddie Tan at once. His black spectacle frames resting on his high-bridged nose and his rounder eyes were the tell-tale signs of his Eurasian heritage – Italian mother and a Chinese father . He worked with James in the Town and Planning Department as Health Inspector.

Su Yin gave a small bow before moving off to the kitchen and making a mental note to feed Ah Hock and the other chauffeurs who had congregated on the lawn by the side of the house.

The sitting room was throbbing with conversation. Su Yin often wished that she could understand everything that was said in English. Everyone seemed to be talking with abandon.

'Can the Malays govern themselves?' asked the District Officer, a stocky hairy Englishman with a brown moustache and a pipe attached to his left hand. 'They are pestering for this, that and the other. The sultans and aristocrats all wanting their land and rights. Look at them – now playing tennis and polo instead of *sepak raga* their own sport. They have embraced the British way of life, it has rubbed off on them.'

'That is a shame in a way,' said Anthony Pendle. 'The gap between the elites and the average Malay chap is widening. Go to the kampong, the village, and you will see them playing their traditional game of *sepak raga.'*

'But what kind of game is that kicking around a rattan ball?' someone asked.

'Don't forget how the golf ball began - as a wooden ball.'

'Yes, that's my point - they haven't progressed.' Someone guffawed.

Another rolled their eyes to the ceiling. 'Surely that's what makes the game distinctive, different from others. Otherwise we might as well be kicking a football as we know it. Move the net to the end of the field and hey presto we have *football*!'

'Talk about golf. It's a damn shame this business of the guerrillas. I can't wait till we can go up to Fraser's Hill to play there again.'

'How many of these communist terrorists, the CTs, are just bandits through and through with no ideological leanings of any sort?'

You mean are they communists through and through or do they just want rid of the British?'

'Wonder when the Chinks, I mean the CTs, will come to their senses.'

'James, what do you make of this? You were with them in the jungle, fought alongside them and now they turn against you so to speak.'

James didn't answer right away. Then he said, 'Many of them took their orders from China and fervently upheld their communist principles. For the rest, they fought with us against the Japanese. When you think about it, they were the ones who sacrificed a lot by fighting from the jungle. The jungle was the only safe place for them. They wanted rid of the Japs. The squatters supplied us with food, etcetera, risking their lives for us. Now they feel betrayed by us by not acknowledging their massive effort. Those who fought from the jungle have returned to the jungle. They think it is the only way to get rid of us Brits. You can't blame them. Especially the young impressionable ones who see no future for themselves out here – no education, no prospects. They turn to communism in the hope that they might get somewhere when they have got rid of us. All the Chinese want is an equitable society. What do we do instead? We evict the squatters from their homes and put them behind barbed wires!'

'You have to admit that lifeline to the communist through the squatters needed to be cut off and Briggs' plan of relocating the squatters far out of reach of the guerrillas is a first-class idea. It's like sucking the oxygen out of their air. Damn good idea!'

'The curfews also seem to be working. It has reduced the attempts of squatters supplying the guerrillas.'

'And death by hanging too.' Someone shuddered.

'I also think that in the first place they were intimidated by the guerrillas to do as they were told. Poor sods – caught between the bastards in the jungle and the Security Forces.'

'There's still smuggling of stuff from Singapore to the guerrillas in Johore. Hell of a job to stop that.'

'It makes me nervous to travel anywhere far or go near the jungle and we are surrounded by jungle! I miss my jaunts to Raffles Hotel, don't you?'

Helen who had been listening quietly spoke up. 'James can't appreciate why I worry about his travelling outstation or when he's late home. There's no telling what could happen if his car broke down in the wrong place.'

Some of the guests had spilled on to the veranda to enjoy the evening air which had cooled down. Su Yin moved quietly amongst them to clear plates and serve drinks. James later came round to Su Yin and whispered in a conspiratorial tone, 'I prefer your curry.' She smiled at him and then saw Ming coming towards her. Su Yin thought that she had grown into an elegant young woman and felt pleased. Wearing a pink and white floral print shift and high-heeled sandals Ming looked slim and very grown-up; her long black hair which was swept up into a French roll showing off her slender neck made her look older than her eighteen years. Su Yin remembered the awkward tomboy who was always arguing with her four older brothers who didn't want her to hang around them when they went kite-flying, cross-country cycling or fishing. She would then cry and run to Su Yin. Ming's tanned heart-shaped face broke into a smile as she approached Su Yin. Smiling back, Su Yin waited for her to speak.

Ming spoke in Cantonese, 'Amah, every dish is delicious. *Aww*, I miss your cooking especially your sticky rice dumplings. Can't even buy good ones like yours in the shop.'

'I am sure you can,' said Su Yin. 'You have grown so tall. I have to look up to you now.' Ming went all shy; a hint of red appeared in her cheeks. Su Yin pointed to Ming's hair, 'This hairstyle suits you.' Lifting a stack of dirty plates from the table Su Yin continued, 'I must take this to the kitchen,' and proceeded to walk towards the kitchen not expecting Ming to follow. To her surprise Ming was right at her heel and carrying her own empty plate and fork.

'It's a pity the children have gone to bed,' said Ming.

As they walked along the corridor Su Yin said, 'Yes, they did ask if you were coming and they weren't pleased that they wouldn't see you. So how is your mother? Is she well?' She looked sideways at Ming who was licking her finger.

In a flat voice Ming replied, 'Alright I suppose. She is not here because her mah-jong group is playing tonight and no way was she going to give that up.'

'So your father asked you to accompany him here?'

'Yes and I also wanted to see you.'

'You have been busy with your exams; that was why I didn't want to disturb you. How did you get on? Do you know your results yet?'

'No not until December. I think I have done alright. I am going to England to study.'

'*Wah!* That is wonderful! You are so clever. What are you going to study?' Su Yin felt proud thinking back to the time she first held Ming in her arms when she was a baby and wouldn't stop crying. Ming's mother had been utterly frustrated and cross. After Su Yin had winded her Ming stopped for a while only to start crying again. Looking at her now she found it hard to believe that Ming was that difficult and irritable baby.

'I'm going to study law,' Ming answered.

'*Wah,* that is very hard, isn't it? But you are a clever girl,' said Su Yin.

They entered the kitchen where one of the helpers was washing the dishes while the other was drying. The soft voices of the drivers talking outside wafted in.

'And partly why Father thought it would be a good idea for me to come tonight is so I can pick Uncle James's or Aunty Helen's brains or anybody else's at the party, you know, like finding out about the country and what I should expect.' Ming sounded annoyed.

'Your parents must be very, very proud.'

'I think my mother can't wait for me to leave.'

'Why do you say that? It is not true. Of course she will miss you very much,' Su Yin frowned.

Ming looked doubtful and shrugged. She suddenly realised that they were not alone. 'Can we meet again please? Can we go and eat at our usual place?'

'Of course when I can get some time off,' replied Su Yin pleased that Ming still wanted to see her. Ming had been devastated when Su Yin left the Lok household and made her father promise that she could see Su Yin whenever she wanted, something her father gave in to. After four sons Ming was the daughter he had secretly longed for. Anything she asked for she got.

Su Yin picked up some clean plates and napkins from one of the shelves and started to make her way out towards the dining room. Ming followed.

'That would be so good. When will you be free? Can I phone you?' Ming was like a child again, following Su Yin around in her father's house.

'Yes, you can,' answered Su Yin and as they were about to enter the dining room someone in the sitting room shouted,

'Hush everyone!'

They turned and saw James turning up the volume of the radio in the corner of the room. Several of the guests had gathered round the radio. Silence fell over the sitting room and rippled through to the veranda. Su Yin and Ming stopped in their tracks. The guests froze with their drinks and cigarettes in their hands, their heads turned in the direction of the radio; the cigarette smoke wafted as the ceiling fans whirred. Then the sombre voice of the English newscaster cut through the silence,

'We interrupt this programme to bring you news that High Commissioner Sir Henry Gurney has been shot and killed. He, his wife Lady Gurney and his convoy were ambushed by communist guerrillas on the Kuala Kubu Road near Fraser's Hill. Lady Gurney survived the attack. Details of the incident are not clear at this juncture. As soon as we know we will bring you more…'

James switched off the radio. His face was pale. No one spoke. No one moved. Then Anthony whose colour had drained from his face spoke, 'Oh, my God, that's terrible. What is going to happen now?'

'But why did he and his wife go up there knowing full well the risks?' said a small voice.

'He would be a sitting duck, armoured convoy or no convoy,' said someone. 'James, you of all people would know how true that is.'

James looked as if he hadn't heard then he said, 'Yes, the guerrillas are crafty. They wait and then they pounce. There is no telling if this was planned. Did they know that the Commissioner was going there? If they did how did they know? They would normally ambush randomly hoping to take what weapons they can from whom they'd attacked.'

'To think that we were just talking about going to Fraser's Hill and how dangerous it was to travel there,' Penny Pendle shuddered.

'What is going to happen now?'

Every head turned around to look at James but James had left the room.

Chapter 13

James tore out of the house, jumped into his jeep and headed directly to the scene of the crime. As he roared through the town and out on to the single-track road through the jungle his heart was thumping. He could not fathom why the Commissioner would have taken that trip. It was foolhardy; it was mad. The mountainous jungle was the most inhospitable place he knew. In parts it was almost impenetrable, a dense webbing of lush vegetation – thickets of bamboo intertwined with tall trees he didn't know the names of, and shrubs such as rhododendrons, bromeliads, ferns, hanging twines and creepers. The only way to move forward was to use a *parang* to cut a path through the mesh of green growth. The intense heat and humidity, sandwiched between the thick undergrowth and the dense canopy of the tall treetops, made it feel like working out in a partially blacked-out steam room. The other problem was the lack of landmarks which made the stretches of hills almost impossible to navigate. On top of that there were snakes, insects and worst, the dreaded leeches that crawled up and clung on to the legs or any exposed area of the body and sucked until they became bloated with blood before dropping off. There had been warnings not to pull them off to avoid the teeth of the leeches being left in the flesh and thus causing infection. Various suggestions had been offered to remove them such as touching them with a burning cigarette end or salt. James remembered that no matter how they came off the bleeding puncture marks would still become infected; he had a few scars to prove it. The jungle was an ideal place for the guerrillas to hide and to conduct warfare from.

The Commissioner had feared the domination of the Chinese people by the communists and had been frustrated by the difficulties of eliminating Chinese support for the communist terrorists. The Briggs Plan was working; it aimed to destroy any support for them by cutting off the supply of food, information and new recruits to the communist camp. Moving the Chinese squatters out of reach of the guerrillas away into secure new villages was having the desired effect. Just as Briggs had envisaged, the guerrillas were now lured out to fight on the home ground of the security forces. But the attacks on the resettlement areas were no longer sporadic and taken by single individuals; they were stepped up and involved more men. And that was exactly what had happened leading to the ambush of the High Commissioner.

The Gap – a narrow winding road that cut through the thick jungle – was the most dangerous spot. James had pointed out before that it was an obvious area that the terrorists would target, where they would lie in wait to ambush any army convoy in order to seize weapons and ammunitions. It was not clear whether the terrorists had known about the Commissioner's trip. Had there been a leak? Planned or unplanned, killing the Commissioner would be the coup, the jackpot, that they had never dreamt of. It was ironic that the same Chinese men that the British had trained at the 101STS in Singapore to fight the Japanese had now turned on the British in such a brutal fashion. By the time James arrived on the scene of the ambush his body was tense with the gush of adrenaline as he remembered his time in the jungle fighting alongside the Chinese. He had every confidence in the new recruits he had helped instruct in jungle warfare; they would know how to cope with the terrain but it was going to be a tough challenge catching up with the slippery guerrillas, let alone catching them.

The full Gap Police Station force was already on site with reinforcements from the British army. Jeeps and army trucks hugged the slope of the narrow road like they had come to an abrupt halt and were abandoned, above him came the urgent clatter of a helicopter circling the area. Men carrying rifles were scattered about like a bunch of turkeys let loose amidst the sound of beating of the bushes. He spotted Assistant Police Superintendent Noordin talking on his walkie-talkie, his brow screwed up tightly. Beside him was a man in uniform, a tall well-built middle-aged man with a bushy moustache whom he immediately recognised as Police Superintendent Colonel MacPhee. He had met him on a couple of occasions, once at the Jungle Warfare School and had thought what a stony face he had. James was surprised at how quickly the Colonel was on the scene. When Noordin saw James his brow relaxed significantly and waved to him. James waved back and rushed up to them.

'Colonel, I came as soon as I could,' said James noticing that worry had creased his stony face.

'We need all the men we can get,' said Colonel MacPhee in a gruff voice. 'Noordin will brief you.'

James reached out and took Noordin's hand.

'Thank you, James,' replied Noordin, an open-faced, fit-looking Malay man in his forties whose usual affable self was now crushed not just by the responsibility of hunting down the perpetrators but the fact that the assassination was committed on his patch. Sweat was running down his brown face. 'I need all the help I can get. Sir Henry was ambushed there.' He pointed towards a cordoned area a few yards up the slope. 'Come, I'll show you.' They started to walk up the hill. 'There,' he pointed to the ditch, 'that was where Sir Henry was shot.' A pool of congealed blood on the grass marked where he had fallen. At the sight of the blood, flashes of images of violent fighting and dead bodies came hurtling at James. He winced and quickly looked away. Noordin started to fill him in on the moments leading to the Commissioner's death.

The High Commissioner and his wife had decided to go up to the elite hill resort where he was known to enjoy a game of golf. His black Rolls Royce was escorted by thirteen policemen in a Land Rover, a radio van and an armoured car. Not long into the journey there was trouble with the radio so that the escort commander had to transfer to the armoured car at the rear leaving the black Rolls Royce to lead the way up to the resort. It was when the convoy was meandering up a narrow one-way towards The Gap, hemmed in by thick jungle on both sides, that a platoon of guerrillas pounced on them and opened fire. The guerrillas were well armed; Sten guns, Bren guns and rifles had been used. No one knew why but as bullets sprayed, the Commissioner was seen staggering out of the car and then he fell face down as he was shot. His body was found in the ditch at the side of the road.

James led a section of the police and army as they fanned out to cover the area. The character of the jungle hadn't changed since he was last in it; it was just as unforgiving and as impassable as walking through giant spider webs. His knowledge of the old routes that he and his comrades had used before came to the fore. They'd hacked through the thicket and James led them to old hideouts where he had camped before – deserted huts and caves - that he thought the guerrillas might be using. But despite their valiant efforts they found no sign of the guerrillas. They had long withdrawn deep into the jungle.

The next day more reinforcement arrived; a thousand British and Gurkha troops and a large number of Malay police swept the area slashing their way through the thick growth and bombing the thickest parts where the terrorists were most likely to hide. It was all in vain.

In the days that followed details surrounding the ambush of the High Commissioner gradually filtered out. His death stunned the country not just because of the shock of realising how far the communist guerrillas had gone but also because of the loss of a good Commissioner. It knocked the morale of the British government sideways and chipped away any confidence the people had in their ability to provide security. Retribution was swift. In the belief that the Chinese in the nearby villages had been helping the communist guerrillas, the police rounded up the Chinese residents to interrogate them. A little Chinese village named Tras, seven miles from the ambush site, suffered the worst fate - all the residents were decanted from their homes, bundled into lorries and taken to a detention camp in Ipoh over a hundred miles away. Not one of them was allowed to return to their homes. James wasn't sure that such brutal measures didn't have the opposite effect of turning the non-communist Chinese against the British and convincing them to join the enemy.

Although security measures were tightened dramatically there was no denying that there was a palpable sense of insecurity. James understood then why Helen had been worried when he was late coming home. He had been blasé; he had been thoughtless and insensitive. The jungle and the Malayan way of life was almost second nature to him. In the jungle he had lived and worked with the Chinese and the *orang asli*, the aboriginals who were born and bred in the jungle. More importantly he had fought with them.

The images of dead bodies returned – bloodied bodies of his fellow fighters riddled with bullets sprawled across the virgin green ferns. The first time he saw one was when another group of fighters from another camp had joined them. Earlier they had gone into the village of Bidor for supplies. Someone had tipped off the Japanese soldiers who came after them in no time. All except one of the Chinese had escaped the Japanese soldiers. They decided to abandon their camp. The leader who was the older brother of the man who had been shot carried his body so that he could bury him properly. When the leader – silent in his grief and his face wet with tears - gently laid down his brother's lifeless bloodied body on the ground James saw that the dead man was not much older than himself.

The sight had shaken him; he had been terrified and it was then that he realised the seriousness and enormity of what he had let himself in for. It was not long after that when they had ambushed a group of Japanese soldiers that he was shot in the leg during the exchange of fire.

He knew the jungle like he knew every line and freckle on his face but he forgot that Helen, although she had acclimatised well, had not stepped beyond the boundary of the city apart from a weekend up to the hill station in Cameron Highlands not long after they arrived in the country. It had been a wonderful respite from the heat and humidity. It was home from home; the air was cool and fresh, fragrant with the perfume of roses from the gardens of the red bungalows that had been built for the likes of them when they needed an escape from the oppressive heat. Since then the Emergency had put fear into the hearts of many especially the Europeans. No one would knowingly stray into the jungle. There were restrictions in place: everyone had to be inside a wired perimeter by nightfall or be fired at, there was no stopping between villages and the carrying of food, money, plastic sheets or anything that the communists might want or need was strictly prohibited. Even the plantation owners were wary and carried guns ready for an attack by the enemy. Most people never thought it would come to this. The fear of something like this happening to him had been so real to Helen. He had been blind to her worries and felt foolish for playing down her fears. The thought of Helen and the children left alone suddenly sent a chill through him. He cursed the guerrillas. The sooner the Emergency ended, the better.

Chapter 14

Just before Mr Lok's car arrived, Helen pushed a dollar note into Su Yin's hand. 'Go and have a treat,' she said softly. Su Yin was dumbfounded when saw the note. She had expected nothing; to be given some time off to spend with Ming was reward enough after the party. At the same time, she was delighted as the money would go towards her savings.

Su Yin looked at Ming across the glass-topped table. She looked her usual self again -wearing a light blue cotton blouse with a matching short pleated skirt and flat sandals, her hair tied up in a ponytail and carrying a small leather purse. She was the young teenager again. Immediately after school Mr Lok's Malay chauffer had driven her directly from school to pick Su Yin up from the MacAlpine's residence and brought them to the coffee house.

'So, what has been happening?' Su Yin asked.

'Not much and yet so much has happened,' said Ming. She seemed distracted by the colourful menu in the middle of the table which she had grabbed to study.

'This is a nice place. Very modern,' said Su Yin.

'Yes,' Ming enthused, 'it is called a "Milk Bar", the in-thing now. They sell ice-creams and 'floats'.'

Su Yin looked around the Milk Bar from the booth that they were sitting in and then at the bench she was sitting on. *Milk Bar*, she repeated softly. It was different from the coffee shop that they used to go to; it was new and clean with mirrors on the walls, there were English songs blaring out from somewhere and the booth idea was foreign to her. It was only two weeks after the tragic death of the Commissioner, yet people were going about their lives as usual. On the streets there were noticeably more policemen.

Shops were opened as normal, trading as before. Schools were operating as if nothing had happened although there was a sense of wariness hanging about. It certainly did not bother the customers in the coffee shop. A bunch of Chinese schoolgirls still in their blue and white uniform with their school bags under the tables all seemed to be bubbling with lots to say over their tall glasses of ice-cream floating on top of some fizzy drink. It warmed her heart seeing the young girls so carefree. At another table was a group of schoolboys laughing as they cast side glances at the girls. She couldn't help comparing their lot with that of her nieces and nephews back in China. Her father had written to say that one of the nieces needed a bike to go to school and that food was getting very expensive due to a shortage.

'What are you going to have then?' asked Su Yin turning to Ming who was still studying the menu. 'Can't be that difficult to choose, can it?' She'd gasped at the varieties to choose from. Even though she couldn't read it she could see that it was a long list.

'*Hmmm..'* Ming tilted her head from side to one side.

'Do they have ice-*kachang* or not?'

'Yes! They have. One ice-*kachang* for you and one coca-cola float for me. That's it!' said Ming smiling, her dark brown eyes sparkling. She waved to a waiter and gave the order. It wasn't long before it came.

Su Yin looked at her bowl of finely grated ice drizzled with green and red syrup and evaporated milk sitting on top of sweet adzuki red beans. She nodded with approval. Ming quickly took a suck at the straw in her coca-cola before scooping the ice cream floating on top.

'Good?' Su Yin asked. Ming licked her lips and nodded. 'Mine tastes good too.'

'How are your brothers? Your youngest brother Kuan must be graduating soon from university?'

'Mother is too absorbed in herself,' said Ming. 'And she doesn't have to work.'

Su Yin was surprised at Ming's unexpected reproof of her mother and quickly said, 'Your mother is a very fortunate woman to have you children and a good husband. She is blessed.' Ming's eyes started to well up. Su Yin reached out to place her hand on Ming's. 'What is wrong? Tell me.'

'I don't blame Mother for being the way she has been,' Ming sniffed. 'She discovered not so long ago that Father has a first wife in China and they have four children.'

Su Yin felt her jaw drop. She could barely get out the words, 'But how do you know this?'

'Mother told me,' Ming replied. 'She had suspected something and then one day a letter came from China. It was for Father..from the woman. She opened and read it. Then Mother confronted Father about it.' She paused for a while. 'Do you know, for the first time I feel sorry for her? You can imagine how Mother feels. She cried for days but she puts on a brave front as if nothing has changed and continues to play mah-jong with her friends.' She wiped away her tears, oblivious to the people and the noise of the chatter around her.

Su Yin leant back in her seat and took a deep breath. She didn't know what to think or say. It wasn't as though the idea of multiple wives was alien to her but still she was shocked. It never occurred to her that Mr Lok would have another wife. And the secrecy of it. She wasn't sure what she thought of him now that she knew this. Was it the fact that he had hidden the truth from his wife that incensed her? She had always held him in high esteem; now it was as if he had come down a few notches. She felt a little sad as well. She had to say something to Ming to console her.

'You don't know what the circumstances were when your father married his first wife,' Su Yin began.

'His father - my grandfather - betrothed him to this girl back in his village!' Ming retorted.

'The thing is he is here with your mother, you and your brothers and sisters. He cares and looks after you all very well.' Ming said nothing but her face was contorted with fury, Su Yin continued, 'Don't be angry with him.'

'How can I not be angry with him? He has lied to us! He kept us in the dark! What sort of man is he? So all the trips he had to make was to go and see her. And all the time we thought it was business!'

'Remember he is still your father and he loves you very much,' she said. Then to her surprise, Ming asked,

'Why didn't you marry?' Her eyes now focussed on her as she waited for Su Yin's answer.

Su Yin took a deep breath. 'It is a long story,' she started. Could she tell Ming the real reason? 'I needed to work to help my family and so I didn't have time to think about getting married. And I am still working!' She let out a laugh. 'I like working. I like looking after you children.' A picture of Ming as a little girl playing with and combing Su Yin's hair sprung up in her mind which made her smile. 'You were so adorable when you were little and you still are. Don't change.'

'People marry and work,' Ming said as she looked at Su Yin with a look that said her reply was only part of the answer. She dabbed her eyes.

Su Yin smiled. 'I always thought you were astute. When I was young it was a choice between marrying someone your parents chose for you or taking a stand against marriage. I chose the latter. We make choices and face the consequences, some good, some not so good. I value my independence too much and to me I made the right choice. Does that answer your question?'

A look of bafflement flitted across Ming's face. 'Oh, I'd expected you to say something like you had been disappointed in love. It's a huge thing to say you are not ever going to marry and stick to it. Then the way I feel now I don't blame you!'

Su Yin smiled. 'Now, as far as your father is concerned don't let what he did alter anything. I know it is hard to believe he is the same man you have always known, but he is. He is a good man.'

Su Yin did a mental double-take: what makes a man good? Was there such a thing as a perfect man, or woman for that matter? A man would say that such a person would be boring; there would be no faults to find and criticise which would make for a dull marriage. Perfect in what way? Did she think that there was such a man, one that would persuade her or convince her to renege on her vow? She thought of her own father. He was a good man; he had been faithful to his wife or at least she thought he had. The point was he and her mother were happy. They were still together and happy. Was it their poverty that had bound them together? Would his eyes have roamed and searched for another woman if he had been wealthy? What about women? Immediately Winnie in the red dress came to mind – a tigress on heat oblivious to boundaries. These were questions that had no answers. She had long concluded that marriage was no guarantee that the man would remain faithful to his wife, that the bond that held a man to his wife was elastic - it could stretch as and when he liked. What about women? She suddenly felt cross with Winnie; *she* had better not try to come between Mr and

Mrs Makapeen. What was wrong with people? Don't they have brakes on their sexual urges? Su Yin looked at Ming who was not much older than her best friend Lan Yee when she took her own life.

Ming was quiet. She looked at her hands as she wrung them and then wiped her tears away. 'If you say so,' she said. She took a sip of her drink. 'What is there to stop him doing it again?'

'I don't know, I am no expert on men.'

Ming hesitated momentarily and looked nervously at Su Yin before she spoke again, 'The reason Father let you go to work for Uncle James is because my mother wanted to get rid of you. She said you were a threat to her. That Father had his eyes on you and she was afraid that he would take you as his wife.'

Su Yin was stunned, her face became stern. 'Don't you dare say things like that. That is not true, can't be. You mustn't say things like that!'

'But it is! I've heard them argue about it!' Ming snapped back, her eyes opened wide.

'You were only a little girl; you could have misunderstood what you heard.'

'No, it was recently I heard them arguing.'

'I don't believe it!' Su Yin felt deflated. She studied Ming's face, she looked earnest. And she had no reason to doubt that she was telling the truth. 'Your mother might have thought that but it doesn't mean your father had any intention of doing such a thing. Your father wouldn't. And you have to believe that. Besides I am only a servant.'

Ming dropped another a bombshell: 'I wish you were my mother.'

Su Yin was stunned into silence and looked around to see if anyone else had heard it. She then fixed her eyes on

Ming who looked like a wilting cabbage. 'You mustn't say that. Never say that again. Think what your mother would feel if she heard you.' Su Yin felt a slight sense of agitation. She didn't know how to deal with this declaration. She certainly didn't want to come between mother and daughter. The thought of that happening appalled her; the guilt would be hard to bear. 'If your mother knew that she would most definitely stop you seeing me. I wouldn't want that. So you must never say that again, do you hear?'

Ming nodded and said nothing. She took a sip of her drink while Su Yin poked at the melting ice in her bowl. For a few moments, the two of them sat in silence and looked at the other young customers chatting like a conference of blackbirds.

'So you must be excited about going abroad?' said Su Yin.

'I suppose I am.'

'Did you speak to Mr Makapeen about it? Or any of the other English people?'

'No, I didn't. I know enough about England. I learn about it in Geography and History and read enough of English fiction. All I need to take with me is an umbrella; it always rains there,' said Ming with a smile. 'Yes, I am looking forward to going.'

Su Yin laughed. 'The rain can't be as bad as it is here. I am glad you are looking forward to it. Grab the chance with both hands and do your very best with it. You are so lucky to have the chance to travel and study. The whole world is open to you. *Wah*, really lucky.' Her mind strayed to all the possibilities and the wonder of it all. 'I want to see you come back with your qualifications. Your parents will be so proud, as I will be too.' Then she chuckled. 'So long as you don't demand a cup of tea in bed when you wake up! Remember your eldest brother did that when he came back from London. A habit he picked up there. I told him that was not the done thing here. We don't even speak before we brush our teeth! Your mother told him what was what and nearly smacked him with a broom!' Ming chuckled. 'The Makapeen family don't do that. Just as well. I would object to taking tea to them while they are still in bed!'

Ming brightened up. 'At least he learnt to cook for himself there.'

Yes, and he was good too. Whenever he was back during his holidays he would ask me to teach him to cook his favourite things.' Su Yin paused. 'So good to see him doing well in banking now.'

Before long Mr Lok's chauffer came for them.

After they parted ways, what Ming had said about Su Yin being a threat to her mother kept playing over and over again in Su Yin's mind. Never in all her time with the family did Mr Lok show any sign of anything other than being a good kind boss towards her. And she was grateful having heard stories from the other sisters how horrid some of their bosses could be. Since the moment she made her vow, she had not entertained a single thought about men or marriage. She had never seen Mr Lok in any other way except as a good employer. His wife was a few years younger than he was and wasn't a bad looking woman. She had a loud voice and always sounded as if she was shouting at the children when she spoke to them. But she was good to them even if at times she seemed cold and distant. When the children came home from school she was either there at home with her friends or away at her friends. The times when she laughed were during her mah-jong sessions with her friends and sounded like a turkey with a sore-throat. It had never bothered Su Yin before nor was she curious about how the couple met. Was it a love-match? Or was it arranged? Su Yin was cross now; how could she look at Mr Lok without this uneasiness even though she had no feelings other than gratitude towards him? Then to her surprise she felt her restraint easing and allowing her imagination to go wild: what if he *did* like her and approached her with a view to marriage? She could conceivably become the third wife assuming that he had a first wife back in China. Being the third wife was indisputably different from being the first in their social and legal status but she would have a strong hold over him. She recalled stories she'd heard about wives and concubines. The last Empress of China herself was a concubine. How she and the other concubines plotted against the real Empress and each other! The dozens of concubines in their various palaces were like vipers in a pit scheming to gain favour from the Emperor for their own survival. Then she remembered a woman in her village who was the second wife. When the husband died the first wife gleefully kicked her and her children out of the house leaving them destitute. At that point Su Yin shook her head hard; she didn't want to think about it anymore. It was just as well that she no longer worked for Mr Lok.

As for children, what Ming had said had both warmed her heart and yet worried her. Ming was the first baby she ever held in her arms. She had wondered what it was like to be pregnant and then to give birth to a child. She couldn't define what being maternal was but she knew she liked babies and looking after them. Ming was the daughter she would have liked and didn't know it until she heard Ming say, 'I wish you were my mother'. She was touched;

she was happy that Ming felt that close to her but she could never come between mother and daughter.

At just seven minutes to midnight the railway line between Port Swettenham on the west coast and Kuala Lumpur was blown up by guerrillas. The explosion disrupted the link to the port which was vital to the export of products such as copra, latex and tin from the hinterland. Another victory for the communist.

Chapter 15

A storm of words was swirling in Helen's head; she didn't know how she should begin. Dinner had been a relatively quiet affair, just her and James. James had seemed tense and distracted throughout. The only time he relaxed was when the children came into the dining room to say goodnight. The cup of coffee that Su Yin had brought to her in the sitting room was untouched. Under the whirring fan she watched James pour himself a glass of whisky and then sink into the chair facing her but looking deep in thought again. Without warning, the words came rushing out:

'It's that tart, isn't it?' Her voice was low and controlled but there was a distinct hurt in it.

James blinked as if he had been rudely woken. He cocked his head, his brow gathered as he slowly sat up. Before he could say a word Helen continued. 'I invited her deliberately to see for myself what she was like. She was dressed to kill in that tight red dress. And you were obviously smitten!' She paused and looked directly into James's eyes. 'To think that all this time I was worried about you thinking you might be putting yourself in harm's way staying out so late. I was so afraid that the guerrillas would get you. And all the while you were seeing her. It's true, isn't it?'

'No, darling!' James put his glass down on the table, walked across the floor and knelt down in front of Helen. He took her hands in his. 'That's not so. I admit I have been seeing her but not all the time, not every time I have been late. I swear. Please believe me, darling,' James pleaded, his face was distorted with remorse. 'Most of the time I was at the security department. There have been so many incidents

– buses set on fire, raids on farms, estate mangers attacked and killed. They have been picking my brains about the guerrillas' activity and their behaviour, which is why it didn't make sense that the High Commissioner would go off to Fraser's Hill like that!'

Helen looked down at his hands clasped over hers and then back up at James again, searching his face, searching for tell-tale signs that he might be lying although she didn't know what to look for as he had never lied to her as far as she knew. In all the time they had been together their relationship had been based on honesty and openness. At least she believed so. Suddenly the thought that he might lie, or have lied to her had sent a ripple of unease and fright through her. The thought that he no longer loved her tore at her heart. She swallowed before she asked softly, her voice shaking, 'Why, James, why were you seeing her? Are you in love with her?' Her eyes welled up with tears. She felt she couldn't bear it if he were to say yes.

James tenderly took her face in his hands, his voice was hoarse when he spoke. 'No, darling. I don't. I'm so sorry. I shouldn't have done what I did. Call it a fleeting fancy, call it anything but nothing can change the fact that I love you very very much... *Nothing* happened.'

'Are you sure? I want to believe you, James,' Helen swallowed a sob.

'Believe me. Please believe me, darling. I love you *so* very much.'

'Do you? Because if you don't...I don't know what I will do. You see... I am pregnant,' Helen looked deeply into James eyes, waiting for his reaction. His eyes lit up, his face lifted as a big smile spread across his face.

'That is wonderful! Oh, that's wonderful!' He bent down to Helen's face and kissed her. 'That is great news!'

He placed a hand on her abdomen and caressed it. ‘How many weeks.. when .. I mean..oh, you know what I mean.’

Helen smiled; for the first time in a long while she felt as if she could breathe easily again. James had responded exactly the same way before when she’d told him about the other pregnancies. Her spirits began to rise, her voice was light, ‘Twelve weeks.’

James did a quick mental calculation and then said, ‘Due June first or second?’

‘Give or take a few days,’ said Helen.

‘Darling, I can’t wait,’ James gathered Helen into his arms and held her tight.

‘Promise me you will always be true to me, to us,’ said Helen.

‘I promise,’ said James.

‘I am so happy Mrs Makapeen! Good news!’ Su Yin said smiling broadly. ‘So good. *Chilllen* know?’ For some time she’d thought that Helen had been quietly winding up inside and she’d wondered when she would snap. She had suspected who the reason for the raised voices was after the night of James’s birthday party – it had to be that Winnie woman. She’d hurried out of the room as soon as she could. Since then Helen had been like a ball of tension waiting to explode. But now, she was like a liberated woman, free of her worries; the strain on her face had disappeared. Su Yin knew for sure that husband and wife had sorted out their problem and she was both relieved and glad. She’d worried about them because she didn’t want them to break up. They were good people, they deserved each other. She had seen them so happy together, so content and she was glad for them. What was it like to be jealous of another woman? She had no idea. Even worse than that, what was it like to stand by and watch some woman take your husband from you with the husband going off willingly? Would Helen put up a fight, go and confront the other woman? What a terrible predicament to be in. Was James really unfaithful? Could men not be trusted? Did they not know what loyalty was? Her mind flipped back to what Ming had told her about her father's secret first wife in China and then her mother's accusation that Mr Lok had designs on her. Su Yin shuddered. She didn't blame Mrs Lok for being suspicious and feeling threatened even though it was unfounded as far as she was concerned. Of the two wives, somehow she was convinced that the one in China could be vengeful and spiteful but probably to no avail. But would Helen turn the same way, all out of love for her husband, all out of fear of losing her man? Su Yin didn't have a clue as to what Helen would do but she would not blame her whatever she did.

As for James, he was not short of women eager for his attention or favours. She had seen how women's eyes lit up when they saw him. She could not help the rise of anger inside; she knew there was no way anyone could stop a man's eyes straying to other women but what did he see in that awful Winnie woman? What was wrong with the man? Couldn't he see what a treasure his wife was? All she hoped for was that James would come to his senses. Su Yin didn't want the family to split up, she didn't want the fingers of unhappiness gripping this family who had become like her own family.

Seeing Helen's change in her countenance - there was a new radiance, her contentment shone through – she felt that all was right again. Now there was the baby's arrival to prepare for and look forward to. Everything was fine again. She was overjoyed.

'No, I haven't told them yet,' said Helen. 'It'll be interesting to see how they react to this,' She then placed her hand on Su Yin's arm, 'Will you stay and look after us especially with the baby coming?'

Su Yin was surprised. 'Sure I stay.'

'Oh, thank you. That makes me very happy.'

'I happy too,' said Su Yin.

'I want my hair to smell just like yours, Amah,' Ellie said as she jumped up onto the edge of her bed. The mosquito net was already let down to cover the bed. 'I love the smell of the frangipani. Please, when you wash my hair tomorrow can we put flowers in the water like you do when you wash your hair? She turned round and looked pleadingly at Su Yin. Ellie, wearing a white cotton nightdress, looked angelic.

Whenever she could Su Yin had always tried to wash her hair with water infused with sweet-smelling flowers like frangipani. Since the night all those years ago when her mother helped wash her hair and then combed it. To her mind it was not just about re-affirming her resistance to marriage, it gave her a few moments of holding on to the thin thread that connected her with her mother. Shutting everything else out she was close to her mother again. She was pleased with Ellie's request.

'Okay. We do *tomollow*,' replied Su Yin as she sat down on the bed and turned Ellie around to brush her hair.

'Thank you!' Ellie was excited. 'I will pick some flowers, no, I will ask Muthusamy to help me. He will know which ones I should pick… if he lets me.' She paused for the briefest moment and then continued, 'I am so excited about Mummy's baby. If it is a girl I would like her to be called Nancy. If it is a boy, I think Bobby would be nice. There is this boy in my class called Anthony. He is very black in colour. He said it is because he is Indian. But he is nice. I like him.'

Su Yin said nothing but continued to brush. Ellie sat very still and surprisingly turned quiet. Then in a small voice she piped up, 'Amah…'

'Y..es,' replied Su Yin. She knew there was something else coming and wondered what it would be as she continued brushing.

'Do you have babies?' asked Ellie.

'No, I got you all. You keep me busy.'

'I know but why don't you have your own babies?'

Su Yin was stumped for a moment. She had never been asked that before and never thought that she would have to explain why she didn't have her own babies. 'You ask so many questions.' Then quickly, 'You happy your *mamee* got baby coming?'

'Yes, oh, yes.' Ellie turned round to look at Su Yin. 'I will help you look after it.'

Su Yin smiled at the little happy face. 'You don't give me *tlouble* will be good.'

There was silence as Su Yin continued brushing the shiny golden hair. Then Ellie's small voice piped up again. 'Do you have a mummy and daddy?'

'*Or* course, I do. We all have *mamee* and *daddee*. My *mamee* and *daddee* live far away.' A lump rose in Su Yin's throat. 'In China. A beautiful place.' As she stroked the silky hair, pictures of the silk factory and each of the family's faces popped up.

'Do you miss them?'

Su Yin felt her eyes moistening. 'Yes.'

'Are you sad that they are so far away?'

'Yes.'

'Don't you want to go and see them? I would be very sad if I didn't see my Mummy and Daddy for a long time.'

'Come. Finish. You go to bed now,' said Su Yin feeling a gap opening in her chest. Ellie leapt off the bed, dived under the mosquito net and made herself comfortable, her hair fanned out around her head on the pillow. She held up her arms to Su Yin. Su Yin bent down to hug her thinking how lucky she was to have such a lovely child to look after.

'I am sure your mummy and daddy are thinking of you,' Ellie said softly, 'and very sad you are not with them.'

Su Yin turned away quickly as her eyes started to fill up.

Chapter 16

Kuala Lumpur city centre was ablaze with preparation for the celebration of the Chinese Lunar New Year whereas a month before Christmas didn't get a look-in. Only the Europeans and the local Christian Chinese celebrated it. At the church gates the pastors and their helpers handed out bags of sweets which attracted children in the houses and shops nearby. Eager children came with hands reaching out for the goodies, not put off by the fact that it was a festival of the western religion.

In the main the Europeans had their festivities in the home with the traditional roast turkey and alternative trimmings of roast sweet potatoes, cabbage and carrots. Helen could not find potatoes which were normally scarce and had never seen Brussels sprouts anywhere in the market. As usual her mother had shipped over a Christmas cake and pudding. No conifer tree for a Christmas tree either, so James improvised and found a large potted hibiscus shrub that wasn't in flower and placed it at the far corner of the sitting room where it could be seen from the entrance to the room. Helen and the children had made small ornaments with gold and coloured paper to hang on the tree and also baked gingerbread men which filled the kitchen with a lovely aroma. Su Yin, who by now had learnt how to roast a whole turkey which Helen ordered from their usual chicken and duck seller, was kept busy in the kitchen.

On Christmas morning Cammy, Lexie, Ellie and Thomas shot out of bed earlier than usual and rushed to look for their presents on the floor around the hibiscus shrub decorated with red bows, small gold and coloured boxes and origami birds. Su Yin was given a box wrapped in silver paper which contained a pair of red sandals that she'd seen and admired when she and Helen were shopping. The year before she was a given a watch. The children had drawn a card for her. Then Ah Hock drove them all to St Andrew's Church, the Presbyterian church in town, where bags of sweets were handed out to the local children who'd flocked to it for the free goodies. As usual Su Yin went along and sat with the family in church. Although she didn't understand most of what was said during the service she liked the music and the singing, something she'd never experienced before and so different from her worship at her temple.

Seeing the whole MacAlpine family together, happy and contented on such an occasion always magnified how much Su Yin missed her family. But Chinese New Year hit her even harder; the distance between her and her own family seemed to have yawned. She would have felt the void even more had it not been for Cheng and Joo who felt the same as she did. She had sent home a box filled with half a dozen jars of Brand's Essence of Chicken for her parents and two tins of milk powder for her new nephew. The money she'd included was not as much as she would have liked and it would be used for buying the special foods for the family reunion meal which would be modest by the standard she had grown accustomed to in the MacAlpine's household. It was the family reunion she missed most. She would give anything just to be able to join them again. Her savings towards the fare was growing as fast as a racing snail. At the last count she reckoned it would buy her a trip that would probably take her a quarter of the way to Canton and that was only a one-way trip. She was sure that once she had redeemed her dress she would be able to redouble her savings. If she had learnt anything at all in all the years since leaving home, it was patience. She would continue to be patient. In the meantime, she was happy that Joo and Cheng and all the other sisters would have their own reunion meal.

With the shops closed for the New Year celebrations, the five-footway became a playground. Happy laughing children dressed in their new clothes were anxiously waiting for the lion dance to start. A group of them had gathered around a man sitting on his stool at his work-box making figurines of animals out of bright red, blue, green and yellow clay. Cut bunches of tall fresh sugarcane were already in place outside some of the shops in readiness for more celebrations by the Hokkien community to give thanks to the Heaven God on the ninth day of New Year. A large platform was being set up in the middle of the market square to display food offerings alongside sugarcane, a reminder of the sugarcane fields which saved their ancestors from the enemies in ancient China. Nearby a group of men were already busy erecting a wooden theatre for the open-air opera.

What was missing were the long lines of firecrackers that were lit at midnight to herald the New Year. Then on the first day of the new year more lines of crackers would hang from the upstairs windows of the shop houses and lit when the lion dance started. Once the explosion of the crackers had stopped the lion would climb a pole to reach the red packet of money at the top end of the line. But in the climate of uncertainty, under the dark cloud of threats from the communist terrorists slithering in the jungle, firecrackers had been banned. Security was visibly increased - Malay policemen and the unmistakable Sikhs with their white turbans patrolled the streets. Even though it was a Chinese festival and the town was well away from the jungle's edge with a large clearing in between where the communist terrorists couldn't hide, the government was not taking any chances.

Every year the sisters' celebration dinner was held at the same restaurant called *High Seas* in Petaling Street owned and run by a fellow Cantonese Mr Ong from Canton who started his business in 1925. His signature dish was steamed seabass marinated in a special sauce the recipe of which he was not willing to divulge. He would burst out laughing whenever someone tried to coax it out of him. Always good humoured, Mr Ong treated them with respect and was always cordial. It was the nearest to a home-from-home. The only problem was getting everyone to meet on the same day since those who worked for Chinese families could not get away on the eve or the first day of the New Year. Su Yin and one other sister who worked for European families were more flexible. This year the day agreed on was the third day of the New Year. As always it was the same ten women who would get together.

All the women were dressed in their new *samfoos* that they had made themselves in their spare time. In keeping with the traditional celebration, they were colourful unlike the black and white they normally wore. Similarly, the restaurant was decorated with red lanterns and red scrolls of gold calligraphy of felicitous words for good fortune and prosperity. The entire restaurant was like a classroom of school children talking and laughing loudly against the background refrain of clanging crockery coming from the kitchen. Mr Ong had greeted them as if they were family and led them to a large round marble-topped table which was laid out with blue and white bowls, spoons, chopsticks and teacups. A waiter quickly appeared with a pot of Chinese tea and proceeded to fill the cups.

Another waiter came and took their order which was much more than they would normally have.

'I know I have said this before,' Joo raised her voice to make sure she was heard, 'but you all will agree that this is so good – to be waited on for a change.'

'Yes, yes,' every one responded with big smiles on their faces and then lifted their cups to drink. 'Another year gone. Wishing everyone a happy and prosperous new year. *Kong hei fatt choy!*'

'I wonder what new dishes Mr Ong has invented this time,' someone said. 'The last time was braised stuffed tofu with salted fish. That was delicious.'

'Yes, I remember. It was so good that I tried to make it for my family.'

'Did they like it?' asked another.

'Yes, I said I invented it myself,' a giggle. 'I suppose I gave it my own twist, added a few ingredients of my own.'

'Like what? Tell us,' someone said.

'I chopped up bamboo shoot and added it to the minced pork, used more pepper to give it a sharper taste - my family like hot stuff, you see. And also added chopped coriander to the mix.'

'Big Sister Ping,' Su Yin addressed the woman sitting directly opposite her, 'what new dishes have you created?' Apart from Cheng and Joo she didn't know the others in the group very well but Ping who was the oldest of them all had a special place in her heart; it was she who took the trouble to welcome her when she first arrived at the *coolie* room. She had always been friendly and warm towards Su Yin and for that Su Yin was eternally grateful and tried to do the same to all the other women who came after her. Ping's youthful appearance, her ready smile and her energy belied her age; nobody guessed that she was almost sixty-two.

'The mistress likes squids,' replied Ping, 'so the other day I tried something different. I minced prawns, seasoned with chopped chilli, salt and a bit of cornflour to hold it together, then stuffed it into the squids. I used toothpicks to skewer together the opening and then lightly cook them in a *sambal* sauce. Not too much sauce, just enough to fry the squids in.'

'Hmmm, sounds interesting. But isn't it a bit big to eat, I mean did you cut up the squid before serving?'

'Yes, and the mistress seemed to like it.'

'Might try that.'

'You are so lucky that your family will try different things. Mine are so fussy. Don't like this, don't like that! So I cook the same old things. I suppose it has its blessing like not having to think too much. I have enough to do as it is.'

Su Yin considered herself very lucky; none of the children she had looked after was particularly fussy. She thought of Ming and was happy that her exam results were excellent, as expected, and she and her family would be celebrating her success.

'But that is just it, you want to experiment and try something new and exciting.'

'The precious children in my family are also fussy. They like this particular Hokkien noodles which you can only get at this stall in Japanese Street.'

'Is that so?' everyone's attention was now hooked.

'Yes.'

Someone asked in a soft voice, 'Japanese Street. Isn't that where the cursed Japanese soldiers would seek comfort in female company?'

'Yes. Although it is not so overt, it is obvious that the same business – brothels – still goes on there. I have to go there every so often to buy the noodles. The brothels have a more respectable front. To all intents and purposes, many of them are coffee shops, even sell *nasi lemak* and Malay cakes for snacks. You see the women dressed in pretty clothes and men with that guilty look going in and out and at all times of the day. But the women sitting at the tables are by no means your average housewife. Their faces are painted, they wear dark red lipsticks and they smoke! They sit with the men and then they disappear behind the shop. Which reminds me,' turning to Su Yin she said in a subdued tone, 'that young newcomer is in the business.' She pulled a sad face.

Su Yin frowned, 'Which newcomer?'

'The one you read the letter for not so long ago, remember? Tall, slim and pretty,' said Joo. 'Surname of Tong I seem to remember.'

'Ah, yes, I remember now.' Since that last time Su Yin hadn't seen her when she had been to pick up her letters. She had wondered about her; it had crossed her mind that she could possibly be snapped up by some brothel owner.

For a few moments no one spoke. Then a waiter appeared with their rice and a platter of sweet and sour chicken which he placed in the centre of the table.

Su Yin noticed that Cheng was very attentive to Wei; she had made sure that Wei sat next to her. She remembered that they had sat next to each other the year before and had got on very well. As all of them picked up their chopsticks to reach for the platter she saw that Cheng was very quick to pick a succulent piece of chicken and put it in Wei's bowl. Wei smiled sweetly at Cheng who looked gratified and proceeded to help herself.

When the platter was empty a waiter came to remove it and while another set down a plate of deep fried king prawns in batter.

Joo spoke. 'Tell me, Big Sister Ping, what are your plans now that the children in your family are grown up?'

Ping licked her lips then said. 'The master and mistress don't want me to go. They have said as much and even the children don't want me to go. The oldest son even said he wanted me to look after his family when he has one. I suppose that is good. I will continue with them until they kick me out or I drop dead first!'

'*Wah,* that is very fortunate indeed, to be valued like that.'

'They are good and kind to me; that is why I have been with them for twenty-one years. They are like my own family.'

'Do you think you will go back home one day?'

'I reckon I will carry on working until I can't anymore then go back to China. My nieces and nephews have promised to look after me.'

'Quite right too after all you have done for them.'

'Do you regard Malaya as home?'

'My heart belongs there in China but I suppose home will be where I am wanted, needed,' answered Ping.

Big Sister Ping, you've got a long time to go before you worry about retiring,' said Cheng.

Someone piped up excitedly. 'I heard that the coolie room might be closed.'

'Closed? What do you mean?'

'Someone said that the person who has been paying the rent for it is not able to do it anymore?'

'That would be disastrous, terrible! That place is our anchor!' Suddenly everyone round the table was lamenting its closure.

'We will have to have our letters sent to our workplace.'

'When the newcomers arrive here where will they stay till they get a job?'

When the topic was exhausted Su Yin interjected beaming broadly. 'My mistress is pregnant again! I am so happy for her.'

'*Aiyahh*, nappies and sleepless nights again! Rather you than me. I remember those days of washing nappies, an endless task!' said Ping.

'Her children are all so adorable,' said Su Yin. 'I'll look after them anytime. One of them asked me the other day if I've got babies. When I said no, she asked why not. That is what I like about them – so innocent and direct.'

'Certainly ask awkward questions.'

More food arrived.

The band of sisters wanted to walk for a bit through the town to soak up the atmosphere, to pretend they were back home in their village again. The afternoon sun was burning, a propitious day for the street celebrations. They put up their umbrellas. Su Yin looked at her watch. Because of the festivities, the curfew was going to be even stricter and James MacAlpine had insisted on Ah Hock fetching her back. She still had lots of time before he came for her. Cheng and Wei had already gone off together in the opposite direction after saying goodbye leaving the rest of the group to stroll, weaving between children playing on the five-foot way.

When they were near the *coolie* room, even though they had collected their letters only two days ago Su Yin said that she would run upstairs to see if there was any mail. She wondered if anyone wanted a letter read.

'I shouldn't think anyone would be there on such day, Su Yin,' said Joo.

'Don't wait for me, you go ahead. I will just run upstairs in case there is someone there. Who knows? Besides Ah Hock is picking me up here, so you go on.'

There was no sound from the room as Su Yin got to the landing. When she entered the room she was surprised to see a figure all alone sitting at the table by the window, her head bowed as if she was looking at something on her lap. For a brief second Su Yin felt as if she was intruding then she said, 'I wasn't sure if there would be anyone here.' The figure spun around. Su Yin recognised it was Mui the young woman she and her friends had been talking about earlier. Mui stood up quickly, surprise and relief on her face.

'Big Sister, I was hoping to see you here. I was beginning to give up hope.' She was wearing a beautiful sleeveless short dress in floral print cotton which was neatly tucked at her slim waist.

'How long have you been waiting?' Su Yin asked.

'It doesn't matter. You are here now. But have you time to read my letter please?' Mui held up two letters. Su Yin pulled out a stool from under the table and sat down, indicating to Mui to do the same. 'I picked them up when I was sure no one else was around. I was hoping I would see you.'

'Why did you wait till no one was around?' Su Yin was puzzled. The whole point of coming to the coolie room was to meet the others. It was usually buzzing with the sisters although there were noticeably fewer newcomers.

Mui lowered her eyes; after a few seconds she took a deep breath and looked at Su Yin who suddenly realised why. Mui said quietly, 'I am sure you must have heard that I am working in a brothel.'

'Yes, I have. And you are not the first. We can't all be domestic servants. I think we have taken all the jobs going,' said Su Yin trying to sound as sympathetic as she could. She patted Mui's arm, 'You can't be afraid of what people will say and people will talk but you can be sure we all understand.'

Mui smiled. When she spoke her voice was calm and assured. 'I am not sure everyone does. But as you said, we can't all be domestic servants. The woman who runs the brothel came here one day when I was here alone and desperate for a job. She asked me if I was looking for work and that was that. I haven't told anyone else about it. It is not something I am proud of but I need the money. I feel I can talk to you because you seem to be understanding and kind.'

Su Yin nodded, unsure what to say. 'Well, I can tell you for sure most of us can sympathise and understand. We've been in the black depths of despair before and we don't ever want to be there again.' She couldn't think of anything else to add. Then, 'Shall we read your letters?'

When Su Yin finished reading and looked up, tears were rolling down Mui's cheeks. She felt her own eyes welling up as she placed her hand over Mui's hands which were clasped tightly on the table. 'You did very well to have given your father a decent burial with the money you sent. Be proud of that.'

'I hope I did,' Mui said softly. 'He was already ill before I left. I didn't really want to leave him but I knew I had to. Who else was going to make sure that they had food? And medicine for my father?' She tried to stem her sobs but they came relentlessly. Su Yin could do nothing else but cry with her as she thought of her own parents. After a long while Mui reached out for the brown mock leather handbag on the table, opened it and pulled out a dollar note. 'This is for you, for all you have done,' she said as she held it to Su Yin.

Su Yin pushed it back to her. 'Don't be silly. There is no need for that.'

'Please take it.'

'I can't. It is too much!'

'Please,' Mui insisted.

Su Yin looked hard at Mui, said nothing for a while and then took the note from her. Mui wiped her tears with a handkerchief she'd dug out of her bag.

'If you need someone to talk to, I usually come here on the first Saturday of the month,' said Su Yin.

'Thank you. I will remember that,' said Mui.

Chapter 17

The temple of Kwan Yin was crowded with people, young and old, quietly moving about in the hall. The air was soaked with the fragrance of incense. At the far end, on the altar draped in red satin were burning joss sticks in large brass holders, plates of pink sweet buns, whole roast chicken, strips of pork and baskets of oranges offered to appease the Goddess of Mercy. In the far corner of the hall a middle-aged nun with a shaven head wearing a baggy grey robe and sandals was chanting softly. Men and women were praying – giving thanks for the past year and pleading with the goddess to grant them a year of prosperity, good health, peace and fortune. Children mimicked their elders, making their own pleas such as letting them pass their school exams. Despite the mass of worshippers there was a reverent hush.

Su Yin, Joo and Cheng purchased joss sticks from a shrivelled old man at the entrance with his box of joss sticks and red candles. They each lit them and started to pray at the altar of Kwan Yin beseeching the goddess to grant them good health for themselves and their families back in China.

They left the temple and passed a Hindu temple that was encrusted with tiers of hand-carved, rainbow- coloured and gold idols. Along the busy street they walked until they came to a small park where they found a bench in the shade of a large Angsana tree. Cheng sat at one end next to Joo while Su Yin took the other end.

'Joo,' said Cheng, 'are you alright? You seem to be very quiet. Not like your usual self. Are you not well? Got a touch of the fever that is going around? This heat is not good.'

'Yes, I noticed you didn't eat much either,' Su Yin said as she leant forward to look at her. 'Is anything wrong?'

Joo looked at a group of children playing in the field next to the single-storey school building. The glass windows of the classrooms still had the criss-cross tapes left over from the time of the Japanese Occupation. She didn't answer. Her hand rose to cover her mouth as if she was afraid that what was coming out might either come out the wrong way or offend the ears of Cheng and Su Yin. Then she swung round to face each of her friends in turn, her eyes intense with earnestness, 'You two are my dearest and closest friends, my sisters,' she said, 'and I value your friendship and respect you very much. I am so afraid that you will think badly of me when I tell you.'

'What could be that bad? We know you, we've known you for such a long time. There isn't a bad bone in you. If anything you are too soft. You let people take advantage of you,' said Cheng.

'What is it? Tell us. We can help, that is, if you want us to help,' said Su Yin.

'Promise me you won't think badly of me,' said Joo. Her desperation showed in her eyes.

'Go on, tell us, 'said Cheng, 'you are beginning to worry me.'

'You remember me telling you about the owner of the grocer shop where I do my shopping?' Joo asked. Her face eased a little.

Cheng and Su Yin nodded. They knew the man had lost his wife a few years ago to some illness. Joo often talked about him. 'Yes?' they asked, their eyes widening.

'He has asked me to marry him.' The look on Joo's face turned to guilt. She waited for Cheng and Su Yin to react. All the two friends could do was stare at her. Their mouths opened slowly but no sound emanated. Joo watched her friends' faces go blank with shock as if she had slapped them. Eventually Su Yin spoke,

'You are not joking, are you?' Su Yin asked. Joo shook her head.

'But your vow,' said Cheng now frowning, 'I mean…I don't understand.'

'Please, please don't judge me,' Joo sounded desperate and anxious. 'Don't think I have gone bad to renege on my vow. Don't you feel lonely sometimes?' Joo's voice turned soft as if she was embarrassed to admit to her real feelings. 'Don't you want someone to hold you? Someone to share your problems and little things like when you see or hear something that makes you feel happy? I feel lonely sometimes and I think I care very much about him, enough to want to spend my time with him and grow old with him.'

There was silence.

Then Cheng spoke, 'You can't break your vow now, can you? Not that I think you mustn't. I simply mean, is it allowed?'

'That's for her to decide, Cheng. Nobody else. It is her life, her choice,' said Su Yin. 'That much I believe. She doesn't answer to anyone else but herself.'

'Even though we made our vows to Kwan Yin?' Cheng added.

No one spoke. Then Su Yin said, 'I still maintain that it is up to you.'

'Thank you,' Joo, her face starting to relax, looked at Su Yin. 'So would it be wrong to renege on my vow?' Neither Cheng nor Su Yin answered. The sound of children shouting and laughing in the field drifted to them. They gazed at them. Joo continued, 'I thought of that nun I saw in the temple. Like us she also made a vow to celibacy. We are like the nuns, aren't we? They in their grey robes, we in our black and whites.'

'I hear they have a good life in the nunnery,' said Su Yin. 'It might be about chastity but not so sure about the frugality.'

We were so young then,' said Cheng, 'but we knew exactly what we wanted. We were so sure. I don't think we can judge you or anyone who wishes to change their mind. Who are we to judge? I have to say that I was concerned when some time ago I heard you say you wondered if that young woman Ah Mui made the right choice. As it happened, she had no choice, or did she, when she went into *that* business?'

'It is about survival, isn't it?' said Su Yin. 'In her case she probably had a choice and she chose that. It pays better and she can work as and when she pleases. Cleaning and cooking isn't everybody's ideal job. She will very likely save enough to pay for her fare back to see her family quicker than I can.'

'With her looks she wouldn't be short of work,' added Cheng.

Joo let out a tiny chuckle. 'Funny how things have turned out. With a face like mine I always thought that if I hadn't joined the sisterhood no man would look at me anyway let alone give me a second look. I was safe from marriage.' Her cheeks turned red. 'And now someone actually wants to marry me.'

'You are worth more than the rest of us put together,' said Su Yin. 'This man knows a good thing when he sees it.'

'And looks aren't everything,' said Cheng. 'How old is this man?'

'He is nearly forty-six,' replied Joo.

'What about his children? What do they think?' asked Cheng.

'They are grown up and have good jobs. He has done very well looking after them since his wife died.'

'What do the children think about his wanting to marry again? Would they think that you are after their inheritance?' Cheng asked.

Su Yin was not surprised that Joo had been proposed to. Apart from being a little tight-fisted - who wouldn't be given her circumstances? - she had all the qualities that would make a good wife. But like Cheng she could not help being suspicious. 'He recognises gold when he sees it.'

'He wants you to look after him in his old age,' said Cheng.

'Maybe… but we have a good rapport. We always have a good banter, right from the start when I first went to his shop.'

'It might all change after you are married,' said Cheng. 'You know what men are like. They chase you when they want you but the second they've got you they lose interest and drop you like a used rag.'

'At least I know what he is like, can be like. It is not the same as with an arranged marriage. At least now I am walking into marriage with my eyes wide open.'

'True. We have seen good and bad marriages. They are not all bad. It will be taking a gamble like everything else,' said Su Yin.

'So..' Joo looked eagerly at her friends' faces, 'are you both saying that you are not angry with me or ashamed of me if I get married?' She bit her lips as she waited for their answers.

'Of course not,' Su Yin and Cheng replied vehemently.

'How long have you been feeling like this, you know, wanting to marry?' asked Cheng.

'How do you know that is what you really want, I mean that this man is the one you want to spend the rest of your life with?' asked Su Yin.

Joo smiled. 'Don't laugh, but when I think of him I feel tingly inside and can't wait to see him or hear his voice again. I want to be near him. He is not the best-looking man but he is not ugly either; there is so much that is good about him. He is kind and considerate. I can't ask for more.' She quickly added, 'He cares about me too.'

'That is so nice,' said Su Yin. 'You know, you are lucky to experience that. Is that what they call 'love'?'

Joo blushed again. 'I don't know. I know I care deeply about him,' she replied.

No one spoke for a while as if they needed a moment to digest what had been said.

Finally, Su Yin said. 'There is such a big element of trust involved, don't you think?'

Joo nodded. 'That's the gamble I have to take,' she said.

'For me it is like stepping into blackness, you don't know what is there waiting for you,' Su Yin continued. 'But that is me. If you are really convinced that it is what you want, then you have to go with it.' She felt her eyes welling up. 'I admire you very much for your courage. I realise it is not something you do lightly.' She reached out for Joo's hand and clasped it tightly. 'It is another giant step you are taking and I hope you will be very happy.'

'Yes, very brave,' Cheng said, 'I agree.' She then threw her arms around Joo and hugged her tightly. 'I am happy for you if this is what you want,' she said through her tears. 'I hope it doesn't mean we can't see you anymore once you are married.'

Joo laughed. 'I am not going to be imprisoned! Of course, you will continue to see me.'

Cheng stroked Joo's face and then her hair. She whispered, 'You won't have to wear your hair up like this anymore.' Joo nodded. 'Or the white and black uniform. You will be the boss lady!' They burst into laughter.

'We must meet this lucky man,' said Su Yin. 'You haven't even told us his name.'

Joo's face, wet with tears, now beamed. 'His name is Tan. As you know he is Hokkien but he speaks fluent Cantonese. In his line of business, he needs to speak all the dialects and Malay. He is very good like that.' She took a deep breath; the tension had gone from her face. 'Thank you for understanding. And for not judging me.'

Back in her room later that night Su Yin felt a sense of relief and gratitude that her life was simple and uncomplicated. Her path was clearly defined; no deviation from it. Her thoughts turned to Ah Mui and her new lifestyle. There was so much she was curious about: what did Ah Mui have to do in her job? How far did she have to go with her clients? What did she think of herself? How long could she keep it a secret from her family? How would they take it when she eventually divulged it, if she divulged it? Would she?

Then she couldn't help feeling worried for Joo; it was a huge step into the unknown. She couldn't voice her worry and fear that her husband-to-be might turn out not to be the nice man he appeared to be. Could she be stepping into an abyss that she couldn't ever get out of? As for herself she had got accustomed to her way of life and not being dependent on anyone else least of all a man. As she started to take the pins from her hair she suddenly remembered the letter in her bag, the one she'd picked up earlier before Joo's confession. The hand writing on the envelope was unfamiliar which got her curious. She turned it over to look for the address of the sender but there was none. She had been baffled and had hastily put it into her bag before rushing to re-join Cheng and Joo.

She took the letter from her bag. The envelope was different from what she normally got from home. This was pale blue instead of white. The handwriting was also different; the strokes were manly and firm, a little clumsy, quite distinct from her father's which were stylish and confident. She knew no one in Kuala Lumpur who was likely write to her. Her initial fear was that it was an official letter from some governmental department to tell her she had to leave the country. She pulled out the folded paper and started to read.

She read it once and then read it again. Slowly the mist began to clear; the picture was coming into focus - the picture of the young butcher's help she saw in the market and then met after he and her brother Keng had finished the boat race. It was Liew the man who caught her eye all those years ago, the man who had stirred her curiosity. A warm glow came over her; she smiled at the memory of that afternoon when amidst the shouting and jubilation at the end of the race which they had won both Fung and Liew came to meet her and Lan Yee. It was so long ago; a different age in a different world. Although she had put him out of her mind the memory had not faded: she could see clearly the young faces, beaming with triumph through the dripping sweat. She could hear the crowd cheering in competition with the sound of the drums pounding in the distance. The two men looked so happy and exhilarated and she herself had been infected with the exhilaration. Then Lan Yee's sweet face smiled at her and she felt the familiar stab of sadness and emptiness.

Su Yin read the letter again.

Dear Su Yin,

I sincerely hope that you will not be offended by my writing to you.
I asked your brother Keng for your address. I hope you are well. It might surprise
you to know that I am in Kuala Lumpur. I would like to meet you again if only
to catch up on what is happening back in our village and what we have been doing all these years. Please telephone me at this number 3018

Your friend
Liew

Chapter 18

On the soft grassy carpet that the gardener Muthusamy had tirelessly maintained, James was running around pretending to be a big bad wolf in pursuit of his bare-footed children screaming as they ran away from him. Thomas was laughing and running to catch up with his older siblings and then stumbling, he picked himself up, still laughing, and tried to run again. From the kitchen window where Su Yin was washing up the dishes she watched them thinking how wonderful it was that father and children were playing together. James had been coming home early or if he was going to be late he would phone to let Helen know which pleased her.

At the side of the lawn in the shade of the frangipani tree, Helen was sitting in a rattan chair with her feet on a stool and looking on with contentment on her face. She was getting bigger and complaining that her feet were swelling. 'This heat is killing me!' she had complained several times – the bigger she got the more intolerant of the heat she became. James had placed a table fan right behind her. Su Yin turned to look at her calendar and worked out that the baby should be due in seven or eight weeks and quickly remembered that Ming would be leaving for England in four months. Ming was happier the last time they met. They had gone shopping together in Robinson's departmental store where Su Yin had only been to once with Helen. It had amazed her seeing Ming buy without hesitation; what she had spent on the umbrella, hand bag and shoes was equivalent to her year's earning if not more. She smiled on recalling how in between browsing, Ming had enthused about what she was going to study; she was going to use her degree in law to fight for women's rights.

'Right children, enough. I'm having a rest,' James said to the children who looked crestfallen. 'I've got to see how Mummy is,' he quickly added. At that the children shot off to do their own thing. Lexie took Thomas' hands and started dancing with him. James limped over to Helen and slumped into the chair at the other side of the table to her as he let out a big breath.

'You must be ready for a cold beer now, you've earned it!' said Helen as she smiled at James. She reached out to take his hand. He took her hand then got up, walked over to her and knelt down before her placing both hands on her abdomen. He looked deeply into her eyes. She was flushed but there was no mistaking the happiness that beamed from her eyes. In her pale blue cotton smock, her short hair brushed back from her face, she was a picture of maternal bloom. She was definitely big now, her bump protruding proudly. James took her hands and kissed them.

Helen caressed his cheeks then kissed his forehead. Her voice trembled as she whispered, 'I don't know what I would have done if it had been you in that Gurney ambush. Thank God you were alright.'

James shook his head as if to silence her. 'You are so precious to me, you, the children and this little one,' he patted her abdomen.

'Oh! It's kicking!' she quickly grabbed James hands to place them over where she had felt the kicking.

'It knows what I am saying,' said James smiling. Addressing the abdomen, 'You do, don't you?' He then bent to kiss the bump. 'Ah, here comes Amah with the drinks.'

Su Yin carrying a tray of cold drinks was walking towards them with the children following behind. James stood up. 'Thank you, just what I need,' he said in Cantonese as he took the bottle of beer from the tray.

Su Yin set the tray on the table. She had specially made a barley drink which was the children's favourite. She poured the drinks which the children helped themselves to and then she handed Helen a glass. 'Mrs Makapeen, good for you. Keep you cool.' She noticed the fine fair hair on Helen's legs, a clear sign that she wasn't now able to bend to shave them.

'Thank you, Amah,' Helen took the glass. 'What would I do without you?'

'Amah,' said Cammy after gulping his drink, 'you should see where I have been doing my target practice.' He led her to where he had set up a tin can on a post that Muthusamy had put up for him. He pulled out his catapult from his pocket, picked up a pebble from his collection on the ground and proceeded to demonstrate to Su Yin.

Su Yin watched then said, 'Cammy, we *kom-pet -ti-shion.'*

Cammy squinted at Su Yin and gave her a doubtful look. 'Okay, Amah, but I warn you, I will trash you.'

'We see,' said Su Yin. At that point the girls came rushing to them holding a kite. Then they heard James calling out,

'Look who's arrived!'

They all turned to see Penny and Anthony Pendle coming round the side of the house into the garden.

Penny Pendle looking like a schoolgirl bursting to share a secret. 'We just couldn't wait to tell you,' she said. 'We've been thinking about adopting and have finally decided that we will do it.' She waited for the news to land as she looked at Helen then James.

Helen gasped. She knew Penny was desperate for a baby but it had not occurred to her that she might consider adoption. 'That is wonderful! Are you thinking of adopting from somewhere local?'

'Yes, it will have to be,' answered Anthony.

'That's wonderful, old chap,' said James as he shook Anthony's hand.

'You are quite sure?' Helen's brow gathered.

'I know what you are thinking: how on earth am I going to find a white baby here?'

'I'm sorry..' said Helen, 'I didn't mean to be…you know what I mean. I have to admit that I'm surprised but I am very proud of you. It will be very noble to take on a child who is very likely non-white.'

'Anthony and I have talked about it and thought hard about it. We've searched our hearts and come to the conclusion that we don't mind what colour or race the child is – Chinese, Malay or Indian. I don't want to wait any longer. I'm not getting any younger. Besides I might as well do some good for some poor unwanted child instead of sitting around doing nothing.'

'You will do more than that I know - you will be a good mother. I admire you for what you are about to do. Oh, this is so exciting!' said Helen as she gave Penny a big hug.

Penny looked lost in her thoughts. Then she said, 'I know I will love it like my own.'

'Penny, I have no doubt about that! But will there be lots of red tape about the adoption?'

'No, I have been told,' said Anthony. 'We have already looked at a couple of orphanages. They'll vet you to make sure you will give the child a proper home etcetera. I don't think they care much about matching colours of adoptive parents and the child; they are just glad to place children in good homes. I've heard some mothers either give away or sell their babies because they can't afford to feed another mouth.'

'Yes, I know,' said Helen. 'That's so sad. I hope you won't have too long to wait. Wouldn't it be amazing if you get a baby at the same time as when this one arrives?' She patted her bump.

Penny smiled as her eyes glistened with tears, 'Wouldn't it be just amazing?'

Su Yin didn't like asking Helen if she could use the house telephone. She didn't want her to think she was taking liberties. She had no choice as there was only a telephone number to contact Liew. His letter had stirred up the homesickness that had been laid to sleep. She felt the familiar deep ache, the longing for her family, to touch her mother and feel her soft cool skin again and take her arm like she used to whenever they went to the market together. She wanted to be her mother's little girl again. She yearned to throw her arms around her and tell her how much she missed her. She so desperately wanted to hear her father playing his flute again, to hear his gentle voice telling her stories.

Then she started to wonder what Liew could be doing in Kuala Lumpur. Had he been there long? Was he simply travelling and this was just a stop? What had he been doing all this time? She felt a slight flutter. Yes, she would be glad to see him and became excited at the thought of seeing him again and hearing news from her family. The night before she had dreamt of her mother weaving silk and had woken up feeling the wetness on her face. She had been sobbing. She remembered that she hadn't wanted her family especially her mother and father to see her tears when she bade them goodbye. She didn't want them to know that she was frightened about leaving to enter the big wide world that was alien to her and sad not knowing when she would see them again. But more than that she knew there was a reason for her dream of her mother weaving the special silk for her. She had decided that she would give the dress to Joo to wear on her wedding day. It was all the more reason for her to act fast – she had to redeem her dress.

She waited until the children were quietly reading their books and doing their homework. In Lexie's bedroom, Helen was sorting out baby clothes that her older children used to wear which had been stored in a wooden Ottoman box. She was looking at a tiny pair of cotton pants which she was holding up when Su Yin knocked on the door. 'Mrs Makapeen,' she called softly.

Helen turned to look at Su Yin. 'Ah, Amah, what is it?' she asked. She looked back at the pants. 'Aren't they just so cute?'

Su Yin nodded. She hesitated and then pulled out a letter from the side pocket of her top and held it out to show Helen. 'A *flend* from my village is here in Kuala Lumpur.' She waited for the information to sink.

'You mean one of the other *amahs*?'

'No, no. It is a man. He come from my village. Here,' she shook the letter in her hand, 'he say he is here. Here in Kuala Lumpur.'

Helen put down the pants and turned to face Su Yin. 'Oh, that's nice! Are you going to see him?'

'I want to… He say to telephone him.' Su Yin waited hoping that Helen would know what she was going to ask.

'Of course! Use the phone. Go and ring him right away!' said Helen.

Later that night on the radio was news that a man in one of the new settlements was caught smuggling food, cigarettes and stolen ammunitions on his way to work in a rubber plantation in Johore. He was hanged. In juxtaposition, a factory owned by a Chinese man had been burned down. The owner had refused to 'donate' to the cause of the jungle guerrillas and to teach him and others a lesson, the guerrillas set fire to the building just after curfew was imposed.

Chapter 19

It took Su Yin a while to get her head round the fact that the man opposite her at the table was Liew, the young butcher's help who had turned her head in the market a lifetime ago. She felt as if her life had been re-wound back to that moment again when they'd come face to face after the boat race. At the sight of him her heart had again fluttered like a butterfly and her cheeks suddenly felt warm.

In spite of the impact of the intervening years Liew had worn well; his appearance belied his age of forty-three. His well-tanned face bore a few lines at the corner of his still sunny eyes, his thick black hair was now cut very short so that it was spiky which Su Yin presumed was to help keep him cool. He had put on some weight, just enough to bulk him a little and he looked fresh in his pale blue cotton shirt and beige trousers. He was just as nervous as Su Yin was when they first greeted each other; to her surprise he held out his hand to her. She had taken it like she had seen her boss and his friends did. At the touch of his hand she felt a warm electric shock. His hand was neither rough nor smooth and his grip was firm. She had to admit she liked what she saw. She was conscious of his dark brown eyes searching her face; what did he expect to find? She hoped that he wasn't disappointed that she was no longer the young woman he remembered. To her annoyance her hand had involuntarily gone up to cover the birthmark on her face which she was convinced was redder than ever and probably flashing like the new traffic lights in town.

Her reaction had taken her by surprise. She had been excited about seeing him again; she kept reminding herself that he was an old friend from her hometown. But she had not expected to be as self-conscious as she had been. Before leaving the house she had been worried about how she looked, brushing her hair more than usual and actually toying with the idea of wearing her hair differently instead of the bun at the nape. She had taken a long hard look at herself in the mirror and wondered what Liew would think of her seeing her as she was now. Then she became cross with herself and quickly snapped out of what she thought was a childish daydream.

Now they both had slipped into an easy conversation like they had known each other forever and were simply picking up where they had left off after a short break, enjoying a cup of tea at one of the roadside stalls where she sometimes had lunch with Joo and Cheng. Her first concern was whether or not he had seen her parents.

'You have nothing to worry about; both your parents are well,' Liew said. 'I saw them a few times when I went to look for Keng to pick him up for rowing.' He paused. 'That was not long after you left. They looked well then and they were in good health when I saw them again not so long ago.'

'That's good.' Su Yin leant forward, she was curious. 'When did you see them?'

'Almost a year ago.'

Su Yin straightened up feeling relieved that her parents were well. She felt a stab of homesickness again, her eyes welled up. For a few moments she was transported to her home and family in China and felt sad for her parents that they couldn't see their daughter either. She looked at Liew; she was touched that he took the trouble to see them. 'Are they really well?' she asked. 'I know that Mother was complaining of a bit of arthritis in her hand. It has to be due to all the years of reeling.'

'She looked well and didn't mention her arthritis at all,' said Liew.

For a few moments Su Yin was lost in her thoughts of her parents; the reassurance from Liew was a balm to her.

'So when did you come here and what have you been doing?' she asked. 'What line of work are you in?'

'I came not long after you left. I did various jobs, you know how it was like, grab whatever work you can get. I was in tin mining to start with. That was hard work. Very different from being a butcher.' Liew smiled, exuding the same sunniness as that first time Su Yin saw him. She felt her heart flip again like it did then. She was annoyed with herself and hoped he didn't notice her reaction. Liew continued, 'I now work in the rubber business.'

'That is a good business. With the price of rubber up again, there's got to be lots of work on the plantations.' Su Yin started to shake her head. 'To think you have been here all this time.' She wondered why he didn't get in touch with her sooner but thought it best not to ask.

'Yes, there is no shortage which is good. I can't complain,' said Liew. 'What about yourself? How do you like living here?'

'I am lucky to work for a British family. They are very good to me. Like you I can't complain. So, tell me, what is it like back home under the new government?'

Liew took a deep breath and straightened up. 'It is not my choice of government but at least there is some structure even if it is not perfect. We are all supposed to be equal. The problem is that everything is under the control of the government which is slightly paranoid to say the least. We have to be careful what we say in case it is misconstrued as criticising the government and that could mean severe punishment.' Liew paused. Su Yin was fascinated; she was instantly reminded of how her father would tell her things, stories of what had happened and she wanted to hear more from Liew. 'The country is not the same any more. You won't recognise the place now. The village has changed a lot. There was much rebuilding to be done. The missionary school was burnt down and all the missionaries expelled.'

'No!' Su Yin was horrified; it was the same school that she had longed to attend but was not allowed to.

'The country has been at war for the last ten to fifteen years.' Liew became visibly agitated. 'First, the eight-year war with Japan in 1937. We in the countryside didn't have it as bad as the cities. The war here in Malaya with the Japanese is nothing like what it was back home between us and them. There was so much destruction. The landscape changed completely. Worse is the suffering of the people. You would have heard of the atrocities in Nanking.' Liew hung his head then nodded as if what he was about to say had finally sunk in after all that time. 'More than two hundred thousand of our people died.'

Su Yin nodded, remembering the time she and the sisters had sat together in the coolie room fearing the worst, feeling terrified and completely impotent as they learnt about the Japanese invasion. She was then glad that her family were far away from Nanking but was afraid it would only be a matter of time before the invaders moved south and ravaged the people and the land. She shuddered. She couldn't imagine herself in the midst of that turmoil. She wanted to hear more from Liew.

Liew continued. 'Then after the Japanese war, we had internal fighting – the nationalist Kuomintang and the Communist. What we want now is peace and time to recover. We've been battered. We are tired. I am not sure if it was better under the Manchu Emperor or worse. From what I understand, under the old system even though there was oppression, people had food to eat. Now under this communist regime food is scarce and worse, freedom is gone. No one dares to speak up. Son is turned against father and brother against brother.'

Su Yin had noticed that her father had been guarded in his letters, had not said much about the government or what he thought of it. Now she understood that he had been careful not to incriminate himself. In his last letter he'd mentioned that he had repaired the roof of the house and had bought more seeds for planting. As for son turning against father and brother against brother she was positive neither her father nor brothers would ever commit such a heinous act.

'You knew my brother Peng was killed fighting with the Kuomintang against the Japanese?' To her surprise she felt her eyes welling up.

'Yes,' Liew said softly. 'Two of my cousins were also killed. I know several people who have friends or family who lost their lives fighting the Japanese. It was a barbaric time.'

'Since then the communist government has hounded my family, questioned them, accusing them of being traitors,' said Su Yin. 'This is what I don't understand: I thought we Chinese – nationalists and communists - were united, fighting together against the Japanese, the common enemy. So why are the communist now treating the nationalist this way as if they were traitors. The same thing is happening here. The communists fought the Japanese alongside the British and now the Japanese have gone they have turned against the British.' Su Yin shook her head. 'I don't know what the communists here are playing at. They may be hurting the British army but they are also making it difficult for us Chinese. It makes the Malays and British suspicious of us. The war is long over and we should get on with our lives. Why can't we live peacefully together? So many lives lost, so much wasted.' Su Yin paused, surprised that she had said so much; she had not realised she'd felt so vehemently about the situation. Realising that Liew was watching her intently she became self-conscious. 'My parents are lucky to keep the farm.'

'Yes, and Keng is doing well,' said Liew. 'His four children are a credit to him and his wife. He is a lucky man.' Su Yin thought she detected a hint of envy in his voice. 'The eldest must be about twelve?'

Su Yin nodded. 'The eldest - a girl – is almost twelve and I have been told she is very hardworking, loves school which is wonderful. Education is the best thing. She has talked about wanting to become a teacher or a doctor even. I hope the government will recognise her ability and support her.'

'If she toes the line, does exactly as they want, she will be fine. Doctors are being sent to work on the land. Maybe by the time she is old enough to be a doctor conditions will have improved,' said Liew.

From what Su Yin had gleaned from the letters from home her father and brothers were of the opinion that they would fare better under the communist government. So on the basis that her brothers' children could lean the same way and conform to the government's edicts there should be no problem. The problem was she didn't know what they really believed in. 'As you said, 'toe the line'.'

'The silk factory where you worked is still there but remains only as a shell of what it used to be. I understand your mother still teaches the new workers how to reel,' said

Liew. Su Yin nodded. 'The production of silk is nothing like it used to be.'

'No, at least some of the women still have a job. When did you leave China?'

'1932.... Exactly a year after you left,' answered Liew, his eyes fixed on Su Yin's face. Su Yin blushed. Liew continued, 'I tried to persuade Keng to come with me but he wanted to stay back to help your father on the farm.'

Su Yin wondered how much better it would have been if Keng had come with Liew. Both she and her brother could at least be a real family here; her homesickness might have been more bearable. Strangely, seeing Liew now and being near to him gave her a sense of being closer to her family and yet it magnified the physical distance between them. 'They seem to be managing,' she said. 'There seems to be so much shortage of everything. How about your family?'

'Food is still in short supply. There was a big flood a few years ago which caused a near famine.'

'Yes, I knew about it,' said Su Yin recalling the panic and worry and how she had to send food home.

'And the government takes their cut of the produce... As for my family, they are all fine. I am uncle to so many nieces and nephews.' Liew smiled broadly. 'Can't keep track of them.'

'Yourself - how many children do you have?'

Liew shook his head. 'None.' Looking straight into Su Yin's eyes he continued softly, 'My wife died during the Japanese Occupation. She was five months pregnant.'

Su Yin felt sad for Liew. 'The Japanese have a lot of blood on their hands.' Although curious about his wife but not wishing to rake up memories and pain she refrained from asking. She had expected him to have enough children to make up a team for rowing. She was right about the envy in his voice. Suddenly the words rolled off her tongue, 'Do you still row?' Seeing his muscular arms she recalled that she had noticed them all those years ago when they stood facing each other briefly at the riverside after the boat race.

Liew let out a laugh. 'No! I don't have time now which is a shame. I cycle a lot instead.' Su Yin had seen the bicycle that he'd parked by the lamp-post near their table. They both picked up their cup of tea, took a sip and then placed their cups on the table.

She looked at her watch. 'I think I'd better go now. The family will be wanting their dinner soon, particularly the children.' As she stood up to go, Liew also stood up. A look of anxiousness came over his face.

'Can we meet again?' he asked.

Surprised, Su Yin hesitated as her cheeks turned red. 'I suppose so.'

Su Yin's curiosity was like a cat that kept poking its head out of a bag. Why did he leave a year after she did? Why had he not married again? Why did he want to see her again? Why had he got in touch now after such a long absence? What did he want? Was she reading too much into this meeting and his wanting to see her again? Her dealings with men were after all very limited. Apart from her employer, fellow employees like Ah Hock and shopkeepers she had nothing much to do with men.

Seeing Liew again had woken up the part of her being that she thought had long been buried. She was shocked at herself; she liked being with him and was at ease after the initial nervousness. Unsure what to make of this revelation about herself she hastily brushed it aside telling herself that it was nothing more than the delight of seeing an old friend from home, and that it made her feel much nearer to family and home. What surprised her was that he'd said he would like to see her again and asked if he could come to the house where she worked to pick her up. That had unnerved her. Her quick reply was, 'I don't think so, I am sure my boss would not allow it.'

Secretly she was pleased.

Chapter 20

'It is so lucky that someone has stepped in and bought the coolie room,' said Joo as she, Su Yin and Cheng sat down in Mr Teng's coffee shop. 'Thank Heaven there are such generous and kind people around.'

'Yes, what would we do if that hadn't happened?' said Cheng who had just picked up a letter from her father to say that her nephew had started work in a factory making electric fans. 'I wonder who has bought it.' The handwritten notice on the wall in the room had not divulged the benefactor.

'A huge relief,' Su Yin added. She had hoped to see Ah Mui but she wasn't there. She wondered if Ah Mui had adjusted to her situation and made friends.

When they had ordered their drinks Su Yin turned to Joo and said brightly, 'Tell us about your preparations for the wedding.'

'I was just about to,' said Joo. 'It is set for the fourteenth day of the eighth month. Needless to say you are both invited.'

'Try keeping us away,' said Cheng.

'What are you going to wear?' asked Su Yin.

'The fashion seems to be a white gown, imitating the European way,' said Cheng.

'I don't know yet,' replied Joo.

'Joo,' Su Yin looked at Joo, 'I hope you won't feel insulted but would you let me make you a gift of my silk dress, the one my mother made for me?'

Joo's mouth opened in surprise. 'I couldn't let you do that... It is too precious.'

'I have no use for it anymore. It would make me very happy if you would wear it.'

'If you really mean it, I would be very, very happy to wear it,' replied Joo as her eyes glistened.

'It would make me happy too,' said Su Yin. 'We are about the same size so there won't be many alterations to make.'

'That is really good of you,' said Cheng. She then tilted her head as she eyed Su Yin, 'I noticed you seem different this morning. You are chirpier, almost carefree. Not been drinking your rice wine, have you?' Su Yin laughed.

'Yes, I have to agree,' Joo screwed her eyes at Su Yin. 'Tell us what's happened.'

Su Yin's cheeks turned pink. 'I don't know what you are talking about.'

'Don't be coy. You can tell us,' said Joo. Both she and Cheng sat up and leant forward in their seats and waited.

Su Yin smiled, 'Alright. I didn't realise it would show. It is worrying. Can't hide anything from you two at all.' She paused and then, 'I don't want you to read too much into this, please.' Joo and Cheng nodded like two schoolgirls waiting for their friend to cough up her secret. 'I met up with this friend from my village.'

'A man,' Joo chipped in.

'Yes. He turned up out of nowhere! I hadn't seen him since I left home and he is here in Kuala Lumpur. When I first saw him – I was about sixteen I think...'

'And you liked him,' said Cheng.

Su Yin blushed. 'He was different from the other boys I had met. He has what I call 'sunny' eyes. He smiles and the place lights up. And you can't help but smile back.'

'You mean he smiles and it reaches out and touches you,' said Cheng with a knowing smile.

Yes, thought Su Yin, but she couldn't admit that to her friends. When her heart flipped again like that first time she was surprised. And she had liked the feeling although at first she'd put it down to the joy of seeing an old friend, her brother's friend, which brought her brother closer to her, as if Liew was standing in for Keng. But she admitted it had spun her head leaving her bewildered. At first she had dismissed it as a normal reaction to seeing an old friend but as time went on it had taken on a different hue. She had actually been playing over and over again that meeting with Liew. She felt good, alive as if she had been given a shot of happiness. What was disconcerting was that she had been so sure she knew where she stood where men were concerned.

'It is simply unbelievable,' she said, 'that after all these years we have caught up with each other. His name is Liew. What is surprising is how much I have found out about him in the short time we met. His father was a chicken farmer and had four sons and four daughters. Liew reckoned that being the youngest of the brothers he was the most wilful and quite a rebel. He was difficult, headstrong and not doing as his parents wanted. So they decided that someone else should teach him and sent him to work for their friend, the butcher. They had hoped that the friend would teach him about discipline and work.'

'And did Liew learn from the butcher?' asked Cheng.

'It would seem that he did. He's knuckled down and is not afraid of hard work. He is working on some rubber plantation here,' replied Su Yin.

'So what did he want with you?' asked Joo.

'Ever the suspicious one,' said Su Yin looking at Joo. 'He just wanted to see me as we are from the same village, you know, as good as family. After all, like us he misses home too. He and my brother were very good friends. They used to row together in the boat races.'

'I might be suspicious and I might be right too. I'll bet he is more than just interested in seeing an old friend,' Joo smirked.

'You've got a one-track mind,' said Su Yin shaking her finger at her. 'There is such a thing as friendship between a man and a woman, you know, without anything else coming in the way.'

'And you would know all about that?' asked Joo.

'My experiences might be limited but I am sure we can be good friends. It doesn't always have to be more than that,' Su Yin retorted.

Cheng squinted at Su Yin. 'Really? Men always want more, don't they? And what would his wife say to that?'

'She died during the Occupation and he hasn't remarried,' answered Su Yin. 'Seeing how he charmed the female customers when he was working for the butcher I was sure he would have married again and maybe even have two if not three wives.'

'You believe him?' asked Cheng.

'What is there not to believe? He has nothing to gain from telling me a lie,' replied Su Yin.

'That's true,' Joo conceded.

'I think it depends on the two persons concerned,' Cheng offered. 'Sometimes the bond that draws them together in the first place simply escalates into something greater that the two of them can't control. Then you either give in to it or walk away from it.' Cheng suddenly blushed when she realised Joo and Su Yin looked puzzled and were staring at her. She continued, 'And I know about that.'

'What are you talking about, Cheng?' said Joo. 'I have a feeling you are going to tell us more.'

Cheng became flustered, looked down and then scanned around to see who was nearby before facing her friends. Her voice and tone were soft when she spoke. 'You know Wei.' Both Joo and Su Yin nodded. 'Aside from the fact that she came from a village near mine we found that we got on very well and wanted to continue to see each other. When I am not seeing you I am with her.' She paused to see what effect that had on Su Yin and Joo. When neither of them spoke she continued. 'We have known each other for some time now. I have mentioned her before.'

Joo nodded. '*Ahh*, now I know.'

Su Yin smiled. 'I thought you two were very affectionate towards each other at our New Year meal.'

Cheng smiled shyly. 'She works for a family on the other side of town as you know. Well, we got on very well to begin with; we enjoyed each other's company and shared the same sense of humour. And then it suddenly changed. There is something that I can't quite define,' Cheng's eyes brightened. 'We've become very, very close. You and I are close; I care about you but this feeling I have for her is different.' She looked at Joo. 'It is probably like how you feel about Tan.'

'Does she feel the same as you do?' asked Joo.

'Yes, she does. I care very much for her,' Cheng's voice quivered, 'in a way that's different from the way I care about you two. Is that odd?' She looked from Joo to Su Yin.

'There is nothing odd about caring for another person,' said Joo. 'In fact I believe we need people to care about. Otherwise what is the point of living? Take us for example. If we didn't care about our family, we wouldn't be here so far away from home and working so hard just so we can support them. It is more than just filial duty. And of course there are different shades of caring.'

'Yes, yes, I want to spend the rest of my life with her,' Cheng's voice lightened with excitement. 'I remember once that one of the sisters mentioned she knew of two sisters who were like a married couple. She said that they did everything together and went everywhere together. Then I thought they were simply two very close friends and didn't understand. Now I know better.'

'I say that as long as you are happy, that's what is important,' said Joo. 'Why complicate matters? Good that you understand now and if this relationship is what makes you glow like you do now then it must be right for you, isn't it so, Su Yin?'

'Yes, quite right,' Su Yin replied. 'Why complicate matters? Listening to you, it's as if you both feel the same way.' She looked at Joo, 'Joo, you care about Tan' then turning to Cheng, 'and you, Cheng, you care about Wei. As for me, I like Liew and am happy to be friends with him.' Su Yin smiled. 'I am happy with that: just friends.'

Both Joo and Cheng looked at Su Yin. 'So who is reading more into it?' said Cheng.

'Time will tell,' said Joo smugly.

Cheng said softly, 'You have to be honest with yourself.'

Su Yin's eyes widened. 'What do you mean by that?' she hit back.

Cheng and Joo were taken aback by her response. Then Joo ventured cautiously, 'I suppose what we are saying is that if the opportunity comes along for a relationship with a good person we should grab it.'

'What is wrong with you two?' Su Yin's voice was shaky. 'Just because you have found your soulmates doesn't mean I have to go down the same route. I don't need a mate like you do. I am quite happy as I am!'

'Su Yin, I am so sorry,' said Cheng panicking, 'I didn't mean to upset you.'

Su Yin was surprised at her own reaction; she could not believe what had just come out of her mouth. She was confused. She was angry with her friends. She felt hurt. More than that she felt she was being disloyal to her best friend Lan Yee who gave up her life for her conviction. She would not demean the vow that they both had wanted to make public together.

Chapter 21

James felt his heart thumping like the hooves of a hundred stampeding buffaloes. A waterfall of sweat was running down his forehead. Back once again in the bowels of the jungle, with Colonel Haines and his soldiers behind him, they were doing their best to advance as silently as they could, treading noiselessly through the mesh of undergrowth. They were some three miles north-east of the area where they had searched for the guerrillas who had ambushed and killed the late High Commissioner. This mission was based on information extracted from a communist-turned-informer by the name of Ah Wing a twenty-five years old man with a nervous smile due more to wanting to please and convince his interrogators than to deviousness. He had been a courier for the guerrillas for two years, shunting between the jungle and the new settlement where he used to live, supplying his comrades with whatever they needed. But more important was the fact that he belonged to the group who were responsible for the High Commissioner's death. And he knew exactly where they had moved to after the ambush. To prove his credibility, he told them about the planned ambush of the British Forces lorry loaded with ammunition that was due to travel on the trunk road from Singapore. He even supplied the name of the driver who was a cousin of one of the communists in the jungle. Just as he had said, it happened the next day at the location near the slip road to Kluang. The army did not take any chances and was ready for it. They circled then swooped down on the guerrillas just before the latter could open fire on the lorry which was not loaded. Five of them were shot dead leaving two to await trial. In exchange for the information that the interrogators wanted Ah Wing was promised protection. Once he'd disclosed the new location of his camp James knew exactly where it was and headed the hunt for it.

He had been in this part of the jungle before. The site of the new camp was about where he and his jungle-mates had hidden before which convinced him Ah Wing was speaking the truth yet he couldn't help feeling suspicious. The ease with which the Chinese - men and women, inside or outside the jungle - changed sides like throwing off a shirt for another one, the British found baffling. But not James. *Spies, traitors, informers* – those were the categories into which the Chinese guerrillas slotted people outside the jungle who were not in their movement. *Woe to their own people inside the jungle who showed the slightest hint of a change of heart,* thought James. The comrades-in-charge were quick to mete out judgement and if those charged fell into any one of those categories, punishment was by execution. James was sure that Ah Wing knew the consequences. And then there were the *oppressors,* the British government and all who worked for them. The aim in life for the oppressed communist Chinese was to purge the oppressors. Despite the huge recruitment of both Malay and British officers to the police force, the communists continued to persecute the police like a malignant cancer resurging with each excision. They'd woven such a large web of informers outside the jungle that it was like fighting ghosts.

His senses were heightened, nerve endings tingling; his entire being was geared ready to act. He gripped tightly the Sten gun he had been issued, poised to open fire. In the steam rising from the ground he listened for sounds of human activity over and above birdcalls, the odd grunting of wild boars and rustling of the leafy canopy above their heads. As he picked his way through the thick growth of ferns, columns of bamboos and curtains of twines, he realised how quickly the jungle had overgrown and now presented itself as undefiled new territory. It had masked the beaten tracks, pockets of bomb-blasted areas - courtesy of the Japanese - and the small clearings where he had once lived with the *orang asli,* the indigenous people who lived in the jungle and whose help he and his fellow-fighters had recruited. Just like the way his own body had absorbed the shrapnel he took in his leg. He was aware too that the soldiers with him were not yet accustomed to the jungle heat and humidity and could wear out quickly. They had already been out for almost an hour since daybreak; it was getting hotter by the minute in the living steam bath. Before the heat paralysed them, they had to move fast to catch the guerrillas.

Half an hour later and a mile further on they came upon the campsite. Ah Wing's information was accurate but all they found were signs of where the guerrillas had been: a cooking area with a heap of ash and half-burnt wood, a bamboo shed with layers of coconut leaves for the roof, make-shift benches and chicken bones strewn about. But there was not a communist soul in sight.

James jumped into the jeep's passenger seat with Eddie Tan his assistant at the wheel. Eddie's role was to help James in the Town and Planning Department and hold the fort when he was called up for what he called his 'jungle duty.' He had already apprised James of the morning's business including complaints and enquiries from local businessmen about their property, planned buildings and land. They were now on their way to investigate the monsoon drains that were shallower and narrower than they should be because the Chinese constructor had scrimped on materials. While Eddie drove away from the British Army Headquarters and navigated the jeep across town James reflected on the debriefing of the failed mission to the jungle. As he'd maintained they were fighting ghosts, chasing smoke and ending up empty-handed even when they had the exact location. There was a depressing sense of collective frustration and at the end of the debriefing all he and the others wanted to do was to unwind under a fan with an ice-cold beer.

As soon as the business with the monsoon drains was completed to his satisfaction, he and Eddie decided to visit *Club One* the watering hole situated in the centre of the city exclusively for men - the expatriates' favourite haunt where they could get a bottle of cold Tiger beer and exchange news with fellow plantation owners and government officers and employees. It was a welcome sight - the ceiling fans were whirring seductively, a palm tree in each of the corners of the room and behind the bar the wall lined with a selection of bottled spirits. James and Eddie made a beeline for a well-chilled bottle of beer each.

James took a huge swig of the beer; as the cold trickled down his throat he felt as if he had received a gulp of oxygen after being nearly suffocated. He rolled the cold bottle across his cheeks. He began to relax as he took a drag at the cigarette between his fingers. He looked around him – white men in white shirts and khaki shorts smoking and sipping beer as though there was nothing to worry about; the only tell-tale sign was their partially hidden pistols tucked in their waists. A picture of the jungle that he had just come from popped up in his head. *Two so different worlds in the space of a few square miles*, thought James as he raised his bottle to his lips and sank back into his chair. The number of casualties on both sides was high, in the hundreds. The communists had become bolder and more aggressive, taking down groups instead of just individuals. The security forces - police and army - and civilians suffered equally although the exact figures were not yet confirmed. *When will this end?* he asked. He loved this country and his family loved it too. He recalled Cammy coming home from school one day looking downcast. When asked what the matter was he looked at James and said that one of his friends said he heard his father saying that the jungle people were shooting 'red-haired' men and his friend thought it might not be safe to play with him anymore. James had quickly and carefully explained the situation saying that his friend was wrong and that the school was a safe place for children which reassured him. The thought of the children being targeted filled him with horror.

James looked at Eddie's face across the table from him; he was without question a handsome man and James was surprised that he was not already snatched up by some woman. His black spectacle frame gave him an air of a school teacher rather than a civil servant. At a quick glance Eddie could easily be mistaken for a Chinese because of his black hair, dark eyes and fairer skin compared to the other ethnic groups. But on closer look his rounder eyes were more deep-set and his aquiline nose instantly proclaimed that he was Eurasian. His Chinese father met his Italian mother when they were both studying at London University. James's mind started to stray; he began to wonder what Eddie felt about his ethnicity which surprised him as he had never paid any attention to it before. People like him and the Chinese rarely considered going into the police force. The Malays were only just beginning to join the force. He reckoned there were only about ten percent of them with a handful of Indians. He found himself looking from the communists' perspective: a Eurasian would be the embodiment of the dual categories that they hated – an *oppressor* (they couldn't tell the difference between British and Italian) and a *traitor. Would the communist derive double delight at the killing of such a person?* James wondered. He shuddered and quickly shook the thought off.

His mind then turned to Helen. He didn't tell her about the jungle-duty before he set out that morning. She would have been ill with worry; she could do without it, not with the baby due very soon. Suddenly he felt a desperate longing to hold her in his arms. He couldn't wait to get home to her and the children.

Chapter 22

Ben was born on the 8th of June exactly a week earlier than expected. If Su Yin had her way Helen would be confined to resting in bed for the first month after delivery and eating lots of chicken in rice wine and ginger to restore her body. But after four children with the family she knew better than to insist on Helen not eating raw fruit or vegetables, drinking cold drinks, and worse, going out of the house. It was her western way again, although Su Yin had to admit Helen was none the worse for it. The upside of this was that she didn't have to cook separately for Helen which meant no extra work for her.

Soft, pink-skinned with wispy blonde hair and sky-blue eyes, Ben seemed oblivious to all around him as his lips clasped firmly round Helen's nipple squeezed rhythmically making sucking noises. Helen seemed content and more relaxed now after a couple of unhappy colic attacks when the baby was irritable and crying. Su Yin had been moved by the wonder of a new life in the tiny form of the baby but she had never seriously wondered whether she herself wanted a baby. There had been countless times when she had held a baby close to her breasts before and had been curious about what it must feel like to suckle a baby – was it ticklish or painful when the little lips were clamped over the nipple and sucking hard? Now as she watched the baby suckling at Helen's breast she was overcome by a haze of emotions she couldn't quite define. She had long resigned to the fact that she would never feel and know what it was like to have a baby growing inside her and what it was like to have the child suckle at her nipples. The path she had chosen precluded this dubious privilege. All the babies belonged to other people, other women who seemed to embrace their role as mother like a flower turning to the sun. She recalled Ellie asking her if she wanted babies of her own but she'd never really answered the question. Instead she had brushed the question aside dismissing Ellie as nosy.

The one time when having her own children came into her thinking had happened in the most bizarre setting. She was then not much older than Ellie. For no reason she had become concerned about death; she had wondered what would she do if her mother died. She was saddened by the thought of losing her mother, of not ever seeing her again. Then she realised the same event would be repeated: *she* would die and leave *her* own children bereft and lonely. She became so distraught that she locked herself in her mother's room. This had frightened her mother who then begged and coaxed her to unlock the door. When she finally did her mother grabbed her into her arms and gave her a drink of warm water as if it would wash away what was troubling her.

Su Yin now quickly trampled the sprouts of curiosity and all the questions that were springing up in her head. She didn't want to be bothered with the unnecessary baggage of the 'what if's'. She *was* content with her life and didn't need anyone, especially a man, to upset her equilibrium. She wasn't sorry that she had snapped at Joo and Cheng. But she was surprised at the force with which her words came out. She hadn't apologised or admitted that she had been too sensitive; she made no fuss about it. She was cross, she was irritated that they had made so much of her seeing Liew. So what about meeting her friend? An old friend from her childhood. What was wrong with the two of them? Had they forgotten their vow? She hadn't, she couldn't. She'd left them in no doubt that she was serious when she said she did not need a mate. All that on top of Helen MacAlpine asking - on the day after she had met Liew - whether she would consider marriage if the right man came along. She had asked tactfully in the way she always did which Su Yin admired. In spite of that she had been abrupt with Helen although restrained compared to how she was with Joo and Cheng. Exasperated, she had simply replied, '*Aiyahh,* I not *interlested,*' and made some excuse about seeing to the ironing.

Helen who admired Su Yin's single-mindedness wasn't just inquisitive. She was afraid to lose Su Yin should she decide to get married and abandon her leaving her without help. Not that she couldn't find a replacement but she wouldn't be able to find someone like her. She would be lost without her; trying to look after the children without Su Yin's help would be like knitting with one needle. The children would also be devastated. They had grown close to her and she knew she could trust and depend on Su Yin to protect them, like the time when Cammy was consumed with fever. Su Yin had insisted on sleeping in his room on the floor beside him, fanning and sponging him down when his body was too hot. After Ben was born Helen had been relieved when her mother wrote to say she and her father couldn't come. Her dear father would have simply acquiesced. It would have been more trouble and stress had they come. It would have upset the happy work harmony that she and Su Yin enjoyed. Her mother hated the heat and humidity, the monotone of the season with no relief from the burning sun, the heat did not evaporate at night to give reprieve so that she could sail into sleep. She complained that the humidity swallowed her like a python devouring its prey. Basically, she didn't like 'this God forsaken uncivilised place', the place God dumped the worst of his creations – mosquitoes, snakes, putrid drains, smelly foods; she hated the stench of garlic and couldn't understand why people didn't speak English. So Su Yin had to cook bland food for her - grilled fish or beef or pork with no sauces and potatoes, food that she considered boring. Her mother was indifferent to Su Yin bordering on rude and couldn't understand how Helen could abide a Chinese person in her house and worse, looking after her children. Unable to cope with 'all these black-skinned people around', she chose to stay in the house. She refused to walk on the streets in town. 'You don't know what you can catch from just breathing in the air. The beggars, the stray dogs and cats,' she complained.

Even the children sensed their grandmother's disdain and although she tried to play the part of a doting grandmother the children could see through her. When she offered to brush Ellie's hair Ellie declined saying that she preferred Amah to do it for her which didn't go down well. They were polite but impatient with her especially when she criticised Su Yin for her cooking - the beef steak was overcooked and tough, the tea she made was like dishwater. Once Lexie asked her grandmother why she didn't like Su Yin. That lit a fuse; she blew up asking Helen how she'd allowed her children to be so rude. So when she wrote to say they weren't able to come - whatever she decreed her father would accept – Helen was overjoyed. She only needed Su Yin to look after her, Su Yin who sneaked the rice wine and ginger chicken into her diet which she had quietly eaten to please her.

Ming followed Su Yin into the nursery where Su Yin started to change Ben's nappy in his cot.

'He is so cute!' said Ming, fascinated by Ben kicking his legs and smiling up at her.

'Yes, he is adorable, just like how the others were,' Su Yin responded.

'Do you think I could hold him?'

'Of course. Here,' said Su Yin. She lifted Ben out of the cot and showed Ming how to hold him, carefully placing her hand under Ben's head so it didn't fall backwards.

Ming sucked her breath in. 'I didn't realise they were so delicate,' she said.

'They are tougher than they look. What is important is good nourishment from the mother during pregnancy,' said Su Yin as she tidied away the soiled nappy.

Holding Ben's fingers and her eyes still fixed on him, Ming said, 'I can't wait to leave home. I wish September would hurry here quickly. Mother is driving me crazy.'

Su Yin did not respond. Ming then looked up at her. 'She is getting worse. I thought it would be good if she and I could go shopping, maybe it would be the one last time she and I could do something together. My friend's mother did that with her. I just want a little time with her before I go away. But no, she is always too busy. Her mah-jong friends come first. It wouldn't be so bad if I liked the friends but I don't even like them. I think that is why I hate the game. It is an addiction now like smoking opium. They should ban it. And then the smoking! Sometimes the room is actually foggy with the smoke. Who needs to go to London to see the smog? We've got it right here in our home.' She forced a laugh.

At that moment Helen came into the nursery. 'Who is a lucky boy?' she said when she saw Ben in Ming's arms. Su Yin was glad of the interruption; she wasn't sure what she could have said to make Ming feel better. 'By the way, Amah, Penny Pendle is coming to visit us today,' Helen mimicked Penny puffing furiously. Su Yin nodded with a smile. Helen continued, 'She has been talking about adopting which I think is a good thing. She will make such a good mother. She wants some advice on what to get ready for the baby. Oh, she is so excited as I am!'

Su Yin turned to Ming and asked in Cantonese, 'What is *adopting?'*

Ming explained.

'Adopting,' Su Yin repeated then looked at Helen. 'Good, good! So many babies nobody want.' There had been too many babies especially baby girls left at the entrance to the convent that she knew of in town. Suddenly in her estimation Penny Pendle shot up on her scale of respect. At the same time she felt cross with Ming's mother for not giving her daughter the attention that she was craving for.

The telephone in the hall rang. In the kitchen Su Yin quickly dried her hands and hurried to answer it. It wasn't often that she had to answer the telephone. James was out at work, the older children were at school while Helen and Thomas were taking a nap with Ben after the midday feed. She didn't want the ringing to wake Ben up.

'*Hallor,'* she enunciated softly into the phone, 'Makapeen *l*esidence.'

'Su Yin?' said a man's voice at the other end which continued in Cantonese, 'Su Yin, is that you?'

Instantly recognising it was Liew she clamped her hand on the mouthpiece, swung round to see if Helen was nearby. 'Why are you calling me here?' Realising her voice had started to shrill, she calmed down and whispered again, 'My boss won't like it! How did you get the number?'

'You told me where you worked and it was easy to get the number from the telephone operator,' answered Liew. Su Yin could hear a smile in his voice.

'But you mustn't telephone me here. What do you want now that you are on the line?'

'I was hoping we could meet again. When are you free?'

Looking behind her again, Su Yin quickly said, 'I am free this Saturday.'

'Good. Can we meet at the same place as we did the last time? We can have lunch. Say, twelve o'clock?'

Desperate to get off the phone quickly she replied, 'Yes, yes, now I must go,' and put the phone down before Liew could say another word. She peered down the corridor to see if she might have woken up Helen or the boys. To her relief there was no sight or sound of any one of them. She rushed back to the kitchen. She was flustered; it wasn't just because she had taken a personal call on her boss's telephone. Hearing Liew's voice and the fact that he had gone to some length to see her again had set her heart fluttering. Just as quickly she chided herself, *Why am I so stupid as to allow my emotions to get rattled like that*? Reluctantly she had to admit she liked the feeling whatever it was called. She then realised that she would have to tell Cheng and Joo that she would meet them later after she had seen Liew.

Chapter 23

At the other end of the broken line Liew smiled. He was pleased with himself and delighted that he was now going to see Su Yin although it wasn't soon enough. He placed the handset on the black telephone cradle and he was grateful for the convenience of the new technology – a wonderful invention he couldn't wait to have it installed in his house when it became available, more significantly, when he could afford it. It was the first thing that he desperately wanted in his new house. The previous house which he'd rented and lived in with his late wife was half the size of this one but after years of living in huts which he had shared with dozens of fellow workers near the port and on the rubber plantation it was like a palace to him. He had felt that he'd no reason to rush into buying his own house; besides the one that he had seen and wanted was not for sale. And then the years of the Japanese Occupation shelved any idea of buying; instead he found himself buying up small parcels of land that owners were desperate to sell which he subsequently sold at enormous profits. He had been more concerned about ensuring that his parents, his eight brothers and sisters were well, comfortable and secure. He refurbished their dilapidated ancestral home and helped kick-start his young nephews and nieces on the path to a good education by paying their school fees. Fortuitously for him, when the Occupation ended and he was ready to consider buying, the owner of the house he had wanted, an English rubber plantation owner, was in a hurry to sell up to return to England with his family. Liew couldn't believe his luck; he snapped up both his rubber plantation and town house.

The single storey, five-bedroomed brick-and-wood house on stilts was painted white with green shutters and doors. It was over-sized for his needs. Set in half an acre of prim lawn dotted with islands of orange canna lilies, bougainvillea bushes with lilac flowers and other flowering bushes which the English owner's wife had designed to achieve a tropical-paradise effect, the house was ideal for him. For the time being it was sparsely furnished with half the house moth-balled and he lived mainly in the large cool room, where he was now, with its highly-polished wooden floor and the slowly-whirring ceiling fan. The six window shutters were closed to keep the sun out. The well-seasoned rattan armchair he was sitting in was his favourite and the solid teak desk was one left behind by the previous owner. In pride of place, at the centre of the wall facing the windows was an old hand-carved rosewood cabinet with inlaid mother-of-pearl that he'd bought back from China. Standing proudly on it was an ivory carving of an old bearded sage holding a staff; it was a present he'd brought back from Canton for his wife Kim. On either side of the cabinet were framed ink paintings done by a Taoist monk he met years ago near Canton. The painting on the left was of gold fishes and the other was of bamboo trees. Rarely he invited friends home; mostly he preferred to take his business associates to restaurants which also solved the problem of cooking although his kitchen was adequately furnished and where he sometimes cooked. The simplicity of the furnishing of the entire house was matched by the silence in it. Once or twice he'd dreamt that the house was filled with his wife and child's laughter only to wake up and be reminded that they were no more.

His mind cast back to Keng's look of shock and disbelief when he first divulged his intention of wooing his sister Su Yin shortly after she had left the country. He was planning to leave for Malaya while Keng himself was already betrothed to be married soon.

'You know she has taken the vow?' asked Keng.

'Yes, but she might change her mind,' he'd insisted.

Keng shook his head. 'I don't think so. If my sister is nothing else, she is very strong-willed. Can be as immovable as the Great Wall.'

Liew smiled. 'I know. That is one of the things I like about her; she knows her own mind.'

'Yes, and that means she is sticking to her decision,' said Keng. A note of pity had crept into his voice. 'You could spend your whole life waiting for her.'

Liew's plan had been to work and save his money before approaching Su Yin. He would need to show her that he could support her before persuading her to marry him. He hadn't minded the hard graft but at times the loneliness swallowed him and that was when he felt discouraged and convinced that he was chasing a cloud. Then when he met his supervisor's daughter at their house for a meal, he was completely smitten by her. She filled the void in his life that Su Yin had created.

Since meeting Su Yin again all his previous emotions, thoughts and memories came rushing back energising every fibre of his being once more. He was more convinced than ever that he had never stopped loving her which was why he sought her out again. He didn't regret his marriage to Kim; he had loved her too. They had been happy together, they were excited about their baby. Would he have bothered to look Su Yin up had Kim lived? He didn't know the answer. Now he had visions of making his home here with Su Yin. It was a dream that his best friend and manager

Lam, his own brothers and Keng had deemed crazy and they thought he was mad.

Liew stood beside Lam who had managed his estate ever since he acquired it. As he looked down between the two rows of oil palm trees that looked like soldiers on parade, a huge sense of pleasure and achievement descended on him. The trees with their fan-shaped leaves looked as if they were bowing before him, beckoning him to inspect them. Nestled at the base of the fans, at the level of his chest, were large grape-like bunches of fruit the skin of which were mostly dark purple but there were tantalising signs of some turning orange-red. When he first came across them, it was the sight of such a glowing bunch that set his heart racing, reminding him of a giant lump of red-hot molten glass. He had been dreaming of this moment since almost four years ago when he was driving past an estate and was struck by the rich deep green colour of the leaves. He'd stopped to investigate and not only was he taken aback by the look of the elegant plants – their leaves shooting up like a fountain from the top of a thick column of a trunk - but the usefulness of the oil that the nut produced decided for him that this was what he should plant in the new piece of land he had bought and that had been lying in wait to be put to good use. The oil from the fruit could be made into soap and margarine which was the new alternative to butter. He gazed now at the bunches of fruit. Each bunch was about the size of his cloth bag of belongings that he carried on his back when he first left his homeland. He reached out to run his hand over the fiery red cluster.

'This is ripe now,' said Lam, a Hakka Chinese not much older than Liew. Lam had always acknowledged that between the two of them Liew was the more business-minded and definitely more astute when it came to seeing opportunities. Like Liew he had worked in the tin mines and rubber plantations and when they met on one of the plantations they struck up a solid friendship that had lasted for sixteen years. Working with and for Liew was the best thing that happened to him. And to be made his manager was more than he could have hoped for. When Liew added the responsibility of the oil palm plantation he was excited. He sounded pleased as he explained to Liew, 'Tomorrow and the day after we will harvest. I've got the men waiting to do it. The lorries and drivers have also been arranged to collect the crop. Then we harvest again in two weeks' time.'

Liew nodded. 'What is the weight of one of these bunches?'

'*Ahh,* easily thirty, forty katis,' replied Lam. 'The yield of the first fruit is usually small to begin with, not as good as subsequent ones.'

'Can I pluck one of these?' asked Liew.

'Yes, yes, here let me cut it for you.' Lam took out his army knife from his pocket and proceeded to cut. 'Looks very good, Boss.' He allowed himself a smile as he handed two pieces of fruit to Liew.

Liew looked at the shiny red nuggets in his hand; they were bigger than the size of a quail's egg.

'Here, look,' said Lam, he had sliced open a fruit revealing two golden halves with a cross section of a healthy-looking stone in the centre. He pointed to the greyish centre of the stone, 'This is where the oil comes from. It looks very promising.'

Liew nodded as he wiped the sweat from his forehead. He was delighted, his heart was dancing. He scanned the plantation, an area of about fifty acres with the trees in neat rows far apart enough so the tips of their leaves didn't touch. Apart from the few creepers curling round the base of the trunks the ground between was as good as weed-free. All the signs pointed to a well-looked after plantation and a promise of a healthy return. He would have to wait until the harvest was collected, taken to the collection point and weighed before he knew what the return would be. The good news was that the price of palm oil was rising; he was gratified that he had made a sound decision in diversifying from rubber.

'You have done a good job,' he said turning to Lam who smiled in appreciation. 'Has there has been any trouble recently?'

'So far, no. The jungle fighters don't come out here. There is nothing here for them to take. Not unless they want to press oil for themselves.'

'*Hmm,* I wouldn't put it past them,' said Liew. He was grateful that neither of his two plantations - this and the rubber plantation - had had any disturbances from them when there had been numerous reports from other plantations of random slashing of rubber trees by the guerrillas.

Lam then added, 'We do get the odd wild boar rummaging around; they are the only intruders.'

Although it was not long after sunrise the humidity under the canopy of the palm tree leaves was rising fast making it very uncomfortable. Liew could feel his shirt soaking with sweat but he allowed himself a few more moments to savour the pleasure of their joint achievement. Then he and Lam walked back to Liew's car, a black Austin 8. He had to make a quick visit to the rubber plantation before going home to shower and then making his way to see Su Yin.

Chapter 24

Any change to her routine especially one that would involve letting Joo and Cheng down would usually irritate her. So Su Yin decided that she would combine both - having lunch with them and seeing Liew again. That way she wouldn't upset her best friends; besides they would get to meet Liew which would please them as they had been dying to know more about him and were clamouring to meet him. They had been pestering her like a fly buzzing around her - they wanted to know exactly how old he was, what he did for a living, where he lived in Kuala Lumpur and so on. When Su Yin told them that they would meet him they were thrilled. Now like two excited girls waiting for the Lunar New Year to arrive they waited for Liew. Bubbling with anticipation they sat at one of the tables in the shade of the tarpaulin awning. A jeep with British and Malay policemen armed with rifles drove past. Several heads turned to look and then returned to their food.

'You think they've been alerted to the jungle fighters' presence somewhere?' asked Cheng her eyes following the jeep.

'Do you think your boss might be involved?' asked Joo.

'I don't know. It is always a worry. My boss lady worries so much. I read that a woman, one of those living in the new settlement, was caught carrying tins of food and writing paper on her way to the rubber plantation,' said Su Yin. 'Under interrogation she confessed to the police that her husband was inside the jungle, that he and his comrades would dress up as rubber tappers and meet her and others who dared to smuggle things like she did. Because she has a few children she has turned informer; that way she lives.'

'Now she lives in fear of the communists! Probably her husband as well,' said Cheng.

'Back to Liew, he has got the courage to phone you at your employer's house,' said Joo, grinning. 'It can only mean that he's keen to see you.' She nodded her approval, 'Not bad. I'm impressed.'

'You shouldn't read so much into this, you know,' said Su Yin.

'I'm not reading anything extra other than what is obvious. He likes you,' Joo responded.

'So he likes me. He's probably homesick- he's got no family here - and wants to talk to a friend from home,' said Su Yin. 'You know what it is like.'

'Whatever you say,' said Joo as she pulled herself straight and raised her head to look for Liew. Since they arrived the other six tables had been quickly taken. Nearby the cook looked as if he was oblivious of and immune to the blazing flames from the wood fire as he performed his magic with the noodles in the wok. The sound of sizzling with intermittent clanging of the ladle against the wok filled the air along with the aroma of fried garlic and soya sauce conspiring to arouse appetite. Joo continued, 'I am hungry. I hope he comes soon. You don't think he might be put off if he saw us three women?'

'I don't think so,' Cheng began, her eyes fixed in front of her. 'I think this man coming towards us might be him. I hope he won't be disappointed that we are here, Joo,' said Cheng. 'Is that him?' she turned to look at Su Yin who was becoming nervous. The man walking towards their table was wearing a light white cotton shirt and beige linen trousers, looking as if he had just stepped out of a fridge.

The white shirt contrasted with his brown muscular arms. His black hair was short and neat. His face was like a new day with fresh promises and it eased into a smile when he saw Su Yin. He strode with an air of assurance towards them.

Su Yin lowered voice which was tinged with threat, 'Yes, now behave yourself, especially you Joo.'

'He looks nothing like I imagined. Better,' said Joo as if she hadn't heard her.

If Liew was disappointed that he was not going to have Su Yin all to himself, he didn't show it. Instead his eyes shone as he greeted them as if he had expected to see them and was completely comfortable. After the introductions were made he sat down on the stool between Su Yin and Cheng at the round table.

'You look fresh and cool for someone who has cycled here,' said Joo. 'How do you do it?' Joo then shook her head. 'I presume you cycled. Su Yin said you cycle a lot.'

Liew smiled. 'No, I didn't. I would have but got delayed at work, so I drove.'

'So you have already worked this morning,' said Joo with a look of surprise but obviously impressed.

'Yes,' replied Liew. He looked at the table and on seeing no food he said, 'What would you like to eat? This is my treat; it is not often I get to eat lunch with lovely ladies like yourselves. We should order. I am sorry to have kept you waiting.' He looked at his watch, 'No,' he said as if to himself, 'I am not late.' He looked up, spotted a waiter and waved to him. The waiter walked to the table.

'That is very generous of you; we are not used to this. We normally pay for ourselves;' said Su Yin.

'Perhaps just this once?' said Liew. Su Yin looked at Joo and Cheng.

'We should be gracious and accept, this once,' said Cheng.

'That's settled then,' said Liew.

'Su Yin told us you work on the rubber plantation,' said Cheng. Joo sat up attentively.

'Yes,' answered Liew but before he could say anymore the waiter was at his side.

'Hey Boss, how are you?' The waiter greeted him with a broad smile that made his eyes disappear. His ease and familiarity with Liew did not surprise Su Yin.

'I am well,' Liew turned to look at him. 'Busy as usual? Business looks good.'

The waiter nodded. 'No let-up. They keep coming which is good. Now what will you have? The usual?'

'Yes,' answered Liew. He looked at Su Yin. 'And what will you have?'

'I will have the fried rice noodles with prawns, no chilli,' answered Su Yin.

'I will have the same,' said Joo.

'And same for me,' said Cheng.

The waiter nodded, repeated the orders and walked away.

'So you drove here. What car do you drive then?' asked Joo

'Just an old car. As long as it gets me from one place to another that's what matters,' said Liew.

'You come here often?' asked Joo.

'Yes, I know the cook. I think his noodles are the best in town,' said Liew.

'He won't tell us his secret ingredient!' said Cheng.

Liew laughed. 'He would lose customers if he did.'

'That's true,' said Joo.

'I was wondering,' said Cheng, 'in the rubber plantation where you work, have you bumped into any of the guerrillas? We have been hearing how they sneak out to look for food or any materials that they might need. Are they a threat to Chinese people or do they just attack the Europeans?'

'They are after the Europeans,' said Joo.

'Obviously the plantation where you work is not owned by Europeans,' said Cheng.

'That's right,' said Liew. 'There has been no trouble but we are always on the look-out. You just never know. If they are hungry enough they might attack anyone.'

'I just remembered, Su Yin, didn't your previous employer own a rubber plantation?' asked Joo.

'Yes, that is right,' replied Su Yin.

'Not the same plantation where you work, is it? What is the man's name again?' asked Joo turning to Su Yin again.

Liew's brow lifted. 'Did you?' he looked at Su Yin. 'When did you work for him?'

'A long time ago. Family name of Lok. Do you know him?' said Su Yin.

'No, but I know of him,' answered Liew. 'A decent man I heard. Haven't met him yet but then I haven't been working long on the plantation. So how many years ago did you work for him?'

Puzzled that Liew wanted to know, she tried to work out how long ago it was. 'More than ten years. I left the family after the Japanese Occupation..in 1946...'

'Su Yin works for a European family now, you know,' Joo interrupted. 'I kept saying before that she was putting herself in danger in case the guerrillas come to the house. They are ruthless! I am so ashamed of them. I don't know what they have achieved so far by this.'

Liew looked distracted for a moment and then said, 'They want them out, they don't want to be ruled by the foreigners,' said Liew.

'But we are all foreigners too, aren't we?' asked Joo.

'I don't know much about politics but do you think the British government will give in to the natives wanting independence?' asked Cheng.

'Yes and from what I've heard and read in the newspapers I do think so but you are safe with the family you work for,' he said addressing Su Yin.

'Of course,' said Su Yin. 'It is about being alert and careful. But we are nearer the town than the jungle so that makes us more difficult to reach.'

'But tell us more about yourself,' said Joo, 'Su Yin said you are both from the same village back home. Are you married?' She felt a kick under the table.

'Not much to tell really. No, I am not married,' said Liew, his eyes smiling at Joo. '*Ah*, here comes the food.' The waiter set down two plates of piping hot noodles on the table and quickly went off for the other two.

'*Hmm,*' Joo inhaled the aroma of a mixture of garlic and soya sauce, 'I swear it is the fried pork fat that gives it that special taste.'

'And his own recipe of sauce, don't forget,' said Cheng. 'It's that jar of black sauce next to his wok, have you noticed?'

'I am sorry Liew,' said Su Yin, 'but as you have noticed, we are interested in cooking and it is only because we cook for a living, amongst other things. We always try something new, something different.'

'That is not a problem,' he said. 'I am interested in cooking myself but as it is just me I don't bother much.' He paused when the waiter brought the other two plates of noodles. 'Thank you,' he said to the waiter and to the women, 'Please eat.'

'Did you come straight to Kuala Lumpur or somewhere else?' asked Joo her eyes fixed on Liew as she picked up her chopsticks.

'I went where there was work. Went first to the port to work as a coolie doing everything from carrying goods to digging..'

'Port? Which port?'

'It is called Port Swettenham, to the west, about thirty something miles from here. It was a good place to start, it was thriving – so many different ships from so many different countries, all carrying different cargoes and we were exporting things like spices, tin and rubber. It was an eye-opener; I got a sense of how big the world was – so many different colours of skin and so many different languages.'

'Yes, but it must have been back-breaking work carrying all those heavy goods and in this heat,' said Cheng. Liew nodded as he picked up his chopsticks.

Su Yin noticed his muscular arm. It struck her that somehow it was an incongruous combination - his tall slim build and the heavy manual work of carrying and lifting heavy goods. His slimness which exuded both gentleness and strength would somehow be more suited to less physical and manual work. She tried to picture him carrying gunnysacks over his shoulders, pushing or pulling trolleys laden with all sorts of heavy goods. Perhaps there was more strength to his build than she realised, after all he was once a champion rower with her brother.

'I was partly drawn to the job because it meant working by the river and sea,' said Liew.

'Liew used to row with my brother,' Su Yin interjected. 'Do you still row?'

'No. I haven't got the time although I should try to make time to do it,' replied Liew.

'So why and when did you go and work in a rubber plantation?' asked Joo.

'Joo, you are asking too many questions. Give him a break. Let him eat,' said Cheng.

Su Yin was not surprised that Liew fitted in with them. She recalled what he was like when she first noticed him in the market back home; he charmed the women customers like he was giving sweets to children. As for Joo and Cheng, they seemed completely enamoured by him. She was convinced that he had won them over without even trying. Then it dawned on her that apart from Joo's husband-to-be they had no men friends to speak of. But was it entirely their fault or did the men set them apart knowing and respecting the way of life those in the sisterhood had chosen? Or had they themselves unwittingly surrounded themselves with a moat that kept the men out? There were the men in the places they went to such as the restaurants and men in the houses where they worked with whom they had good rapport but they weren't friends like the sisters were. They were not people they would open their hearts to. Being with Liew now was a breath of fresh air; it was like opening the window wider for a bigger better view. Suddenly she felt happy that she knew him and that her friends too have now met him. But more to the point, she reckoned, Liew was interested in being friends with them and seemed very much at ease with them. Besides he didn't appear to mind being grilled by Joo. Which was a good thing as she was learning more about him.

Liew then spoke, ‘I have an idea. You must let me take you to the riverside and then to the port. Su Yin, I don’t know about you but I miss the canals back home and to be near the water was why I went to work at the port.’

Su Yin looked at Cheng and Joo to see what they thought. They were nodding their heads.

‘I think that is very thoughtful of you,’ said Cheng. ‘That would be a treat for us.’ She looked at Su Yin who appeared unsure what to say. Conscious that her friends were waiting for her to respond she said meekly,

‘Yes, it is very generous of you but won’t we be taking up your precious time?’

‘No, not at all,’ said Liew.

‘If you two are up for it,’ she looked from Joo to Cheng, ‘then yes, we accept your kind offer.’

Chapter 25

Su Yin needed to get her red silk dress back. The urgency to redeem it from the pawnbroker had become greater now that she had promised it to Joo. She had been surprised when she found out that neither Joo nor Cheng had a silk dress, that their mothers didn't make them one. She had assumed that all mothers made one for their daughters especially as they worked in the silk factory. Knowing that alone - that her mother not only weaved the silk but also sewed the dress for her – made her value the garment even more. But although it was a precious gift she was never ever going to wear it herself. What occasion would there be for her to flaunt it? No great parties like what the MacAlpines threw where the women came to show off their finest garments. No formal function that would require her to wear an exquisite dress like that. Besides, her place was backstage, behind the scene and serving; if she was required to be extra smart she would wear a newly starched and pressed white *samfoo* top. The highlight of her outings was the Chinese New Year lunch with the sisters and not one of them would dream of wearing anything more colourful or fantastic than a muted pastel *samfoo*. If she did turn up in her dress she would be laughed out of the restaurant; they would think the Malayan heat had finally got to her. She could hear them saying that she now had 'air in her brain' – she had gone mad.

Joo was about Su Yin's size in height and weight although Joo conceded that her breasts were marginally bigger. That was after Cheng had described them as melon-size compared to Su Yin's that were pomelo while her own were fried-egg size. Su Yin was sure that Joo would look fantastic in it but she had taken some convincing to accept the dress. 'Cheng and I are as good as your family here,' Su Yin had said. 'So, as your sister I give you my dress. Besides I think your husband-to-be is very nice. I know it doesn't matter what I think but I approve of him.'

'It matters! It matters what you and Cheng think of him. I am so glad you approve. But how can I take your dress from you? It is your mother's gift to you,' Joo argued.

'When am I ever going to wear it?' replied Su Yin.

'You never know. Look at me,' Joo appealed to Su Yin, 'I am getting married. Did I ever think it would happen?'

'Well, we will see. *If* and *when* I need to I will borrow it from you,' Su Yin laughed.

In the end it was agreed between the two friends. Joo was delighted that she would not need to depend on her future husband to provide her wedding dress. Seeing the happiness on Joo's face, as if she had been promised a pot of gold, made Su Yin even more determined to redeem her dress quickly.

As Helen had not objected to Su Yin taking the time off she had planned to go after she had fed the family and be back in time for her afternoon story on the transistor. The kitchen had been scrubbed, the pots and pans washed and dried and the floor swept after lunch and there was only a little of the ironing left to do which she knew she could finish in no time at all when she returned.

She had decided to take the bus to town turning down Ah Hock's offer to drive her and she didn't tell Joo and Cheng what she was up to. She felt her purse that was in her bag; it had the right amount of money that she had carefully counted along with the pawnshop's receipt neatly tucked in the notes. She couldn't wait to get her dress back. Once settled into her seat on the bus her thoughts leapt to

Ming. At the farewell party that her parents laid on for her the night before, both she and Ming had shed a few tears when they finally hugged and said goodbye. Thinking of Ming's leaving had engendered a mixture of emotions. She was both sad and happy that Ming was embarking on her new venture. Ming looked beautiful and was actually excited about taking her next big step, thrilled about flying and couldn't wait to see England with her own eyes. Watching her go around to say good bye to her relatives and friends Su Yin had felt a sense of pride in having helped raise the young and confident woman from birth, the daughter that she would have liked to call her own. At the same time, she couldn't help remembering her own journey, when she had to leave her family. She had a glimpse then of how her parents must have felt when they had to let her go. She didn't have a gift for Ming but she had a huge store of love and affection for her which Ming knew she could count on. Su Yin was beginning to miss her already.

Her mind then wandered back to the boat trip that Liew took her, Joo and Cheng on. It had been a wonderful treat beginning with the drive in his car and then sailing down the river in a fishing boat that he'd somehow managed to get hold of. For Joo and Cheng it was an adventure; for Su Yin it was like a trip home. From where they set off in the boat she saw that the river bank was lined with the thick green leafy canopy of mangroves propped up by tentacle roots in the brown water. Against the blue backdrop of the cloudless sky, the meandering edge looked like a dragon languishing in the life-sucking heat. Once she was in the boat she was immediately buoyed by nostalgia and exhilaration. The sight and smell of the salt water and the sound of the waves lashing against the side of the boat transported her back home; she was lost in the memories of the landscape criss-crossed with rivers, of the boat races and the gazebo where she and Lan Yee used to go. It stirred up the same old yearning for home but she felt strangely content at the same time. She couldn't help suspecting that Liew's presence contributed to her sense of contentment; she had felt comfortable and relaxed. With the Malay boat-owner in charge of the sailing, Liew was quietly in control and seemed to enjoy pointing out landmarks to his guests as they approached the port where he once worked. The port had now burgeoned into a heaving mini-town with many docked ships the size of which she had never thought possible before. But the moment that stood out was when the boat suddenly rocked causing her to lose her balance. All four of them had been standing in the shade of the awning with the wind sweeping past and she had been quite lost in her reverie when a large swell from a passing vessel rocked the boat. She swayed and tilted backwards and instantly felt Liew's hands on her bare arms. His hands were strong yet gentle, without any hint of callus; his grip conveyed a sense of masculine protectiveness. To her surprise it suddenly woke up feelings that she didn't think she would ever experience. She was embarrassed that she liked what she felt; she liked the warmth of his touch. Even thinking about it now made her blush making her wonder again what was happening to her. Unconsciously her arms crossed to place her hands on where Liew's hands had so firmly held her.

It was still raining when the bus stopped at the top end of the road where the pawnshop was, a couple of streets away from where she and her friends met each month. The rain was fortuitous: it was in her favour for not many people would be out in it. It wasn't as if lots of people in town knew her but she didn't want to be seen. There would be the one or two people who might recognise her such as Mr Teng the coffee shop proprietor or one or two of his workers. She held her umbrella low over her head as she walked briskly in the rain towards the pawnshop, afraid in case she bumped into someone who might know her. Although she hated what the pawnshop stood for – the place where she had to exchange the most precious gift from her mother for a few dollars - she had to console herself that it had enabled her to send more money to her parents when they desperately needed it. Not for a second had she dreamt that her dress would come into use like this; what would her mother think if she knew the truth? She would never need know, Su Yin thought. Deliberately she avoided the five-foot way; instead she walked cautiously on the road with the deep drain alongside it. Holding her umbrella low over her head, she walked until she came to the front of the pawnshop. Her heart was pounding like a drum in her chest with the anticipation of retrieving her dress. More than that, it was the thought of freeing herself from the burden of the debt. She closed her umbrella and, just as she had hoped, saw that there was no one else on the five-foot way on either side of the shop.

When she looked into the shop she saw the proprietor, a bespectacled middle-aged man with a bald egg-shaped head, sitting behind the glass counter his right hand poised over his abacus. He was a picture of respectability wearing a white shirt and baggy brown trousers. He looked up over his spectacles at her; with quick flicks of his fingers he finished what he was doing with the abacus and then wrote in his open notepad. As she stepped through the open door into the smell of stale cigarette he removed his spectacles and smiled at Su Yin, revealing a top gold-capped tooth. Su Yin forced a smile. She didn't like him the first time she dealt with him, she didn't like him any better now. The fact that he was also Cantonese had made business easier. She now wished that she had brought Joo or Cheng with her.

'I have come to redeem my dress,' said Su Yin as politely as she could and leant her umbrella against the counter.

'*Ahh*, good,' the proprietor said, taking the receipt from Su Yin. He studied the receipt as Su Yin scanned around the shop searching for her dress expecting it to be hanging somewhere. There were all sorts of artefacts – leather belts, shoes that looked new, a bicycle leaning against the shelves of Chinese vases, books, lacquered boxes, cameras and many other items. She became worried when she couldn't spot her dress. Had he sold it off? Panic streaked in. She didn't understand why the man didn't get up to fetch her dress for her. She wanted him to hurry. The money was in her hand, all ten dollars; she was all ready to hand it over as soon as she got her dress. She wanted the exchange to be quick.

'I don't see my dress,' said Su Yin glaring at the proprietor.

'It is at the back, don't worry. I haven't sold it. I knew it meant a lot to you,' he said still smiling. He then stood up. 'Come with me. It is hanging at the back in a cupboard.' He walked through the door behind where he had been sitting. Su Yin followed him into what was a dark storeroom. The creaking door shut behind her. She caught a whiff of the smell of mothballs. He switched on the ceiling light. The walls were lined with cupboards with all sorts of stuff spilling out of them. Su Yin scanned the room for a cupboard that held her dress. On the floor was junk of all kinds imaginable including a kerosene lamp, a small bronze Buddha, another bicycle, wooden crates and an unmarked granite headstone. Su Yin expected that the room beyond where they were, was where his wife or workers would be busy working although there was no sound of movement or voices. Outside the rain had not given up, it continued pelting down. She was impatient to get what belonged to her and go home quickly. Then she saw the cupboard hidden in the far corner. Her heart lifted.

The proprietor sauntered over to it and opened it. He took out a folded red dress which Su Yin instantly recognised as hers. Relief flooded through her like a cool breeze on a humid day; she was overjoyed as if she had found her lost long friend. She reached out to take it in one hand as she handed the money in the other to him. To her surprise he waved both hands away.

'*Aiyyah*, not so fast. The price has gone up,' he said looking at Su Yin to see her reaction.

'Why?' cried Su Yin.

'There is a time limit and after that the price goes up. That is the way it works.' His eyes were still fixed on Su Yin.

Su Yin's heart sank. Every cent she had earned had been carefully allocated and it had taken her nearly two years to save up for this. 'How much?' she asked.

'Another twenty percent which is not much, as I normally charge thirty,' he said. 'In the first place I gave you a very good price because I like you.'

It meant another two dollars. She knew it would take her at least another three months before she could save that much. Despair overwhelmed her whole being; she felt at a loss. Suddenly she was aware that he was moving closer towards her, holding up her dress which was rightfully her property if he had taken the money she had ready to give him. He wasn't much taller than her; his face was just above hers, his eyes narrowed as he continued to look at her. She could smell the mixture of coffee and cigarette on his breath when he spoke.

'We could come to an arrangement,' he said, his voice had turned raspy.

It took Su Yin a few seconds to understand what he meant and the first thing that came to her mind was where was his wife? She panicked. She shook her head and before she knew it he had grabbed her waist and pulled her towards him. Su Yin pushed him away and struggled to break free from his grip but he was stronger than her. As he pushed her against the cupboard she saw the glint in his eyes. He was like one possessed, possessed with the intent and determination of getting what he wanted. He pressed even harder against her. Su Yin could not breathe; she tried to scream but even if she could the rain would drown her cries.

Chapter 26

At last Ben had drifted off to sleep after his feed. He was such a hungry baby that Helen had to give him a bottle in addition to the breastfeed. She gently lowered him into his cot careful not to break the sleep spell and waken the rest of the children who were having their afternoon nap. Feeling a sense of relief, her heart leapt at the sight of his angelic face framed by fair curls. Ben's colic seemed to have disappeared and he had been a much happier baby as a result. She felt blessed – 'my cup runneth over' came to her mind; she was quite sure her family was now complete. Gingerly she let down the mosquito net over the cot, picked up the bottle from the table and went to the kitchen. Not expecting to see Su Yin in the kitchen she was surprised and when she saw the state she was in she gasped.

'What's happened, Amah? You are soaked!' she cried. Alarm rushed in, she could feel her heart galloping. Su Yin didn't respond. She was standing by the sink dripping with water, looking like she had stepped out of the shower fully clothed. There was a vacant look on her face as she stood frozen to the spot holding a towel. Helen put the bottle down on the table, grabbed the towel from her and started rubbing her down. 'Come and sit down.' She guided Su Yin to the stool by the table and noticed the red dress half out of Su Yin's cloth bag on the table. 'What happened?'

Su Yin did as she was told and sat on the stool still looking blank and distant. 'Bad thing,' she mumbled. 'Bad.' She kept staring at the space in front of her as if she was in some place else.

'What bad thing?' asked Helen. 'Are you hurt?'

A small voice from the kitchen door called out,' Mummy, what is the matter with Amah?' It was Lexie looking puzzled and concerned.

Helen turned to her, 'Go get Daddy, quickly. And stay in your room.' Without any question Lexie turned around and shot off down the corridor. James appeared in no time his face contorted with concern. He bent down to Su Yin.

'What's wrong? Amah, what happened?' he asked. When Su Yin did not answer he looked at Helen. Helen shook her head. 'Has she been out?' James asked. The first thing that shot into his head was that Su Yin might have had a brush with the guerrillas. There had been reports of skirmishes and rumours of the guerrillas desperate for food and venturing out of the jungle to the edge of towns to steal. They had relentlessly gnawed at the security and had managed to attack an English plantation owner. Had they assaulted her because of her working for him? It was irrational – how would they know? He became angry.

'Yes,' said Helen, 'she said she had an errand to do. She kept saying 'bad thing'. Can't get anything else out of her. She doesn't look hurt.'

James then spoke in Cantonese as if he was coaxing a child, 'Amah, tell me what happened to you? Have you had an accident? Are you hurt?'

Still staring, Su Yin shook her head. 'I could not fight him off,' she started. 'I hit him.' Without looking at James she continued, sounding as if she was tightly wound up, 'He was strong. He tried to cover my mouth.' She screwed her face. 'Bad breath -smell of cigarette and coffee. I hit him. Then he crumbled to the floor.'

Helen could only look on as they spoke. 'What is she saying, tell me!' she said to James when she saw his face tense even more. James didn't answer her. His mind flew to all kinds of possibilities, his eyes widened as he continued to probe, 'Who is this man? Where did it happen?'

'Pawnbroker in town,' said Su Yin. 'I think I might have killed him.'

'What is she saying, tell me please,' said Helen. When James repeated what Su Yin had said she clasped her mouth then let out, 'Oh my God!'

James turned back to Su Yin. 'Tell me exactly what happened,' he said. 'Where did you go and who did you meet?'

Su Yin hesitated then slowly the words came out. She told him how she went into the shop anxious to retrieve her dress and when she'd told how the pawnbroker led her into the inner part of the shop she stopped abruptly.

'Then what happened?' James asked. Was it worse than he thought? 'What did he try to do? What did you do?' His voice shook; he felt his fury mounting taking him to a place he had been before a long time ago.

Su Yin screwed her brow as if she was having difficulty trawling through her memory and then gradually the words came, 'I think I grabbed something... yes, the small Buddha statuette from the side and I hit him on his head with it.' Suddenly as if she had woken up from a nightmare she said quickly, 'Yes, that was what I did. When he fell I grabbed my dress,' pointing to the dress in her bag on the table, 'and ran out of the shop! I don't know if he is dead or not. I didn't stop to find out. I just ran. I wanted to get away from him as fast as I could!'

'It's alright,' said James, his heart was pounding furiously. He was now unable to keep the anger and panic in his voice. 'You did the right thing. Tell me again where this pawnshop is.'

As soon as Su Yin had told him he turned to Helen and told her what Su Yin had said. 'See to her. I am going to phone the police.'

Su Yin looked at him in horror. 'Will I go to prison?' she asked.

'No. No, you won't! Helen will help you get dry,' said James as he hurried off to his study to make the call.

'Oh, Amah,' was all Helen could say. Her heart ached for Su Yin; she had never seen her so flat and so lost. Against her better judgement, she hugged her. Su Yin let her and then started to cry.

'So..so *solly*,' she stuttered.

After a few moments Helen released her. 'Don't be silly.' Her eyes fixed on Su Yin's she pointed at the area below her waist, 'Did the man hurt you?'

Su Yin shook her head vigorously, 'No! No!' and then she wiped her tears away with her hands. 'I hit him!' She picked up an imaginary object and then swung it in front of her.

'Thank God for that!'

James returned to the kitchen, his face was taut. 'Amah, you need to come with me to the police station to report the assault.'

Su Yin gasped, her eyes widened. 'No, no, I won't! I don't want everybody to know!'

'It's alright, nobody else will know,' James's tone had softened but was firm. 'This man has assaulted you and he should be punished.'

'No, I won't. You do what you have to, but I won't go to the police.' Su Yin stood up and ran her hand over her wet hair. Then in English she said, 'I go change,' and pulled off the towel that Helen had wrapped round her shoulder. 'Then I cook.' She glanced up at the clock on the wall.

Helen looked from Su Yin to James then back to Su Yin, 'There's no hurry, Amah. Really, there's no need to rush,' she said gently.

'I fine. Thank you.' Su Yin now looked embarrassed. 'I go change now.' She gathered up her cloth bag from the table, gently pushing the dress in and started to head out of the kitchen, her wet clothes clinging to her skin.

Helen knew better than to try to stop her.

In her bedroom Su Yin rushed to open the window. The cool night air that greeted her caressed her face; she welcomed it after working herself into a heap of heat. Despite her earlier shower she was perspiring again and would need another one. She inhaled deeply. As she let out her breath she was surprised at how calm she now felt. Looking after the family, making sure that they were fed had helped to diminish the afternoon's incident. For one brief moment she was annoyed that she'd missed her afternoon soap opera. She'd scrubbed the aluminium pots and wok like she was scrubbing for her life. If they had skin it would have long been rubbed off. She scrubbed and scrubbed and with each furious movement she'd cursed herself. Perhaps she should have asked either Joo or Cheng to go with her knowing she had not liked the man the first time she met him. What was wrong with her? Why didn't she do that? But she didn't want her friends to know she had pawned her dress and certainly she didn't want Joo to know she had to redeem it specially for her. Suddenly she recalled the image that had flashed before her when she was defending herself: in a hall full of women sitting at rows of long tables, all their faces were turned to her as she walked in; they were all very solemn. The image was like a black and white photograph. Who were these women? Were they her sisters? Were they judging her? Or were they sympathetic towards her? She didn't know what it all meant.

She had heard enough of rapes during the Japanese Occupation; along with the other women she had lived in fear of that ever happening to her. She'd survived the ravage of the country without any harm to herself and in that moment when she was faced with the possibility - shocked that it was one of her own countrymen - she was determined that no man would defile her like that. The aggressiveness of the pawnbroker's action had frightened her, the blind obsession of satisfying his need with no thought of the consequences had startled her. Every fibre of her being rallied to her defence; she'd fought him off. She had been shocked at her response; she had never hit anyone before apart from the one time she'd swung round and accidentally hit Lan Yee when they were little and playing. She recalled that when the pawnbroker grabbed her she knew she had to do her utmost to fight off the beast and to get out of that place. She wasn't going to allow him to force his will on her. Not while she had breath in her. She had suffered enough loss – she'd lost her best friend Lan Yee, she'd lost her brother Peng. She was not going to lose any more now, not her dress and most of all her virginity. No one was going to take it away from her. Least of all a man like that vile creature in front of her. *And not against her will*. Once he fell away – and he'd fallen like a cockroach that had been flicked off - she flew out of the shop like a bullet clutching her bag with her red dress in it close to her chest. She ran as fast as she could, this time not caring whether anyone saw her or not. But how she got the bus – the conductor had frowned at her when she got on the bus dripping like a soaked sponge – and then walked back to the house was all still a blur.

The questions kept darting at her. Why had that happened to her? What had she done to deserve it? Had she said or done something to encourage the evil man, something that might have misled him into thinking she was willing to 'come to an arrangement' with him to waive the extra charge that she had incurred due to her lateness? The fear that pierced her entire being when he'd grabbed her with his filthy hands and pulled her towards him was still vivid.

But she was not going to make it public by going to the police. She couldn't cope with the publicity, the shame. Besides she was unhurt and that was a blessing. As for the pawnbroker Mr Makapeen and the police could do whatever they wanted with him, let them handle it. Suddenly the thought of her going to prison or worse, being deported, terrified her. Mr Makapeen was still not home yet. *What was he doing?*

To her surprise she wondered what Liew would have done if he had been around. Would he take the law into his own hands and deal with the man? Worse, would he think badly of her? *I can't harp on this, I have to get over this, I can't let this cripple me, I have to move on,* she told herself.

She moved to her bed where her bag was lying and took out the dress, giving it a shake before spreading it out on top of her bed. The sight of it in its sumptuous splendour filled her with joy, dulling the horror and fright of the assault. She knew she would fight anyone who dared to take it from her. With the palm of her hand she gently stroked the dress to smooth out the creases. Feeling the soft silk that her mother's hands had touched and handled for a long time as she painstakingly wove it for her, she felt close to her mother again. A sad smile slowly appeared on her face; she remembered how excited she was when her mother, after handing her sister Mei her wedding dress, turned to her and held out a folded dress. 'Here, this is for you,' she had said in the tone, packed with love, that she had come to recognise as one her mother used when rewarding her.

She was stunned into silence like a lid had been dropped on a pan of bubbling boiling water. Her eyes widened as she stared first at the dress then at her mother who was holding back a smile as she watched. 'For me?' she'd asked. She'd been surprised that her mother had sewn her a dress. She knew she had spent hours on the weaving machine to produce the silk cloth but she thought it was only for Mei's wedding dress. Then when she opened up the dress and saw that it was made in the style she had suggested, she was speechless. She'd been sure that her mother would not have approved of her suggestion. Her mother had quietly acquiesced and made both Mei's and her dress in the style they wanted. Above all she had made it for her in spite of the fact Su Yin was not going to be married.

Eager to see how it would look on her and wondering if it would look as good as it did on the model in the newspaper where she had seen it before, she'd dashed into her bedroom to put it on. When she saw herself in the mirror she was flabbergasted- it was the most flattering piece of garment she had ever worn. She could see why the fashion-conscious elite in Shanghai raved about the new design; it was cut to follow the smooth contours of the body and the side slits which came up to the knees or higher showed off the legs. More than that, her mother had embroidered gold peonies to sweep down the left side of the dress. She felt she could float away like a balloon filled with air of ecstasy. So much love and affection had been woven into that dress.

Su Yin couldn't see any damage done to the dress and was relieved that it had not been tainted by the smell of cigarettes. She would still give it a gentle wash. A light cool breeze oozed in; the dress would dry quickly. She would press it in the morning. She was determined that nothing was going to contaminate the precious happy memories associated with it.

Chapter 27

One evening not long after the sun had set, a Chinese man was caught carrying a bundle of clothes and a gunnysack of sugar, salt and rice on his bike heading for the jungle near the village of Bidor on the route to Cameron Highlands. When he was caught and questioned by the police he claimed that he was only taking food to his mother-in-law who was sick. But he was unable to produce the mother-in-law and was promptly arrested. There was yet another attempt to attack a European rubber plantation owner in his own home which failed. The alarm had been raised by one of the owner's workers. The worker, a Malay man, was outside clearing up at the end of the day's tapping of rubber when he spotted movements - 'shaking shadows' he'd said - between the shrubs. When he realised the ominous cause of them he flew into the house to alert the owner. Immediately shots rang out from the house and soon the terrorists disappeared leaving a trail of blood behind.

It was against this background that when James saw the state Su Yin was in what immediately sprung to his mind was that the guerrillas were involved. On discovering that it wasn't so, his worry swung to anger once he learnt the cause of her distress. He was instantly taken to a place that he'd run from a long time ago and old feelings against his own father were rapidly raked up. To his surprise images of what his father did to his mother came hurtling back: he saw his mother shrinking away from him as he lashed out at her with his strong right hand. It wasn't frequent; most of the time he was quiet and gentle. But when he had downed a few whiskies or when something upset him at the shoe factory where he worked, he would take it out on her. For James, seeing it happen once was too much for him to bear; the first time was when he was six and small. But when he stretched into his full height he didn't hesitate to stand in front of his mother when his father became unreasonable. He didn't know what he would do next when his father became abusive again; would he punch and knock him down? To everyone's surprise - mother, father and himself - that act of defiance and challenge actually woke his father up to his own heinous behaviour. He changed; he didn't touch another drop of whisky and had not laid a hand on his mother since that day. Nothing was ever said about the matter. Somehow James knew that he didn't have to worry about his mother any more when he left to come to Malaya.

The shock and terror in Su Yin's eyes stirred him and he was determined to deal with the perpetrator. Twenty minutes after he had driven to the police station and spoken to his friend Police Superintendent Noordin, they and two English and a Malay policemen descended on the pawnshop to find that the proprietor had got up from the spot where he had fallen. He was in a daze and was rubbing his head where the Buddha statuette had landed. When the police charged him with sexual assault he didn't deny it. He was then handcuffed and bundled off into the back of the police van.

It was another fine warm morning. There was no trace of the heavy rain from the day before; there was a fresh feel to the air which had not yet been saturated with moisture. Some three hours earlier Su Yin had watched as the sun emerged above the trees; it was the best time of the day for her - a quiet time for her to gather herself as the new day began, before the chaos of the day took over. But this morning was different as a huge sense of gratitude enveloped her; she was safe and unharmed. She had felt her equilibrium restored.

The tears had washed away the debris from the day before. It was another brand new day. There was no question of her not going out into town again to see Joo and Cheng. She had the dress all ready to hand over to Joo and she was excited about it. She couldn't wait to see Joo's reaction when she presented her the dress.

A breeze rushed past. She could hear the rustling of the leaves in the garden; her senses were heightened, accentuating her gratefulness that she was alive and well. She had just taken two mugs of black coffee to Muthusamy and Hassan who were now taking a break in the shade of the frangipani tree in the garden. Looking out of the window in the kitchen as she finished washing up the breakfast things she could see the two men chatting amiably as they intermittently wiped the sweat off their foreheads. Behind her Cammy, Lexie and Ellie were sitting at the table. Earlier Cammy was hysterical, dashing about the house searching high and low for his running shoes at the same time as Ellie was in and out of different dresses fussing over which she wanted to wear. Now Cammy was engrossed in his homework while Ellie in the pink frock she finally decided on and Lexie, with their colouring pencils spread out on the table, were busy drawing and colouring in their sketch pads. There was a lot to be thankful for. Earlier when she had gone to get Lexie out of bed, Lexie had sat up quickly and asked softly as if she was afraid Su Yin would break like a piece of delicate china, 'Are you feeling alright, Amah?' Her large eyes were filled with concern. Lexie's thoughtfulness had touched her. She had not expected a young child like her to be concerned for her.

'I fine,' she'd replied.

'Oh good!' Lexie's face broke into a big smile and she threw her arms round Su Yin leaving her to wonder how one so young could not only be empathetic but genuinely concerned and able to verbalise it as well. As she hugged Lexie back she felt a renewed surge of strength and determination to let nothing hold her back. Now Lexie was as industrious as a worker ant creating a work of art.

'You said you were going to draw a dog,' said Cammy looking up from his book and studying Lexie's picture of a house, a large tree and flowers.

'There,' Lexie pointed to the tree, 'it is hiding behind the tree!'

'Oh, Lexie,' Cammy rolled his eyes.

'It's only a small dog so it is well hidden,' Lexie insisted.

Ellie looked over at Lexie's picture. 'If you draw a little thick line here,' she said, her finger touching the side of the tree, 'then you can see its tail.'

'That's a good idea,' said Lexie, her eyes brightening.

'What colour is the dog then?' asked Ellie.

'I think it is a brown one,' replied Lexie smugly. 'Thank you, Ellie.'

Su Yin heard a knock on the back door and turned to see a smiling Ah Hock holding a flask in the doorway.

'Good morning, Ah Hock!' the children called out in unison which brought out an even bigger smile on Ah Hock's face.

'*Ahh*, good morning,' Ah Hock responded.

'Did you know it's school sports day this afternoon!' said Cammy.

'Yes, I know. You going to win!'

'I'm going to try. I've been practising hard,' said Cammy. 'You saw how fast I ran around the house yesterday morning. That was the best I think. Ahmad my friend is probably the fastest, not just in my class but in the whole school. He's the one I've got to beat.'

'You can beat him,' said Ah Hock. 'You concentrate,' he started to run on the spot and screwed up his face, still holding the flask in his hand, 'and run fast as you can as if tiger chasing you.'

Ellie and Lexie giggled. 'You look so funny,' said Lexie.

Ah Hock laughed with them then turned to Su Yin and spoke in Cantonese. 'This is from my wife.' He held the flask out to her. 'It's herbal tea. She said that this weather was not good. Too hot and wet, not good for health. This tea will cool your system and restore balance,' he said.

Su Yin felt a little flustered at first although it was not the first time he had brought her gifts - rice dumpling, mooncake and other cakes at Chinese New Year - from his wife whom she had only met a couple of times. 'Thank you very much,' she took the flask from Ah Hock. 'She is very kind. She is right; it is very probably what I need. I hope I am not depriving you by taking this from you.'

'You don't have to worry'' Ah Hock chuckled. 'When my wife cooks she cooks enough to feed the village.'

'She is very kind. Please tell her I appreciate this.' Su Yin felt a sob rise in her throat. She suspected that they were feeling sorry for her after the incident the day before. It had gradually come back to her that Ah Hock, coming out of the house, had seen her as she ran up the drive to the house and she had run past him without a word. She was convinced that Ah Hock didn't know the details – James MacAlpine would not have divulged them - and it made her feel very grateful that they cared. More than anything it reminded her how her own mother would have done exactly the same thing for her. Her voice shaky, she continued, 'How is she? I hope she is well.'

'Oh yes, she is very well. Still happily working in the primary school, cooking for the children; she loves the children,' replied Ah Hock, with a discernible hint of pride in his voice.

They were not blessed with children and Su Yin often wondered about them. She had always held that children were the glue that bound the man and woman together, notwithstanding the man's roaming eyes. How did they manage to stay so close and devoted to each other after such a long time together. They'd been married for twenty-four years, or, as he'd told her more than once, when he was twenty-two and his wife was eighteen and was the prettiest delicate girl he had ever met. Su Yin wondered if her 'delicateness' had anything to do with their not having children. How was it that he hadn't run off to find another woman to bear him children? Ah Hock was indeed a rare specimen and his wife a very lucky woman.

'She is very lucky,' the words slipped off her tongue and she became embarrassed wondering if Ah Hock suspected why she had said that.

'Yes, she is. The children love her back. They are always calling out for her, 'Aunty this, aunty that. *Ahh*, enough of that. I am ready when you are,' said Ah Hock as he started to move away from the door. 'First you should have a drink of the tea before we go.'

'I will have some now. I won't be long.' Su Yin picked up a cup and poured out a little of the brown coloured drink the smell of which reminded her again of her mother. She drank it.

‘What does it taste like, Amah?’ asked Ellie looking up from her book, ‘It looks like very muddy water.’ She screwed her face.

‘Nice. Good for you. You want some?’ Su Yin held her cup out to her.

Ellie shook her head vigorously and pulled back, ‘No, thank you.’

Su Yin smiled. She washed and dried the cup. ‘Be good. I go out now. She then picked up her cloth bag and went to knock on Helen’s bedroom door which was slightly ajar.

‘Come in,’ Helen responded.

Su Yin walked into the room to find Helen in bed cradling Ben in her arms.

‘Mrs Makapeen, I go now?’ Su Yin could see anxiety in Helen’s eyes as they searched her face. She smiled to reassure her.

‘Of course,’ said Helen, her concern undiminished by Su Yin’s smile.

Su Yin stepped into the passenger seat. Ah Hock was already sitting behind the wheel in the car. She noticed his Nanyang Daily News folded on his side. It struck her then that the incident might be reported in the news. ‘May I borrow your newspaper when you have finished with it?’

‘Certainly,’ Ah Hock replied.

Neither of them spoke much as they meandered through the busy town. It was an easy and comfortable silence, as if they had both mutually agreed on it. Strangely Su Yin found the scent of Ah Hock’s *Brylcreem* reassuring. Her bag with the dress now wrapped in brown paper laid on her lap. Once again the sense of gratefulness filled her; the people around her including the children had been so thoughtful and caring. Unusually Helen had got up early to check that she was fine when she started work in the kitchen. She was surprised when Su Yin told her she was going out to meet Joo and Cheng as normal. It was the same when James came into the kitchen for his cup of tea; he had looked askance at her, trying not to make a fuss. And then he explained to her what had happened to the pawnbroker.

The weather had crisped up again; the sun was bearing down from a clear blue sky. The shops on either side of the road were again heaving with shoppers browsing the displays of goods on the five-foot way now in the shade of awnings. Su Yin gazed out at the cars in front; cyclists were idling alongside them to the rhythm of the ringing of their bells. A cyclist had a young boy sitting on his crossbar while a girl looking unperturbed sat on the rack behind with her arms around him. Another had a stack of boxes and bundles towering above him strapped on his rack. Su Yin was quite lost at the sight when suddenly she became conscious of her heart racing. The front of the pawnshop had just come into view. She averted her gaze. The image of the owner's face leering at her, next to her face appeared; his eyes were piercing, his breathing heavy, his breath foul, his weight pushing against her. She shuddered. She hoped Ah Hock didn't notice it. She realised that he had no reason to avoid going this way to meet Joo and Cheng. She took a deep breath. No, she told herself again, she was not going to be intimidated by the vile man or the assault. She had been through war, she'd been through fear for her life when the Japanese soldiers tortured some of the people in the village. She had survived and she was not going to let that insect of a man cripple her. *Especially not when she had fought and stood against subjugation by men.* To be frightened now would be giving in.

She wasn't sure what she would do if she saw him again. Would she scream, point to him and tell the world what he had tried to do? And yet she didn't want the publicity. She didn't want the world to know she had been molested. Thank Heaven, he was held in custody. She was relieved that she didn't kill him. His licence to practise was taken away from him. She felt no pity or hate for him. He was just rubbish to be thrown away, left to rot and be forgotten. And she was sure she had done just that. She felt another shudder go through her. In that instant she knew she would not, she could not, let him and his action stifle her. She took another deep breath and then slowly breathed out. The car glided past the pawnshop and then eased right to avoid a slow-moving bullock-drawn cart. A Malay policeman on patrol came into view and the irony struck her: in her moment of terror and need when she should have shouted *mata-mata* for the police - the first Malay word she had armed herself with in case of emergency- she didn't.

'We will go to the coolie room first?' said Ah Hock.

'Yes, thank you.'

Chapter 28

Dear Su Yin,
Thank you very much for your gift of money which arrived in time for our New Year celebrations. I don't need to tell you how we wished you were here with us. But as long as your mother and I know that you are well and happy, we are happy. I am not able to do as much as I used to in the field but your brother Keng has been a great help and joy to me. My concern is for his daughter who seems to be swayed by the current politics. She reminds me of you – very inquisitive and prone to day-dreaming like how you were when you were her age. And she has a wilful streak. She asks about you a lot and hopes to meet you one day soon. She tells me she is studying hard so she can become a doctor.
Your mother's arthritis is much the same but she does not complain. She is still teaching the younger ones in the factory to reel silk although her sight is not as good as it was.
We are all well. You take care of yourself.
Your father

Su Yin heard the sound of footsteps and looked up from her letter. To her surprise and delight Mui was there standing in the doorway. She had only seen her twice since she received news of her father's death. She couldn't forget how Mui had sobbed when the news was read out to her, how her slender body shook; she'd thought she would die too. 'Life is so cruel!' she said. Then she whispered through her tears, 'At least he didn't know what I do for a living. I need to send more money home so my mother can afford more burnt offerings when she next prays to him.' Looking at Su Yin she said, 'He never got to enjoy the money I sent while he was alive.' Su Yin had cried with her; there was nothing she could say to console her; she thought of her own father too wondering if that was how it would be for her – not being able to say good bye properly. When they met again Mui seemed more collected. The time after that she had seemed more confident than before.

Each time Mui was dressed in an outfit that Su Yin could only dream of. This time she was wearing a short orange cotton A-line dress which showed off her smooth legs. She couldn't understand how Mui could look so impeccable and fresh. At the back of her mind was the reminder that Mui needed to look good and attractive all the time whatever the weather. She reckoned that it was one of the prerequisites of her job.

Mui beamed at Su Yin. '*Ahh*, Big Sister Su Yin. So lovely to see you again. I was hoping that I would see you here.' She opened her handbag and pulled out a letter. 'Are you well?'

'Yes, I am well. Good to see you too. I was beginning to wonder about you,' said Su Yin. As Mui walked to the table to pull out a stool to sit down, she added, 'I see you have a letter too. Would you like me to read it?'

'If you don't mind,' said Mui. Her fair unblemished face was clear of make-up apart from a light touch of lipstick. Su Yin approved; the young woman sitting opposite her did not need any enhancement; she was blessed with a perfectly beautiful face, the melon-seed shape accentuated by her shoulder-length black hair that turned in towards her chin. Under her thin eyebrows which arched gently, her dark brown eyes looked serious but when she smiled they twinkled and she showed off a set of pearly white teeth. It was a wonder that she had not been snapped up by some man. But the circle of men she moved in, her clientele, would mostly be Chinese immigrants who had come to seek their fortune here and who might already be married, their wives and children eking out a living back in China. What were the prospects of finding a single respectable man of reasonable means among that lot? And what matchmaker would think of presenting her with her tarnished background to mothers seeking a chaste hardworking virgin for their son? The matchmaker would have her own reputation to consider. At least Mui was in a position to pick and choose her man *if* she wanted a husband. Not a bad position to be in, Su Yin reckoned. Then the thought sneaked in: Why take on the unnecessary trouble and burden of a husband if she was able to support herself? Su Yin was surprised that she found herself wishing a good decent man would make Mui an offer of marriage and take her away from her way of life before she became too embroiled in it. Suddenly Liew popped into her head; he was one single respectable man who could conceivably do just that if he got to know Mui. He was considerably older but nevertheless attractive and still fit. Her mind strayed.

Mui opened her envelope and then handed the letter to her. Su Yin snapped out of her musing, took the letter and proceeded to read it out loud.

'…….I have made sure your father is not deprived in the other world. I offered lots of food and burnt a lot of gold paper for him. He always said you were a good daughter, as good as a son….' Su Yin read on and when she had finished she was pleased to see a look of satisfaction on Mui's tear-stained face.

'That is good news. My brother has always been interested in things mechanical. It is good that he is now able to study this course that he wants. So he wants to design and make machines.' Mui smiled then said softly, 'It makes what I am doing worthwhile.'

'You have made such a big difference to his life.' Su Yin patted Mui's hand.

'Yes, I am very gratified.' Mui opened her handbag and took out a dollar note but before she could hand it to her, Su Yin quickly put up her hand and said, 'No, please. I don't need payment. I am very happy to help.' Her face turned serious to emphasise her point.

Mui looked at her pleadingly. 'But you must. I would have to pay that man who normally charges for it.'

'I am not that man,' Su Yin said firmly.

'I am really grateful, not just for reading my letters but for your friendship too.' Mui looked down at the handbag in front of her and then at Su Yin. Her eyes became sad, 'I don't have many friends outside work. You can understand that women would not view me as a friend, more an enemy, a husband snatcher.' She chuckled, 'Even a devil!'

'Ignore them,' said Su Yin.

'I try.'

Su Yin wanted to say that it would get easier but hesitated. 'We have to grow a thick skin sometimes. We mustn't let what other people think or do stifle us,' she said as she made a mental note to heed her own words. Then what came out of her mouth astonished her; until now she'd had no intention of telling anyone, not even her best friends Joo and Cheng. 'The other day I was assaulted by this man…'

When Su Yin finished telling her what had happened to her in the pawnshop she was surprised that her eyes were dry, she didn't cry. She had recounted it in a matter-of-fact manner, the words had flowed out like a river that had been unblocked. It had been easy opening up to Mui.

'Big Sister,' Mui began softly, 'I understand. I am so sorry it happened to you.' Then she paused. When she resumed her voice took on a hard edge, 'What I do most of the time is allowing someone to do just that to me. The difference is that I am paid for it.' Her face was solemn. 'The trouble is you don't get used to it, you just become numb to it.'

Su Yin felt a jolt; a wave of sympathy swept over her. The horror of different strange men with their different predilections clawing at Mui's body, making demands of her body while she pretended to not mind at the very least, was beyond her imagination. She shook off the images that leapt up in front of her. Her own assault was nothing compared to what Mui had to bear time and time again every day. She was sorry she had made such a fuss over it. The two of them sat there in silence; any awkwardness or shyness they felt earlier dissipated. Su Yin felt a bond developing between them.

'If you had a choice, would you continue in this job?' asked Su Yin. 'I know you were desperate to get a job right away, weren't we all?'

Mui didn't answer right away. 'The money is good.' Suddenly she perked up and looked anxiously into Su Yin's eyes, 'Would you be seen with me outside this room? I mean, would you be embarrassed to, say, have lunch with me in a restaurant or something?'

Su Yin frowned. 'Of course not. I wouldn't be embarrassed, why would I?'

The anxiety evaporated; Mui's face brightened, 'Thank you. Thank you.'

'I am meeting my friends for lunch. Why don't you join us?' said Su Yin pleased that the thought had occurred to her.

'Your friends, would they not mind?' Mui asked timidly.

'No. They would be glad to meet you again.'

When Su Yin saw the letter from Liew at the coolie room she was pleased. He'd asked if they could meet. Her first reaction was not to see him, her unfortunate experience came to the fore. She thought of excuses: she was too busy; her employer would not give her time off. But, she stopped herself in time. She reasoned with herself, what did Liew have to do with what happened to her? Not seeing Liew would be allowing that one blip to dominate her life. It had nothing to do with him. He wasn't to blame; she could not lump him with the likes of the pawnshop owner. He was in a class of his own – good and trustworthy. And there was a pressing reason for her to see him: she had to get him and Mui together. If anyone could get Mui out of that horrible job he could. He was financially secure. And from what she could tell, not only did he have a good well-paying job he was sensible with his money. If he could afford a car then he was in the position to provide for a wife and family. He just hadn't found the right woman to marry or *had he*?

She decided that she would be direct and ask if he was looking for a wife but how could she? How could she ask such a personal and private question? And what if he did have a wife and a bunch of children back in China even though he had said he wasn't married? Another thought crept in: she could find out by asking her brother Keng. She smirked inwardly; Liew could easily be found out. But he would know that, so why would he even bother to lie to her?

She shook her head. She had become too cynical. Then she wondered how she could engineer a meeting between Mui and Liew without making it too obvious that she was trying to match-make?

Now she was a woman on a new mission. She would meet Liew.

Chapter 29

'Don't you like the watermelon, Ellie?' Helen asked as she watched Ellie push the cubes of watermelon to one side of her plate of cut melon and mango.

'Not really. Please may I leave it?' said Ellie.

'Of course, you may,' said Helen.

'I prefer the mango.' Ellie put a piece into her mouth.

'Children,' said Helen looking around kitchen table, 'this afternoon Aunty Penny is bringing her baby to visit.'

'Oh good!' said Ellie. 'Another baby.'

Lexie asked, 'Is it a boy or a girl?'

'A girl,' answered Helen. 'She is called Julia.'

Ellie frowned, 'Mummy, did her baby pop out of her tummy like Ben did out of yours?'

'I don't think so, silly,' Cammy piped up. 'Her tummy was never huge like Mummy's was.'

For a few moments Helen did not speak. Then she said, 'Aunty Penny and Uncle Anthony have adopted this baby.'

'What does that mean?' asked Lexie.

'That means that because the baby's real mummy is not able to bring her up herself she has decided to let Aunty Penny do it.'

'Is it like Amah looking after us?' asked Ellie.

'No. Aunty Penny is the baby's new mummy now and will look after the baby.'

'But why can't her own mummy look after her?' said Lexie.

All three children's faces turned to Helen. 'Well,' she said, 'sometimes it is because the mummy cannot afford to keep the baby because she is poor.'

Lexie immediately asked, 'Why did she have the baby if she couldn't afford to look after it?'

'You are too young to understand,' said Helen. She looked at Thomas who was busy chomping his food. She reached out to him to wipe his mouth. 'What is important is that we welcome Julia when she and Aunty Penny arrive. And I don't want you asking too many questions when they come.'

'Julia's a nice name,' said Ellie. 'She can be a playmate for Ben.'

'Yes,' said Helen brightly, relieved that they had moved on from the adoption, 'and we have a present here for her. Do you remember we bought a dress for her?' At that point Ellie ran off to her room and returned holding up a brown teddy bear.

'Julia can have Coco,' Ellie said.

'That's nice of you,' said Helen. 'But are you sure about it? You won't miss it and cry for it?'

'No, I won't,' Ellie replied. 'Julia can cuddle Coco when she misses her real mummy.'

As the strains of Tchaikovsky's Piano Concerto No.1 faded out, Su Yin turned the transistor radio off. She put away the ironing board and the piles of pressed clothes. As she looked out of the window on the way to the children's room she saw a blue Mercedes coming up the drive and recognised that it was the Pendles' car. She could hear the children talking in the sitting room with Helen. She quickly put the clothes down in the first room she came to and hurried to tell Helen that Penny Pendle had arrived. She then rushed down the steps at the front of the house where the Mercedes had stopped. The news that Penny had finally got her new baby had filled her with admiration for the couple and she too was eager to meet the baby. She could hear the children racing behind her to meet the new addition to the Pendle family.

Penny's Malay chauffer had hurried round to open the car door for her. Lexie and Ellie shouted, 'Hello, Aunty Penny!' Penny looked up from the baby in her arms wearing the biggest smile Su Yin had ever seen.

'Good afternoon, Mrs Pendle. I help?' said Su Yin; she noticed that her new servant girl had not come with her.

'Good afternoon, Amah. Thank you and how are you?' said Penny still smiling.

'I fine, thank you,' replied Su Yin. It was the first time Penny had ever asked about her welfare. She couldn't help wondering if she knew about the pawnshop incident and was feeling pity for her or if somehow 'motherhood' had caused a change in personality. Before Penny could answer, the chauffer reappeared with a wicker basket of the baby's things which she promptly took from him and stepped away to let Penny out of the car.

'Penny! How wonderful to see you and Julia,' Helen called out as she came down the steps. 'You know the children have been so looking forward to this.' Lexie and Ellie were craning to see the baby. Penny lowered the bundle in her arms to show them.

'Children, this is Julia,' said Penny.

'*Aww.* She's so cute!' said Lexie rubbing Julia's hand. 'Look at her Mummy, she's looking at me! She's smiling!'

Helen looked. 'Yes, she's lovely,' she said. 'Come, let's go inside.'

Satisfied that Ben had fallen asleep Helen gently lowered the mosquito net over the cot. Ben was lying on his side, his eyes were shut and his thumb was still in his mouth. Helen turned to Ellie. 'Now young lady, your turn to go to bed.'

'Mummy, Julia and Ben are so alike, aren't they?' said Ellie looking up at Helen.

Helen's brow screwed up like a crushed ball of paper. 'What do you mean?' she said. Regretting the sharpness in her voice, she quickly added in a softened tone, 'All babies look alike, darling.'

'They both like sucking their thumbs. Look,' Ellie pointed to Ben who started to suck at his thumb.

Helen turned to look at Ben. 'I see,' she said softly. 'Yes, they both like doing that. Come on, time for bed.' She swung Ellie around towards the door. 'Amah is waiting for you in your room. I'll come and say good night later.'

Ellie ran off to her room to find Su Yin tidying her clothes in the wardrobe. 'I will be quick, Amah,' she said as she grabbed her pyjamas from the bed and started to change. Once she'd changed she leapt on to her bed.

Su Yin sat down beside her and began to brush Ellie's hair. Much to her surprise Ellie remained quiet. Wondering what was going through the little girl's head, she waited as she continued brushing. Then,

'Amah, will you always look after us?' said Ellie.

'Of course. Why you ask?' replied Su Yin.

'Because I want you to look after us all the time until we grow up,' said Ellie.

Chapter 30

Su Yin chose to meet Liew again at the same place as before when he came to meet her, Joo and Cheng for lunch. Nearly all the tables were taken but they were sitting at one well away from the edge and under the awning, shaded from the midday sun. There was just a hum of chatter against a constant background of the clanging of the cook's wok and the waiters calling out the orders. She had been very excited at the prospect of meeting Liew again. When she saw him she felt a sense of satisfaction that she was on the right course. She thought that Liew looked as good as he always did and was affable as ever. She pictured him next to Mui and smugly admitted to herself that they made a plausible couple. The almost twenty-years difference in their ages would not be obvious. Besides, which man wouldn't prefer a younger woman to an older one, she asked herself. A younger one would do him proud, boost his ego and perhaps reflect his virility. She had no doubt that he could keep up with her youthfulness. Once they had given their orders Su Yin decided that the best course was to get straight to the point and asked if he was looking for a wife and would he be interested in meeting Mui.

Liew blinked back his surprise and then Su Yin saw a smile dancing in his eyes.

'Su Yin,' he said as if he was about to correct a child, 'I feel very strongly that I must say this. I am very touched that you are concerned about my welfare. But I fear that you have totally misunderstood me. I am not sheltered in any way from women, believe me I have had a few advances from eager matchmakers. And I have humoured one or two and gone along with their suggestions but that was all.'

Su Yin gasped, feeling she had made a horrible mistake. She shook her head. 'I am so sorry if I have offended you. Really, I didn't intend to. I have no doubt that you have no trouble finding a partner. Look at me, here I am asking you the same as a matchmaker would. I was merely thinking of my friend. You would be such a good catch...' Su Yin stopped herself as her hand shot up to cover her mouth. She blushed.

'You flatter me.' His eyes didn't leave Su Yin's face. He became serious and his voice grew hoarse as he continued, 'Would I be a good enough catch for you?'

Instinctively Su Yin looked around to see if anyone else heard what he'd said. A waiter shouted another order to the cook. She was dumfounded. She couldn't answer as she tried to digest what she had just heard Liew say. *What exactly did he mean*? Her heart pounded as she searched for the words. Then she said, 'I don't know what you mean by that.'

Liew leant forward, 'I mean, will you marry me?'

Su Yin screwed her brow and looked hard at him. 'You are not making fun of me, are you?'

'No, of course not! Perhaps I should explain, start at the beginning,' Liew paused and took a breath. 'I was heart-broken when you took your vow. You didn't even give me a chance to prove to you that I could and would be a good husband to you if you had married me. That's because I *care* so much for you, I would never hurt you or be untrue to you.' He swallowed before he continued, 'But of course even if you hadn't taken the vow what did I have to offer you materially? I didn't have any money. I was put to work for my uncle to get me on track, to teach me discipline.' He paused. 'Then after you left I was devastated. I knew I couldn't give you up. No one could compare with you.'

Su Yin felt her cheeks becoming hot and was sure the red scar on her cheek was now very prominent. 'Now you are embarrassing me,' she said.

'It is true. I wanted to be near you, that was why I came to this country. I also wanted to make some money so that I could have something to offer you. Yes, I did marry but it was partly because I didn't think it was at all possible for us to get together. I had given up hope. And the proof that I would be true to you is the fact that I've not been tempted by any other woman; that's why I am still unmarried. I have met lots, believe me. But none could rise to your standard. Since Kim died I felt I had to find out how you felt about me and if you would have me as your husband.' Liew searched Su Yin's face as he waited for her response. 'Please say something.'

Su Yin looked up at Liew; she put her hands against her cheeks and shook her head. Her heart was still pounding. 'It's as if you've just thrown a lit match into a box of crackers in front of me. I didn't expect this. Now you've flattered me. I don't know what to say. It is all too much for me to take in.'

'Say you will let me take care of you,' Liew looked pleadingly at Su Yin, his hands on the table desperate to reach out to touch her.

'I don't know you that well. And you don't know me either. So how can you be so sure?' Su Yin quickly looked away conscious that his eyes were making her wobbly.

'I know you enough to want to spend the rest of my life with you. The first time I saw you it was as if you were imprinted on my brain… you had taken permanent residence in my heart. And it wasn't that I was living a dream. I came here to find you and here you are, just as I remembered you.' His voice took on a tender tone, 'Only you have blossomed so...' A waiter appeared at their table with two plates of noodles. 'Thank you,' Liew looked up at the waiter who nodded then walked away.

Su Yin was grateful for the interruption; her head was spinning. She felt as if she had been lifted onto a cloud and was floating away. Never in her memory had she felt like this before; she was confused as well as happy and embarrassed. She remembered vividly how her heart had somersaulted and how blissfully light she had felt when they met at the boat race back in their village.

For a long while neither of them made a move to eat. Then Liew picked up his chopsticks and gestured to Su Yin to do the same.

'I have changed,' said Su Yin. 'Besides I still don't know you.' Then against her will the words tumbled out, 'Yes, I have enjoyed your company but how do I know that you don't already have a wife back at the village? With enough children to form a team to compete in the boat race?' She looked at him half expecting him to squirm and wriggle out of the corner she had put him in.

'So why did you want to fix me with your friend?' Liew smiled.

'I don't know – it just seems that she has a rough deal..' Su Yin bit her tongue; she couldn't tell him what she did for a living. Liew said nothing but nodded as if he understood. She shook her head. 'This is not turning out the way I'd planned. So answer me, do you or don't you have a wife back home?'

Liew shook his head emphatically. 'No. Your brother Keng can back me up – I haven't got a wife and children back home.'

'What about a wife in another town here in Malaya?'

Liew's brow knitted; he thought for a moment then said, 'I have connections in other towns.'

Su Yin's heart started to sink. *I am a fool,* she thought.

Liew continued, 'I have property – a shop, a house - here and there.'

Su Yin couldn't speak as relief and surprise flooded in.

'I wouldn't lie to you. I have waited a long time for this moment to ask you.'

'My family needs me,' she said. 'Not just my own family but the family I am working for.'

'I have enough money to provide for you and me and your family back home,' Liew's voice was confident. 'You have no worries there. As for the family you are working for, they can find someone else although she won't be as good as you. And I am sure they would hate to lose you.' He smiled.

Su Yin lowered her eyes. 'It is not just about money either. I can't, even if I wanted to. I made my vow.'

'I don't mean to belittle your vow but your friend Joo is getting married soon. She too made her vow.'

Su Yin looked hard at Liew. 'That is her choice.'

Chapter 31

Mr Teng's coffee shop was buzzing as usual.

'Have you noticed,' asked Cheng, 'that there seems to be fewer girls coming over from China? Definitely fewer girls who have taken the vow. In fact, Wei was telling me that some of them come offering themselves for marriage.'

'Yes,' replied Su Yin. 'How things have changed. We are at the mercy of the economy.'

'Many are going elsewhere like Hong Kong which is nearer home,' said Cheng. 'Wei's sister is there working for this very wealthy businessman in the film-making line.'

Joo piped up, 'Have you heard? Someone by the name of Sam Liew Hin has taken over the coolie room. Su Yin, it is not your friend Liew, is it?'

'Really?' said Su Yin. She thought hard. 'I think it could be him.'

'You mean he is in the position to do so?' asked Cheng whose jaw almost hit the floor when Su Yin nodded. 'He has money and is generous as well.'

'*Wah*, we've got him to thank! I never thought..' said Joo.

Looking at Cheng, Su Yin quickly interjected, 'Tell me, how are you and Wei getting on?'

'We are getting on just fine,' Cheng smiled. 'We meet as often as we can which is not often enough. But tell us about your wedding plans, Joo. Three more weeks to go to wedding.'

With the attention turned on her Joo became visibly excited, bubbling like a boiling kettle. 'Thank you again, Su Yin, for the beautiful dress. You have no idea how grateful I am. Every morning when I get up the first thing I do is look at it hanging in my wardrobe and think how lucky I am. It is so exquisite and I hope I do it justice. And you will never guess: I didn't expect this but my boss's wife told me that I could get ready in their house on the morning of the wedding!' She let out a big breath. 'It will be so good to do that. I was getting worried. I admit that I was a little depressed by the fact that I have no home, not my parents' home or my own, to get dressed for the wedding. Most of all I am sorry that my parents won't be here to see me marry.' She swallowed then smiled. 'At least now I can dress up and leave my boss's big house as if it were my parents'. It is important, isn't it?'

'Of course. You can do it just like other brides.'

'Will both of you come and help me? I need you two by my side.'

'Try stopping us! Of course, it goes without saying!' said Su Yin.

'Your boss and his wife have been invited too?' asked Cheng.

'Yes. They have been very good to me. The wife can be a bit grumpy but at least she is fair. 'If I am honest, I shall miss them, and the children.' Joo looked into the distance. 'Fourteen years is a long time and yet they seem to have flown by.'

'Yes, you have a new adventure ahead of you,' said Cheng. 'I admire you for grabbing it with both hands as you have. Takes courage which I am not sure I have.'

'Are you not nervous though, honestly?' asked Su Yin.

'Of course I am nervous but I also believe that I owe it to myself to make the best of what life brings. Ask me again in a few months after I am married and perhaps I will give you a better answer.'

'Joo, will you still be able to come and meet like we've always done?' asked Su Yin.

'Without a doubt. Tan is not going to imprison me!' Joo smiled. 'He has promised me that. You see, this is the difference between now and when we were very young and starting out. I know the man I am going to marry, not very well yet but at least I know what he looks like and what sort of person he is from what he has done and achieved.'

For a few minutes no one spoke. They quietly sipped their coffee.

Turning to Su Yin, Joo then asked, 'So tell us what is Mrs Pendle's adopted baby like?'

'I don't know what she was expecting,' said Su Yin, 'but I was expecting a Chinese or Malay baby. I think this one is mixed race. I would say it's Chinese mixed with European. Very pretty large eyes and a small pointed nose not like the knob-noses we have. Dark brown eyes and her hair is brown with strands of gold. She is adorable.'

'Don't suppose the adoption people would say who the parents are,' said Joo.

'I don't know. These Eurasians are good looking people like that Mr Tan who works with my boss.'

'Is the baby's mother Chinese or European I wonder? said Cheng. 'I wonder what the story is there. Chinese parents object to mixing with other races not just Europeans.'

'When two people are in love colour or race doesn't matter, does it?' asked Joo. 'Love should transcend everything.'

'Says the bride-to-be,' Cheng chuckled. Joo smiled shyly. Cheng then turned serious, 'To some, family name and honour come first. And then there is the matter of keeping the family line pure. Take my boss for example. He is very cordial and friendly to the European business men that he deals with but he will not abide intermarriage with them. His children have been well and truly drilled on that front.'

'Never mind races, some are even opposed to inter-dialect marriages!' said Joo. 'They maintain that a couple of different dialects are like "one is a chicken and the other is a duck. How can they communicate? And what have they in common?" they say.'

They both lay eggs!' exclaimed Cheng at which all of them laughed. 'Seriously though, it is very brave of the couple to take on such a child. They must surely know that people would wonder.'

'Wonder about what?' Joo frowned.

'If the husband has been naughty,' replied Cheng with a mischievous glint in her eyes.

'What do you mean?' said Joo.

'What I mean is, could the husband have gone with a Chinese girl and unbeknown to him he is the father of the child that he and his wife are adopting?' Cheng explained.

'Then I would say this husband has a clear conscience,' said Joo. 'Otherwise he might be worried in case he was the father. Think of the poor child; maybe nobody else would have a mixed-race baby, she is at the bottom of the pile, the one that gets left. Nobody wants her because she is mixed. There are all sorts of reasons –'

'I know, I am just being wicked; no harm done,' Cheng turned to look at Su Yin. 'Anyway, what have you been up to?'

Su Yin looked embarrassed. 'You could say I was trying to match-make.'

Joo laughed. 'Who for?'

'For Mui and Liew'

'*What*?' exclaimed Cheng.

Su Yin shook her head. 'I don't know why I presumed that they needed me to bring them together.'

'Why?' asked Cheng. 'Do you mean that maybe he visits the brothel regularly and has already met Mui. Maybe they already have a relationship.'

No, no, I meant that he is quite capable of finding a woman himself. I am *so* naïve,' said Su Yin.

Joo raised her brow. 'So what did he say when you tried to match-make?'

Su Yin didn't answer.

'No don't tell me,' Cheng interjected. 'I can guess. He asked you to marry him instead.'

Su Yin's mouth opened. 'How do you know?'

Cheng shook her head in disbelief. 'You can be so blind sometimes. Anyone can see he is crazy about you.'

'What did *you* say to him?' asked Joo.

'I didn't answer him but I think he knew what my answer was.'

Oozing impatience Cheng muttered, '*Aiyahh!*'

'When we took our vows,' Joo started, 'we didn't do it lightly. And we did it for good valid reasons, one of them being that we were scared of walking into a marriage with our eyes blindfolded, not knowing who we were marrying. We were young and taking the vow was the only way to assert ourselves. Our situations have changed; we are older now and we are able to decide and choose for ourselves what we want in life. Nobody can take that from us. I grant that for some of us the choice isn't there but for you it is there. Liew is a good man -'

'How do you know? You've only just met him,' said Su Yin.

'Do we ever really know anyone very well?' asked Cheng. She quietly placed her hand on Su Yin's and looked directly into her eyes, saying softly, 'Not all men are bad.' Su Yin held her look.

Joo continued, 'Liew is one of the good ones. And he works hard at his job on the rubber plantation. What I am saying is that you have two choices – there is Liew on the one hand crazy about you, waited all these years to finally pluck up the courage to propose and on the other hand the same job as you are doing with no end in sight.'

'So is that what you think of our jobs? And that is why you are marrying Tan?' As soon the words came out Su Yin clasped her mouth in horror and quickly added, 'I am sorry I didn't mean it like that. I know you two care very much for each other. I am sorry.'

'But it is true,' said Cheng, 'we will continue working as domestic servants until we aren't able to do it anymore either because we've been sacked or we are too old. Look at Ping; she is still working at her age and there is no sight or sound of her stopping. Both Wei and I have resigned ourselves to that and we are quite content as long as we have each other. I don't suppose it matters so much now but when we are older we'll need companionship if not true love and companionship.'

Joo nodded. 'I am glad you agree with me. I know I've set a bad example, but in the end, it is my life and I have to choose what makes me happy. It is not just about financial security although you have to admit it is important. It is a gamble but I won't know if I don't take the step and find out what is there waiting for me.'

'That's right. I don't know if Wei and I will change how we feel about each other but at the moment we are committed to each other and just enjoy being together. We can't tell you what to do but maybe you should consider giving Liew a chance?' Cheng asked softly. 'More to the point you do like him, don't you?'

Su Yin felt her cheeks warming; she said nothing, her eyes fixed on Cheng as if she was carefully formulating her answer.

'You *do* like him. You yourself have always said that what's most important is being able to choose. It is obvious what you should choose too,' Cheng added.

Su Yin nodded. 'Choice comes with consequences.'

'We're living the consequences of one choice,' said Cheng. 'It doesn't mean that we can't change our minds; there is nothing wrong with that. Is there? We can choose to change our minds.'

Su Yin took a deep breath. 'I know you are concerned for me but can we forget about me and focus on Joo's wedding instead?'

What would her parents and the rest of the family say if she reneged on her vow? She was sure that none of them would disapprove but even if they did, it was her life and she had always done as she had pleased. She was *wilful,* as her father had called her and he would not be surprised or try to stop her if she had made up her mind on something. But the trouble now was she could not decide.

She turned her thoughts to Liew - what sort of a man was he really? Was he true to his words? Somehow hearing that he was the new benefactor who had taken on the coolie room didn't surprise her. She realised that she was no longer self-conscious about her red scar on her cheek when she was with him. What alarmed her was that he had awakened a tenderness in her. It suddenly struck her that the closest she had ever been to a man physically was when the revolting pawnbroker grabbed her. The thought was quickly snuffed out by Liew's strong fingers clasped round her bare arms when she'd lost her balance during their boat trip. The warmth of his fingers had sent an electric current through her. She became self-conscious; the feel of his touch lit up a glow inside her. Liew was nothing like the pawnbroker; they were as different as night and day. She knew they were different but what characteristics would constitute virtues that a woman should look for in a potential husband, she asked herself. She thought of James MacAlpine. A woman couldn't ask for a more loving and caring husband. He was kind and generous not just to his wife and children but also to her, a mere servant. He was without airs and that made him special. As for faithfulness, she hesitated. A strong sisterly protectiveness stopped her from opening her mouth when Cheng had wondered if a European man had been naughty when they were talking about Julia, Penny's adopted child. She couldn't tell Joo and Cheng that the thought had crossed her mind and she'd noticed Helen's reaction when she saw the baby. She couldn't bear the thought of James being smeared with scandals.

There was such a lot to consider before any woman stepped into a life-long contract with a man. At her age she had had more time than most women to think about marriage. She wished that she had the same confidence as Joo and not be restrained by fear.

She could still see Liew's face when she told him that she could not marry him. Disappointment and pain clouded his usually sunny eyes. She had never seen him like that before and was immediately sorry for what she had done. But she could not retract what she had said. In the silence that ensued he recovered and composed himself.

'My proposal was a bit sudden; you weren't expecting it,' he said. 'Think about it, take your time. I will wait. If it is fear of the unknown, what being with me would be like , then you have nothing to fear because I will do everything in my power to look after you. But I don't think it is fear.'

'What is it then?'

Liew looked into her eyes. 'It is your loyalty to Lan Yee. I know how close you two were and how devastated you were when she died. Maybe her death precipitated your taking the vow, I don't know. You think you would be betraying her if you turned your back on it now.'

She had been furious; how dare he presume to know her motives and reasons for her vow. Once the anger had diffused and she had calmed down she conceded that there might be some truth in his perception. She'd said nothing.

And that was how it was left between her and Liew.

Thinking about it now, perhaps he was right. Perhaps it was the fear embroiled with loyalty to Lan Yee that had cemented her resolve not to marry. The strange thing was she missed Liew and wished that he was there with her.

She recalled that when she was a little girl she'd heard stories of eunuchs but had no idea what one was, except that they were boys who were castrated on the order of the emperor and who worked in his palaces of his many wives and concubines. She had once called her brother a eunuch when he pulled her pigtail. Their mother was furious. 'Don't you ever call anyone that! They may live well but they have a bad life.' She didn't explain why - why a bad life if they had everything they could want such as luxurious living conditions, good food, fine clothes and maybe even travel when the emperor's wives or concubines travelled.

But when Su Yin got older she understood: the boys' testicles were removed and they grew to become men stripped of their manhood. No wonder they were bitter and harboured anger and hatred. They couldn't function as men; they could not procreate. She couldn't imagine her brother like that. Now she compared herself with the eunuch, like them her emotions were all there, her desires, her need for love, human touch and embrace. And like the eunuchs, she was impotent; she was unable to bend with the wind.

Su Yin sighed.

Whatever her reason was for not wanting to marry there was no hurry to decide what she should do. Her position in the MacAlpines' home was secure and she was content.

Chapter 32

Su Yin never thought she would attend another wedding after her sister Mei's wedding. Who would have thought that one of the sisterhood would actually get married? They were such a strong and determined group; they had the older ones in the group to look up to for encouragement. They had zealously focussed on maintaining their self-sufficiency and self-reliance without recourse to dependence on men. They had stoutly upheld their vows of celibacy. The memory of her friend Lan surfaced again; she who'd rather die than marry after turning her back on marriage. What would she have thought of Joo getting married? Would she have been disgusted that Joo changed her course or would she have understood and accepted that change was not a sign of weakness? Su Yin didn't mean to be disloyal to either sister by siding with one against the other. There were times she felt that Lan went too far to make her point and yet she admitted it took courage to stand by her conviction. Or was Lan foolish? Was there not another way out of it? Run away from home perhaps? Whatever, she was not around now, her absence a testament to the strength of her conviction. Was Joo or any of them bound by duty or loyalty to adhere to their commitment? Surely above all, the goddess Kwan Yin - goddess of mercy and compassion – would understand especially as Joo had found happiness. Kwan Yin surely could not deny Joo that.

But Su Yin had forgotten that some of the sisters had no choice; they had had to turn their backs on their pledge of spinsterhood. They had to take what was on offer when openings for domestic servants were few and far between because of the huge influx of women workers from South

China. Some even had to offer themselves as brides for the burgeoning Chinese male population that far outnumbered the women. Su Yin lamented the reality and - for those without alternatives- the irony of resisting marriage only to then offer themselves as brides in order to survive. Others had to work in brothels. Mui, her new friend had to do just that. What would Kwan Yin say to that? Mui had resigned herself to that way of life 'for the time-being at least' according to her. Who could say who was the better off? Financially Mui easily won hands down. She was convinced that as soon as she could afford it she would get out of that business. Su Yin was sorry that her attempt at matchmaking for her had failed. Joo was doing something of her choice which was the most important; no one was forcing her against her will and she was marrying Tan, a man whom she had come to respect and like very much.

Su Yin looked at Joo who was completely transformed. She thought anyone who didn't know her would not suspect she had been a domestic servant slaving in the kitchen at the beck and call of the family she was working for. She worked up to the last day of notice the week before; she had worn the white and black uniform for the last time and now was on the threshold to be elevated to the heights of the wife of a businessman. No more *kowtow*ing to anyone and no more taking orders from her employers who showed their gratitude by insisting that Joo should get ready in their house and that the groom could come for her on the wedding morning.

She looked radiant; the curves of her lips were emphasised in cherry-red and a hint of rouge highlighted her cheek bones. It was the first time she had ever worn make-up and Su Yin could see that she was very self -conscious apart from knowing that she was the centre of attention. 'Look at me!' she'd whispered earlier to her and Cheng when she got close to them, 'I look like I am ready to go on stage at the street opera,' which made them giggle.

Her hair was now combed and piled up on the top of her head studded with a few diamante flowers, showing off her smooth neck instead of it being hidden by the bun that she had been wearing all her working life. The night before she had discussed with Su Yin and Cheng what she should do about her hair. She had thought long and hard about it; any change would symbolise the breaking of her vow. They'd reminisced their experience of the night before they took their vow, how they'd washed their hair with water infused with pomegranate and then the hair ritual when their mothers combed their hair for the last time. They recalled their chants:

'First comb for luck...
second comb for longevity...
third comb for contentment....
fourth comb for safety...
fifth comb for freedom...
sixth comb for courage...
seventh comb for self-belief and finally
eighth comb for health.'

The three of them then became very sombre and emotional; that particular night marked the beginning of a new road, a new life and it seemed a life-time ago. They had come so far down the road. They had got used to being without their parents especially their mothers but it didn't dull the pain of their absence which also served to magnify the importance of the closeness of the three friends. And now they had come to another crossroad which they had not anticipated. After a few moments of silence, Joo piped up, 'Well, I think that on the whole we have had most of those wishes, don't you?' Cheng and Su Yin nodded. 'I can't believe this is happening to me. I hope I don't wake up and find that it is all a dream,'

'It is real and it is happening,' said Su Yin. 'You will just be taking a different path from us two. And as long as we can continue to meet as before I won't complain.'

'I will always meet with you.,' said Joo as her eyes welled up. 'Promise me you will always be there for me as I will for you.'

They promised.

Joo could wear her hair any way now; she could try out the new permanent waves that was the latest fashion or she could cut it short and have a fringe. But she decided that she would do neither yet; instead she would keep it long as it was and put it in a ponytail to begin with.

The red silk dress fitted her beautifully after the waist was taken in a little. Su Yin was thrown off balance when she first saw the dress on her. This was the second time she had seen the dress worn in public. As she beheld the bride a strange feeling of sadness mixed with happiness had shot through her as she was reminded of the time she wore it during the ceremony of her pledge. Wearing high-heeled shoes Joo stood tall and gracefully elegant 'like a film star' she heard someone in the crowd say. There had been audible gasps of admiration and a ripple of '*Wah! So beautiful'* across the hall when she first arrived at the groom's house. Su Yin herself was among those who were spellbound by the sight of her. She noticed the red silk shoes that complimented the dress. In spite of her thirty-eight years Joo looked as good as any bride half her age. She did the dress justice. She was glad, glad and proud that Joo was wearing it and showing off her mother's handiwork which would otherwise have been kept hidden in her box tucked away under her bed.

Joo knew nothing of what had happened in the pawnshop. Fortunately there had been no mention of it in the *Nanyang News.* Su Yin said nothing to her about redeeming it either. She couldn't bring herself to tell her what the pawnbroker did. When she'd made Cheng promise not to breathe a word to Joo and then told her what had happened, Cheng was horrified beyond words. Her eyes bulged and her chest blew up. She was livid. 'Son of a tortoise! The devil!' she'd cried. 'Why didn't you tell me? Why didn't you ask me to go with you? Are you alright? You are not hurt in anyway are you?' After Su Yin had reassured her she continued, 'How dare he? Who does he think he is? He should have his testicles cut off and thrown to the dogs!' She became very agitated for some time and when she'd simmered down she said, 'You know I remember hearing about that son of a tortoise. His wife left him about a couple of years ago. He was probably sex-starved or was that why his wife left him? Of course, I won't tell Joo. She would be mortified.' Fortunately for Su Yin, the whole incident was now a speck in the horizon of her memory.

The tea ceremony was about to begin. A row of five chairs had been arranged for Tan's elders in the front room of the family house which was a large wooden house on the edge of the city. The spacious house was well kept and cool which was a good sign to Su Yin – Joo would not have to work like a slave cleaning and tidying up after the others. Here, Joo would live with her parents-in-law and the two step-daughters who were nineteen and twenty; the three older sons lived and worked in other towns. Su Yin wondered how the dynamics would work in the new set-up when Joo moved in; she realised that the old fear of being at the bottom of the rung in the new family hierarchy was stubbornly embedded in her. That had been one of the reasons for tenaciously hanging on to her independence. How would Joo cope with the loss of her freedom and her independence? Like her Joo might have only earned a pittance but at least she could say it was her own money and hers to do as she wanted. Now that she was married would she have to hold out her hand to her husband for money? Perhaps he would give her a huge allowance like Mr Lok did for Mrs Lok whom she considered an artful woman, one who would use anything to her advantage such as making her husband pay for keeping her in the dark about his first wife. Joo wasn't that sort of person. Su Yin reckoned that the trade-off for Joo was a home to call her own. She would never be homeless, not unless her husband threw her out which seemed as likely as the sun rising in the west. Especially after she noticed the way he looked at his new bride.

Su Yin had briefly met Tan's children who seemed very accepting of Joo and happy for their father. The two daughters were well-educated and Su Yin hoped they were open-minded enough to allow Joo into their lives. She had no doubt that Joo would adapt quickly because of her generous nature. And she would fit in with Tan's family's business given her shrewd way with money. Su Yin could picture her helping in the shop surrounded by gunny sacks of rice, beans and sugar, serving her customers and bewitching them with her lovely smile. That together with her charming and easy manner would make her a great asset. Su Yin smiled at the thought of her now being the boss-lady sweeping in the day's takings; she could be learning to use the abacus to count the money next. She hoped that Joo would be valued and not simply be regarded as an extra pair of hands.

Su Yin liked Tan much more than she had expected and wasn't surprised at his generosity in inviting all Joo's friends to the wedding. She looked at the new bride and groom standing side by side. Tan, looking very smart in a western-style cream-coloured suit that he had hired from a local tailor's shop, could not stop smiling and at times looked slightly dazed as if he couldn't believe his good luck in finding such a beautiful bride. From the few times that she had talked to him before now she had formed the opinion that he was thoughtful. In spite of her shield of cynicism she conceded that Tan was genuine and really cared for Joo. Standing near the bride and groom Cheng and Wei were beaming at each other, a picture of contentment and she wondered if they too were as good as married in spirit.

Joo looked happy although she was nervous in the amidst of the chatter of the throng of relatives and friends and clatter of the whirring fans working at full speed.

'Did you know she was an *amah* until now?'

'Yes, her friends are the same.'

'Tan is very lucky to have a good woman to look after him now. He has waited long enough.'

'She is the lucky one to be able to find a husband at her age and a good catch I daresay.'

'So how old is she then? She looks very young.'

Then it was time for the tea ceremony.

Holding the wedding teacup in both hands, Joo very gracefully bowed as she served each of the elders in her new family. First it was Tan's elderly paternal aunt, a stern-looking woman, with silver hair combed back and tied into a bun at the nape. She smiled at Joo as she handed the new family member a red envelope after she had taken a sip of the tea. In contrast, Tan's father who was served next had a happy face and a loquacious nature. Sitting next to him was Tan's mother wearing a silk pastel blue floral *samfoo* and a look of contentment. Her face was tanned and wrinkly but something in her eyes said she was happy. When she smiled she revealed a missing front tooth.

Su Yin decided that Tan's parents were amiable enough and they had welcomed her and the other sisters warmly. As in-laws go, they were more than a reasonable lot, much better than one dared hope for; something told her that they would be kind and good to their new daughter-in-law. Her initial worry for Joo was unfounded.

Secretly, she allowed herself a feeling of smugness that Joo was wearing the dress her mother made.

'This is probably the only wedding we will attend for the rest of our lives,' said one of the sisters at the table. The others, their mouths full, simply nodded their agreement. The large restaurant was filled to capacity with the wedding party and bustling with loud conversations. There were at least eleven tables of ten which to her mind was a favourable sign: Tan's family was not short of money. From a corner the sound of little children laughing filtered through and then at the sight of the waiters appearing with the first dish a gentle chorus of approval coursed through the restaurant.

'Su Yin, Joo's dress is absolutely beautiful,' said Ping. 'Your mother is a very good tailor as well as weaver. The cut is just so right.'

'Yes, lovely dress. And Su Yin herself isn't too bad at sewing either,' said another. 'Look at the outfit she is wearing; it is very well made.'

'Not as good as my mother's,' said Su Yin. She was pleased that she had decided on the wearing the newest of her three *samfoo*s– a red floral one. After a pause she said, 'Is none of us daring enough to wear a dress like what the modern youngsters wear?' She looked at the faces around the table. One or two shook their heads.

'*Aiyahh,* my legs are so white, they would look like they didn't belong to me if I wore a dress!' said one which brought a laugh.

'Go sun your legs before you wear one!'

'I prefer to cover my legs. They are not nice anyway.'

'Never thought about it. Are we not too old for it?'

'Or are we just too stuck in our ways?'

'Yes, look at us. We might be wearing coloured and patterned *samfoos* but anyone would easily guess we are the white-and-black army.'

'That is true.'

'It is more economical to make a dress than a *samfoo*. See how much less fabric is needed.'

'Yes, worth considering.'

A waiter came to clear the empty dish and another brought the next course of deep fried king prawns with the delicate aroma of garlic and chilli. The discussion quickly swung to the golden battered prawns which were garnished with a sprig of spring onions and coriander leaves.

Cheng savoured the prawns. Then in a lowered voice directed at Su Yin who was beside her she said, 'I know for sure Joo is going to be happy.'

'I agree with you,' replied Su Yin. 'These prawns are good,' she licked her lips, 'just the right amount of seasoning.'

Cheng's eyes were now fixed on Joo who was sitting at a table at the centre of the restaurant. She was smiling at something Tan had said. 'She is courageous and I admire her for that.'

Something in her tone made Su Yin spin round to look at Cheng. 'What are you getting at?' she asked.

Cheng didn't answer right away but continued chewing without looking at Su Yin. Then, 'It takes courage to change your mind about something. Self-belief, courage, that's what our mothers wished for us.'

'What are you talking about?' Su Yin was glad that the other women at their table were engrossed in their own conversations and busy eating.

Still not looking at Su Yin, Cheng said, 'Simply that if circumstances change, we might have to change with them. I am sure the goddess Kwan Yin will understand.'

'I think you have been drinking too much of that rice wine again,' said Su Yin feeling the prickles of a rising irritation.

As Cheng reached for another prawn on the platter she pointedly said, 'Maybe.'

Chapter 33

Su Yin heard James whistling as he walked along the corridor before he bounced into the kitchen.

'Hello, Amah, how are you?' he said in Cantonese. 'Smells good. I am ready to eat.' He walked to the fridge and opened it. He took out a bottle of Tiger beer, got the bottle opener from the drawer and proceeded to open it.

Su Yin beamed at him; it always reminded her of how her brother Keng did just the same when she was cooking, coming in to sniff to find out what was for dinner. Like Keng he would hover around briefly to chat and watch her cook. And she'd detected something new in James's attitude, it was as if he was protective of her. Out of the blue he had given her a salary raise without making any fuss which had surprised her. When she had told him thinking that he had made a mistake over the amount, he'd quietly said she was due it. She was pleased to see him looking cool and carefree like a helium-filled balloon dancing in the breeze. He had changed from his work clothes into shorts and a short-sleeved shirt hanging loose outside his shorts. 'I am well,' she said as she stirred the shallots sizzling in the wok. 'Cooking sea bass,' she pointed to the freshly cleaned fish on the worktop, and next to it a heap of shredded ginger and cut spring onions.

'Great! What are you going to do with it? Steam or fry?' James drank his beer.

'Steam with shallots, ginger and spring onions.'

'Good. How is your family? Latest news?'

'They are well. Another grandson for my parents, would you believe? That house is going to burst.'

James smiled. 'Your parents must be very happy. Is it another boy?'

'Yes.'

'Look at the children out there,' he said as he peered out of the window. Cammy was perched between branches of the old hibiscus tree aiming his catapult at unsuspecting targets while Lexie and Ellie were playing hopscotch in the shade of the frangipani tree. Thomas was showing Ben something in his palm. 'They were so enthralled by the Pendles's baby girl. She is lovely, isn't she?' They had seen the Pendles earlier in the morning when they were in church for the Sunday service.

'Yes, she is,' Su Yin looked at James; his face was open and smiling not like someone who had a guilty conscience or a secret, she thought. 'Mrs Pendle is very kind-hearted and the baby is very lucky to have her for a mother,' replied Su Yin pushing the brown crisping shallots to the side of the wok before turning off the gas. She gestured to James that she had to get on with seasoning the fish.

'Right, I will get out of your way,' said James. 'I'll go join the children.'

As Su Yin spread a mix of fried shallots, chopped garlic and spring onions over the seabass it struck her that James had nothing to hide or be ashamed of where the baby Julia was concerned. He wasn't guilty of any misdemeanour. Cheng had been mischievous suggesting that either Anthony Pendle or James could have been involved. And she felt guilty that she did have a tiny tip of a doubt even though it was ever so briefly. She could shake off her initial misapprehension now.

Su Yin thought that there was a wall of ice between James and Helen during dinner. Even the children were quiet, not their usual happy talkative selves and were now in their bedrooms. She sensed immediately that something was wrong. As soon as she had served the food, she returned to the kitchen to wash the pots and wok. She didn't hear raised voices in the dining room which could have been bad or good. She couldn't help thinking that Helen was bottling up whatever was troubling her. For several weeks now since Penny brought her baby to visit she had suspected that something was not right with Helen. She had been distracted and impatient with the children. Did Helen somehow also have the same suspicion that Cheng raised about the father of Penny's adopted child? The day before when Cammy had accused Lexie of stealing his marbles and the two had started arguing, Helen, like a bolt of lightning, screamed at them which stopped them in their tracks. As was her wont Su Yin kept out of her way. It was not her business; hers was to serve and wait on them but she didn't like shouting and she couldn't help her feeling of disquiet. Helen was no saint and could lose her temper but she always recovered herself very quickly and all would be right again.

As Su Yin scrubbed the pans, her parents who were never far from her mind came to the fore. They seldom rowed because there was no time to do so. And when they had finished work at the end of the day they were too tired to argue. Perhaps that was the advantage of being poor. Besides she couldn't imagine her father raising his voice over her mother's to make his point. She had come to accept that this friction between couples was part of the package of marriage which was an aggravation she could do without. Liew then came to mind. She was conscious of her heart doing a skip and a warmth flushing through her body. She *liked* the feeling. But what would it be like to be married to him, to live with him for the rest of her life? She had been used to the freedom to be and do as she liked without worrying about someone else, something she would find hard to relinquish. Perhaps, she thought, this selfishness on her part would militate against a happy union. Suddenly she heard a car engine start and then silence in the dining room.

James had rushed out the house. She did not see Helen trying to stop him.

Chapter 34

1952

After stitching Ellie's teddy bear's ear back on, Su Yin packed away her sewing things into her needlework box. The day's dust and sweaty stickiness had been washed away by the afternoon downpour. The initial smell of the earthy steam when the rain first hit the arid hot ground had evaporated leaving the air fresh and cool, tinged with the sweet scent of frangipani. As always the sight of the crescent-shaped moon surrounded by a sprinkling of silver stars lifted Su Yin's spirit. There was no denying that the buzz from seeing Liew in the afternoon before the rain was still there and it had been distracting her from her duties since she came home. Liew had insisted on bringing her home as the heavens promised to open. She accepted only because Ah Hock was busy driving Helen and the children. Liew drove her to the backdoor, and *not* the front door, at her request. It was strange, she thought, that although she had been in his car a few times she still didn't feel it was right and proper. It wasn't that she was bothered by what people might think of her - a single woman and an *amah* at that, being driven around by a single man. She didn't want to give Liew false hopes. She was happy to meet him for a chat or have a meal as old friends would do. Liew on the other hand was adamantly concerned about her safety as the communist terrorists seemed to have stepped up their attacks and had even ventured into the built-up areas. His concern had touched her; it made her feel as if he was holding her again like the time he did on the boat.

Su Yin walked to her chest of drawers. Next to her photographs and mirror was a new addition: a small blue and white vase that Ming had given her when she came to see her. It wasn't the gift but her thoughtfulness that brought tears to her eyes. She hadn't expected it. She studied the vase again; the delicately embossed white images of ladies in long flowing robes carrying water urns against a blue background couldn't be more different from a Chinese vase. Ming had explained that it was a typically English product - *Wedgewood*, she remembered Ming calling it. She liked it. Besides she had not possessed such a pretty and delicate vase before.

She then picked up the mirror, stood under the bright glow of the ceiling lamp and peered at the face in it. She conceded that the way her hair was combed back from her forehead and tied in a bun made her look a little austere. Joo's new hairstyle - short and softly waved – made her look years younger, augmented by the bloom of pregnancy. Sixth months pregnant, she looked like she was made for it; she was so proud of her protruding abdomen and still disbelieving that she was going to be a mother. Su Yin couldn't help feeling a tiny bit envious. She examined closely the mirrored face for wrinkles and to her delight there was none noticeable. She removed her gold pin from her hair and then shook her head to loosen her hair. Lan Yee was right – the pin was a constant reminder of her. *So you don't forget me,* she had said when she bought it in the shop. Su Yin now wondered if Liew was right that her loyalty to Lan Yee was holding her back from deviating from her path, a path that seemed like a fixed and deep trench that she could not get out of. He had not pressed her to give him an answer since he asked her to marry him. 'I have waited for twenty-three years, I can wait a bit longer,' he'd said when she told him that she didn't know what she wanted. It was incredible, unimaginable, that someone like him could feel so strongly for her. She had been stumped then as she was now. In between she had once wondered how things would have turned out if he had agreed to see Mui. To all appearances Mui was doing well, always looking beautiful and smart, as if she didn't have a care in the world. But Su Yin knew better. She started to brush her hair.

Although Su Yin still met with Joo and Cheng as they had done for years she admitted to feeling lonely sometimes, vaguely ostracised, which she felt was part of the reason she continued to see Liew. Cheng was happily and firmly attached to Wei; they were like a wedded couple and she had to admit she was happy for them. She had arrived at this stage of the road which she had never for a second envisaged would happen. When she committed herself to celibacy she hadn't thought that far ahead. All that mattered to her then was her independence. Looking at Ming she had been amazed at the change in her. Bounding with the joys of adulthood, freedom and independence Ming exuded quiet confidence. Her first year at university, the long spell away from home and her parents seemed to have instilled an appreciation for her family; she was noticeably more conciliatory towards her mother. What Su Yin found gratifying was that Ming still thought enough of her to specially come to the MacAlpines' residence to see her. She had talked with certainty of her future after she graduated. Had she, Su Yin, not been just like that at her age even if all she had to look forward to was work in the silk factory? Where and whom was she going to turn to in her old age? Was she jealous of them – Joo, Cheng and Ming? She thought of the others in the sisterhood. What were their plans? How far could they plan for? Look at her. She *had* planned; it was all going as planned until these distractions popped up like spots on a teenager's face. She had asked Cheng, 'What is the point of living? We work so hard to enable our relatives to live and maybe enjoy life a little. They do well - marry, have children, and look forward to grandchildren to play with in their old age. We could bask in their success but what do we have to look forward to?' *What was to be her legacy?* She didn't like this sense of self-doubt seeping in which sometimes nudged her into mild melancholy. Her mind had been swarmed with questions all jostling for precedence for answers.

Joo was happy with marriage. Her contentment was there for all to see: her face glowed with joy. She didn't have a single regret at all; she wasn't even worried whether people would laugh at her being pregnant at her age. Now all she had to do was wait for her baby to arrive. Tan didn't want her to tire herself helping out in the shop. Hers was clearly a case in favour of marriage.

Su Yin recalled the night before when Ellie had shouted for her in the garden, 'Amah, come quickly!' She had run to Ellie thinking she had hurt herself, only to find that she had spotted a butterfly resting on a calla lily. Its wings were orange and black like a tiger's coat. 'Isn't it beautiful?' Ellie gushed softly.

'Yes,' she'd answered and wished that Liew was there to see it too. Suddenly she was propelled into comparing herself with the silkworms she looked after a lifetime ago. Was she like one of these worms spending all its energy spinning silk threads to make its cocoon shell, to then not only give up its silk but lose its life too in the process. The crusted cocoon in her drawer sprang to her mind. Was she to be stifled mid-life, never to become a butterfly to fly and be free, to feel the wind beneath her wings lifting her through the air? The questions swarming in her head had left her feeling disorientated and bereft and she didn't like it.

Now at thirty-nine Su Yin felt she was set in her ways and it would be difficult to un-set them. She was sure that after all the years of independence and self-reliance, it would be impossible to bend her will. She recalled her mother always saying to her when she was little, 'So headstrong! Nobody would want you for a wife!' Could she allow herself to be subsumed by a man? If he was serious about marrying her would he understand and accept her need for freedom? Would he allow her to be her own woman? Or expect her to be subservient, and be nothing more than his appendage?

Her foibles had become clear to her with the years: her impatience – she couldn't stand to be kept waiting; she was strict about punctuality and a respecter of other people's time. Waiting for her employers and their children was one thing; she was paid to do that. Outside of that she could so easily be infuriated if she was kept waiting. What was Liew like? So far he had been on time, turning up at the appointed time and place. But was that simply a show to impress? A few weeks ago he brought a bunch of palm oil nuts to show her; he was clearly excited. It was his child-like marvel at the structure of the tiny red fruit and what it could yield that she found endearing. Then when he took her to his plantation to see the rows and rows of the trees that produced the nuts she was transported into another world.

Liew had gradually opened up about his wife to her. She could see that he'd cared very much about her as he recounted how he came home to find her gone and the house turned upside down. The crying neighbours told him that she along with a few other women had been taken by Japanese soldiers. The worst was when they found the women's bodies the next day on an abandoned farm and he saw that his wife's abdomen had been slashed open revealing their dead unborn child. He had had nightmares since while his heart hardened against the evil perpetrators. His voice quivered when he said, 'It was a boy.' Inwardly Su Yin had cried for them. When she looked at Liew she could picture him as a good father, more understanding and patient than most. He was quietly big-hearted as well. When she, Cheng and Joo thanked him for buying the coolie room he merely shook it off as if he had only treated them to a plate of noodles.

Cheng had called her intransigent at Joo's wedding dinner. 'Why are you blind to other things that are on offer to you like a good man's love, a proposal of marriage and financial security?' she had asked shaking her head, perplexed. Su Yin knew that Cheng cared deeply for her just as she did for Cheng. Perhaps Cheng's concern was based on knowing that her own future would not be lonely; she had Wei to share and enjoy her old age with when the time came. But what about her, Su Yin? There was the Hall back in the village in China where there would be other geriatric residents like herself, but wouldn't it still be incomplete without a partner, a soul mate?

Su Yin had been thinking a lot of Liew alongside questions popping up like the first shoots of bamboo after the rain. When she went to sleep he was there in her thoughts and when she woke up she'd be thinking about him. She missed him when they were apart. What was it about him that she liked? She thought of his touch again and she had wanted so much to stroke his cheek when they were facing each other at lunch. *Was this what her sister Mei called love, this emotion that makes you feel and act irrationally?* Was this 'love' an essential ingredient in the recipe for a good marriage? All the marriages that she knew of back home were arranged and love didn't come into it. If the couple were lucky they would grow to care and love each other like her parents did. They were like *yin* and *yang*, two pieces of one neatly slotted together. Were they *soul mates*? Helen and James were clearly different; they loved each other before they were married. Even they had their ups and downs but they were happy and were now planning to celebrate their wedding anniversary. Su Yin chided herself for imagining that James could be the father of the Pendle's adopted baby. If Helen had had the same suspicion it was obviously now banished.

So what was the glue that bound husband and wife together? There had to be a huge element of trust. *Love* and *trust*. The sadness was that there was no guarantee that those vital elements were in all marriages. Yes, she was afraid. She didn't have the courage as Cheng had pointed out.

While she didn't have the courage, she reckoned that as long as the MacAlpines were happy with her and were willing to keep her on in their employ there was no urgency or need to change tack. To plunge into the unknown which might turn out to be disastrous was a fate worse than what she had tried to escape by not marrying in the first place. Look at Sister Ping their oldest friend, she reminded herself, she was still working and well looked after by the family she'd worked for for the last twenty-two years. They had promised to keep her on until she was no longer able to work. Su Yin suspected that apart from Ping's good nature it was her exquisite culinary magic that bound her to the family. Anyone could wash, clean, iron and sew but to be able to cook well raised a servant's worth several fold. At the last meeting of the sisters for the New Year dinner, Ping had reaffirmed that she would stay on with the family and had been very upbeat about her future. Many of the older sisters she had known of had gone the same way. The prospects didn't seem so bad, Su Yin thought. She considered her own cooking ability to be a little above average but as long as it was good enough for the MacAlpine family, it was good enough for her. There was nothing wrong with the monotony of the job, the same day-in day-out routine, the same unwritten order of duties, the afternoon soap operas, meeting her sisters and Liew, and finally looking up at the night sky. It was a far cry from her childhood fantasy of standing up for her father and her family like warrior Hua Mu Lan; it wasn't quite like fighting the battle against the marauding hordes of invaders. But it was synonymous with security and she could not spit at that. Besides there was something more to it than just working for the MacAlpines; she cared about them, they were like family to her and young Ben was a handful of pure delight now that he was walking and learning to talk.

On the other hand, it would be less lonely to have someone to share her life, a companion, a true friend. They wouldn't have to be man and wife. But what man would want that? What man would deprive himself of his dues in a marriage? Instantly her mind darted to her body. It was slim with no hint of excess fat, not unattractive in comparison to some women of her age. Underneath her baggy old sleep *samfoo* her breasts were still supple and firm without the support of the new cotton brassiere she had recently acquired as a replacement for her usual cotton vest. But was her body still fit for child-bearing? Feeling Joo's baby kick was the most extraordinary experience; her palm almost connecting with the baby in her womb, she felt the thrill going through her. It was as if the baby was saying, 'Yes, I am here'. She had been moved, overwhelmed. Although she had held many new-born babies she had never felt an unborn child like that. Had her womb given up and shrivelled after years of waiting to bear fruit? She wasn't sure. She had heard that the mistress of one of the sisters gave birth at the age of forty-one, her eldest child being twenty- three years old. The image of her hunchback great grandmother sprung to mind; what if she became bent like her? Who would want her for a wife or to work for them then? She quickly flung away the frightening possibility. Then suddenly, to take its place, like a thief springing out of nowhere the memory of the attack by the pawnbroker pounced on her. The first thought was: *What had the man seen in her?* Or was he so sex-starved, as Joo said, that any woman was prey and was it purely bad timing and her bad luck that she was there? She would never know. The last she heard through one of the sisters was that the man had moved away to another town. She still avoided that part of town whenever she could.

Su Yin sighed, shook her head at the turmoil of her thoughts, took one last brush of her hair and turned to the mirror. She studied the image in it. Her long silky hair now fell forward and covered her red scar on her cheek. The scar didn't bother her anymore when she was with Liew. She'd looked for wrinkles around her eyes and found none that would bother her. Her skin was still smooth and clear apart from it being a shade darker than she would like. *I am still young*, she thought. *Maybe I should spread my wings and fly like a butterfly.*

Chapter 35

'Amah,' said Cammy licking his fingers after swallowing the last bite of prawn fritter, 'I have to say I wasn't sure about this fish at first but I must say it's good. A bit sour,' he screwed his face, 'but good.'

Su Yin couldn't help but smile at Cammy's youthful diplomacy. Although fussy he was willing to try any food she put in front of him. His absolute favourite was prawn fritters which had almost disappeared from the plate between him and his sisters who were less inclined to try. But she had cooked the mackerel in chilli and tamarind sauce at their mother's request when she had asked Helen what she should cook. It had piqued her curiosity; Helen MacAlpine tended to crave for sour foods when she was pregnant. But when she was serving it, Helen had only wanted a small portion which was unlike her as her appetite was generally good.

'The fritters were delicious,' piped up Lexie. She tilted her head timidly as she always did when she wanted something she wasn't sure she should have, 'Is there any more, Amah?'

'You've had enough, Lexie,' said Helen, her voice was curt. Lexie pouted. Ben, sitting in his high chair next to Helen was busy shoving a piece of mango into his mouth.

Su Yin hesitated for a few seconds. 'Too much not good for you.' She pointed to her own throat. 'Make sore*thloat.*' Lexie did not look at her and continued sticking her puckered lips out.

Her hair tied back in a ponytail, Helen's tanned face was glowing after an afternoon out in the garden with Penny and Julia. The children had had a fun time. Cammy was engrossed with his new wooden top that he had bought with this pocket money and was showing off after Ah Hock had earlier shown him how to spin it. Between fussing about Ben and Julia and playing hopscotch and annoying Cammy, the two girls Lexie and Ellie played catch-up, and danced and sang with Thomas. Ben and Julia toddled about on the grass while their mothers exchanged news as they looked on. Su Yin served a big jug of chrysanthemum tea but Penny would only drink tea with milk. She noted again that there was no resemblance between the two toddlers whatsoever. Apart from the fair hair there was nothing to make anyone think they were related. Now in the dining room, despite the ceiling fan spinning sedately, the room felt airless. But Su Yin suspected that it was not just the heat that was making Helen restless. James had gone off again to Kota Tinggi, to the Jungle Warfare School. He had been away for three days. Helen was always edgy when he was away on such a mission.

'Mrs Makapeen, don't *wolly.* Mister Makapeen can take care of himself,' Su Yin said softly as she took Helen's plate away from the table.

Helen looked up at Su Yin, she forced a smile even though her eyes were watery. 'I know,' she said.

'Mummy,' Ellie called out, 'after dinner can we go out into the garden again for a little while?'

Helen hesitated. She looked at the children's faces with their eyes fixed on her and eagerly awaiting her response. She put on a mock stern face and then said brightly. 'Yes, you may but only for a short while.'

'Yay!' the children chorused except for Ben whose eyes lit up and darted around at his siblings as he banged his table-top.

Out in the garden the air temperature had suddenly dropped. In the long shadow of the evening sun the children ran about chasing each other and kicking Cammy's ball as if they had been locked up for days inside and this was their first time out. Lexie was steering Ben as he tried to run after the ball. Cammy kicked his ball towards Helen who was looking out at the distant sky.

'I wish Dad was here so I could show him what I learnt at football practice today,' said Cammy walking to her.

'I know, darling,' Helen put her arms around Cammy. She looked up at the sky again. A thickening band of grey clouds had appeared in the horizon. The coconut leaves were twisting furiously as a giant gust of wind tore across the garden. She shivered as she whispered, 'I wish he was here too.'

The rain pounded on the corrugated zinc roof as if a horde of wild horses were galloping endlessly across it. The noise in the mess was deafening. James had known heavy rainfalls – sudden short downpours -but this one was persistent and had dragged on like an energetic long-winded nag of a fish-wife. It had gone on for three days and three nights without a break. In all that time, he and the rest of the residents had been holed up in the various huts of the Jungle Warfare School. The rain had been anticipated as it was after all the season of the north-east monsoon but no one had expected such a voluminous and continuous downpour. Even the Chinese cooks were shaking their heads, their faces glum with gloom and fear of what the deluge would cause. Just before dinner one of them had said, '*Wah*, rain never so heavy before.' He shook his head again and then proclaimed, 'Going to flood *lah*.'

Captain Douglas swirled the brandy in his glass then took a puff of his pipe. 'Well, this lot is getting a good introduction to the local weather,' he said, referring to the fresh-faced young soldier recruits, fresh from the temperate climate of Britain. They had not had long to acclimatise yet; their skin was pink from sunburn.

'Nothing like being thrown in at the deep end, eh?' said James. It was not the open ground warfare that the young recruits had been trained in back home, in the lush green and pleasant pastures. He had taken them into the jungle for six days. His task was to teach them survival in the jungle and to deal with enemies of a different kind. Under the thick canopy of the leaves at the top of the several hundred feet tall trees, the new arrivals had been plunged into the darkness of the tropical jungle. It was sometimes indistinguishable from night time depending on the thickness of the canopy. Not only did they have to learn to adapt quickly to the hell-hole of humidity but they had to look out for traps set up by the guerrillas, traps like the ones James had helped build during the Occupation. Apart from the guerrillas, there were the deadly insects, and snakes. He warned the recruits of the slimy black blood-sucking leeches that would find their way through every opening of their clothing to latch on to their flesh. The soldiers had to learn to resist pulling them off. He was gratified to see how quickly they learnt; one of the soldiers who was attacked by a couple of the leeches had shuddered and squirmed at the sight of them but quickly reached for his cigarette to burn them off.

When food ran out James pointed out plants that were edible such as bamboo, yams and coconut palm. Turning bamboo trunk segments into cooking utensils, cooking rice if they were lucky enough to have some. They were fortunate to come across a wild boar which they killed and roasted over a fire. Then when the rain started it prompted the building of shelters with bamboo and palm leaves. All in all it had been a satisfactory exercise and he was pleased. The men were as exhausted as he was by the heat and humidity and secretly James was pleased to be back in the relative comfort of the mess. They had started to feel as if the rain had soaked through their skin. A couple of days back in the lecture room would re-energise them.

'Looks like you managed to get back in time just before this,' Captain Douglas's eyes rolled up to the noisy ceiling. 'Almost of Biblical proportions, wouldn't you say?'

'Look at it this way: this rain will either keep the CTs in check or flush them out of the jungle,' said James mindful of the fact that the state of Johor was a hotbed of communist aggression.

'Cook who comes from K.T. informs me that the last time it rained this hard and flooded the town was back in thirty-two. It was calamitous,' said Sergeant-Major Moss.

The Captain's brow creased. 'We should be on standby. The water is rising fast.'

At 0409-hours news broke that the river had overflowed its banks; the most immediate parts were now under water which meant that many areas of the town of Kota Tinggi were flooded. The water was rising so fast that the bridge linking the south to the north bank was rapidly disappearing under the tide.

In the bleak light of the new dawn the soldiers pushed out in their boats towards Kota Tinggi just over ten miles away from the School. The town was half submerged in water; people were stranded or trapped upstairs in their wooden houses where the ground floors were immersed in dirty brown water and their furniture floating about. What was once a dusty road into town was no longer to be seen as James and a couple of soldiers headed for town in their motorboat. They passed the school field now a lake of water with the school buildings sitting on the edge well above the water level. The school had been designated as a rescue centre. As they slowed they saw the top half of a single row of houses behind a deserted petrol station.

Pointing to the houses James called out to the soldier manning the boat, 'Let's see what's there!'

The boat turned left and advanced towards the brown tin roof tops and as they neared the first of the houses they heard a girl's frantic cries.

'Over there, sir!' shouted the soldier over the noise of the engine. He carefully manoeuvred the boat between truncated coconut palm trees - its leaves nodding in a sombre mood - and young tree tops that looked like floating balls of leaves. The girl's cries got louder as they approached an open window above which was a cage hanging from the eave with a bird in it. Looking through the window James saw two teenage girls in their pyjamas sitting on top of a table surrounded by brown water, the tearful younger girl clinging onto the older one. They had been left at home by their parents while they went to work in the plantation before the flood separated them. Close to them two rattan chairs bobbed up and down, against one wall was a tall cupboard with books, clothes and cooking utensils piled on top. When the girls saw James their eyes widened in disbelief, the older girl turned and hugged the younger girl. Then they turned to smile their gràtitude at him and the soldiers.

James and one of the soldiers quickly picked up the girls and when they were safely on board, he then took down the cage before steering to the next three houses which they discovered had already been evacuated. They took the girls directly to the rescue centre which was bustling with cooking and feeding those already rescued then swiftly proceeded to the town looking and listening out for any distress calls. The rain had stopped. The town was now a lake; the top storeys of shophouses stood out in the brown murky water with their rusty corrugated tin roofs. Broken off branches of trees, rattan baskets, empty gunny sacks, newspaper, wooden boxes and stools now roved above what were once the town's streets. Men were out in rubber dinghies busy trying to retrieve some of their belongings from the water. Children waved and called out from windows as James and his team cruised through the flotsam. James approached them to check that they were safe. To the older residents the flood was nothing new, they had experienced flooding before although not on this scale. They knew what to do.

James and the soldiers then decided to move away from town towards the Malay *kampong* which was closer to the edge of the jungle. Here the water level had not risen to the floor of the half a dozen or so wooden houses on five-foot high stilts dotted in the area. There was no one in sight, the residents were inside, shut off from view. Then a man came and waved at one of the windows. 'We okay,' he shouted.

'Good,' James shouted back. Beyond the houses he could see that the thinned part of the jungle that was on a slope. He looked around, scrutinising as he did so. Something began to niggle him. Instinctively he drew his gun tensing as he did so. Then he heard the sound of the first gunshot. As he pulled his trigger another shot rang out. He collapsed.

Chapter 36

The heart-piercing scream that shot through the house when Helen was informed by Captain Douglas that her husband had been killed still resonated in Su Yin's head. Torrents of tears then came at a soul-shattering rush and force. Su Yin, feeling as if a hand had punched through her chest and ripped out her broken heart, did not hold back her own tears as she held Helen in her arms. They had stood there in the hallway shaking with violent sobs until they became aware that Cammy, Lexie and Ellie were tugging at them, looking utterly bewildered and frightened.

For days after that Su Yin would sometimes forget and expect James to bounce along the corridor into her kitchen and then open the fridge to get his beer. And each time she realised that he would never ever be there to do that again she wondered how she would get over his death. In front of the children she would suppress her tears watching them moon around the house like deflated balloons. They seemed lost especially Cammy who had become withdrawn and quiet. 'I miss Daddy, Amah,' Lexie and Ellie had said to her when she was brushing their hair. She didn't know what to say when they'd asked why their father had to die. They would start to cry and she would join them, inwardly railing against the cruel fate that took their father away from them. Her tears were for the loss of a very special human being, James, and in the chaos of emotions she thought of her best friend Lan Yee and her dear brother Peng.

For days Su Yin went about her work mechanically with her head in a daze, as if she was in a dream. Yet she was acutely aware that she needed to be strong for Helen and the children. Robbed of her life partner Helen was suddenly left holding all the loose ends of financial and household matters. Su Yin admired her, was amazed at how she quickly reined in her tears, pocketed her grief and conducted the sobering business of organising James' funeral while she steered the children out of Helen's way. Helen carried herself with such dignity and calm that it made Su Yin wonder where she derived her fortitude from. In response Su Yin felt obliged to put up the same resilience, if not for herself then for Helen and the children.

Now sitting in the front pew of a packed church that was respectfully silent except for the kindly tones of the English vicar, Su Yin stole another sideway glance at Helen to her right. Wearing a white cotton frock – she had deliberately chosen a white one - Helen was as serene and still as a tranquil lake on a windless evening. Throughout the service her face was dry, her eyes fixed on the wooden coffin in front of her. She stirred only when Ellie or Lexie on each side moved to cling closer to her. She had wanted all the children to be there to say goodbye to their father. With Ben on her lap Su Yin held him to her tightly in one arm as if to smother her own sobs, her other arm clasped around Thomas who was fidgeting and looking around at the people behind him. Next to him Cammy was sitting up straight with his head bowed. Su Yin reached out and stroked his shoulder. Cammy did not budge.

'…he was without doubt a brave man,' the vicar's voice rang out. 'Aside from his achievements he was a warm kind man and a loving husband. He had always said how lucky he was to have met, fallen in love with and married Helen.' He paused. 'When the children were born he said he fell in love all over again with each one. A more devoted father you couldn't find. James MacAlpine…'

On hearing his father's name Ben shot up in Su Yin's arm and called out, 'Daddy!'

In that same moment Su Yin heard Helen burst into tears.

'What will you do now?' Liew asked Su Yin as he leant across the table at their favourite noodle stall.

'What do you mean?' Su Yin replied, conscious that she'd sounded curt and defensive.

'I mean that I presume your boss lady would be considering returning home to be nearer her family..' said Liew.

'I'm sorry, I didn't mean to snap at you like that,' said Su Yin stirring the noodles on her plate with her chopsticks with no intention of eating.

'I didn't notice,' said Liew. He took a sip of his tea. 'You have been through a tough time.'

'I knew what you meant,' said Su Yin. 'It is just that I didn't want to face up to it. Not yet. Not until my boss lady tells me that they are going and gives me notice.' She felt her eyes welling up. She had always thought, believed and hoped that she would bring up the five MacAlpine children like she brought up Ming. She would have gladly and without hesitation dedicated her life to look after them and their mother. She knew that the tide of fortune had turned, that it wasn't to be and she lamented it. 'I have to confess that my boss's death came as a huge shock. He was such a decent man. I saw myself continuing in this position forever, until the children grew up, until I grew old.' Tears trickled down her cheeks.

Liew nodded as he reached out and patted her hand. 'So what will you do when they go home?'

Su Yin put her chopsticks down and took a handkerchief from her bag. She dabbed her eyes and blew her nose. 'Look for another position, what else?' she answered softly. Although the thought of looking for another job was daunting she'd reminded herself that she was no stranger to crisis or change.

'Marry me,' Liew said softly as he looked straight into Su Yin's eyes.

Su Yin blinked then held Liew's searching eyes. For a few moments she couldn't find her voice and when she did it trembled, 'You are very kind and generous…'

'That has nothing to do with it.' Liew's voice was firm. 'I love you very much and I want to spend the rest of my life with you. I want to look after you. You've looked after others all your life and now it's time you let me take care of you.' His face had become flushed, its muscles tight with intensity.

Su Yin felt her cheek turning warm. She looked down briefly and then raised her eyes to meet Liew's which were ablaze with anxiousness. 'I still say you are kind and generous,' she whispered. She then looked away towards the street and saw a thin old beggar man hobbling along the street with his coconut shell. She stared at the man for a few moments watching him shake his coconut shell as he approached some passers-by. Panic hit her; *I could be out begging on the street like that man if I couldn't find a job,* she thought. It was clearly crazy to turn down a proposal from a man who obviously loved her and would offer her the world. Marrying Liew would wipe out all financial worries and remove the burden of her family from her shoulders. Without thinking she reached up to feel the gold pin in her hair. She took a deep breath. Biting her lips she turned back to Liew and in the softest tone she could muster she said,

'Thank you very much for your offer. I am very honoured and flattered. I don't wish to appear ungrateful…'

'Then say yes!' said Liew, his eyes wide with eagerness and hope.

'But you know that I cannot,' Su Yin's voice had risen to match his. She quickly turned it down, 'You know the reason why.'

Liew's face remained taut. 'Yes, the vow you took. That was so long ago. Things have changed. Circumstances are different now. Besides you've upheld your vow long enough. Surely you can, surely you are entitled to change your mind. No one would judge you.'

'I was only sixteen when I took the vow,' Su Yin said slowly. 'People would say I was too young to know what I wanted to do for the rest of my life.' She paused. '*But I did.* I knew why. I have no regrets at all; not then, not now. I also know now that there are good men around like yourself. You don't make it easy for me. Please understand that it is not you; I have to be true to myself. I will muddle along...'

Liew leant forward again, his voice punched with earnestness, 'Come, come and be my housekeeper. Come look after me and my home.'

Su Yin shook her head. Her eyes appealed to him to understand.

Liew's face twisted with disappointment. 'Is the thought of looking after me so horrendous?'

'Not at all,' Su Yin replied.

Liew shook his head. He placed his elbows on the table, then clasped his hands in front of him and rested his chin on them. His face was solemn as he stared at the table. Neither of them spoke. Su Yin knew she had hurt him but didn't know what to say. She was afraid he would get angry;

he looked as if he was struggling to recompose himself. She watched as the muscles of his face gradually set into a mask of sadness. A sense of helplessness overcame her. After a long while, to her surprise, a small smile started to steal across his face.

Liew looked up at her. 'Years ago,' he explained, 'your brother Keng warned me you were stubborn.' A little twinkle appeared in his eyes. 'He told me that once your mind was made up you stuck to it. I think he said you were as immovable as the Great Wall.'

Su Yin smiled with relief. 'I have been told that I could be as stubborn as our father's buffalo.'

'I remember saying that I admired a woman who knew her own mind,' Liew continued. 'Keng also said I could wait for a lifetime for you to change your mind…I might do just that.'

'No, don't! You mustn't,' Su Yin pleaded. Looking into Liew's eyes her heart started to flutter. 'You must know that I care very much about you too, that I am very fortunate to have your affection. Will you promise me this: if ever I am in trouble, if I ever need help I can come to you?'

Liew inhaled deeply and gently took her hand. 'You know I will always be there for you. Always.'

A month after the funeral, while Su Yin was wiping the table after putting away the dry crockery, Helen came into the kitchen. She looked drawn and tired, the wrinkles under her eyes were prominent; the sparkle in her eyes had dimmed. Su Yin knew immediately that she had come to tell her of her plans for the future and she was determined not to pile on Helen's grief by getting upset. She felt her pulse quickening.

'Amah, would you sit down for a minute?' Helen pulled a chair from under the table. Su Yin put her tea towel down by the sink and sat down facing Helen. 'I have decided that the children and I should go home to Scotland. We would be near my parents. It would be better for us, for the children especially.' Helen's eyes started to glisten as her face reddened. 'I am so sorry about this.'

Su Yin nodded vigorously. 'I know, I know. Better be with family.'

Helen nodded in response. 'I am so sorry to lose you. You are like family to us. I know the children will be devastated to leave you. I haven't told them yet.'

Su Yin nodded again unable to say another word as she struggled to fight back her tears.

Helen continued, 'I know you will worry about getting another position. But you mustn't worry because Penny has said that she would very much like you to work for her if that suits you.'

'Mrs Pendle?' Su Yin was surprised. For no particular reason she had always thought that she would be the last person Mrs Pendle would want to work for her. And it had not crossed her mind to work for her either. Mrs Pendle was not like Mrs Makapeen but Mrs Pendle had gained some of her respect seeing how she had done a good job of raising her adopted mixed child.

Helen looked anxious. 'Yes. Would that suit you? Would you like to work for her?'

'Yes, yes. Thank you,' said Su Yin, relieved that she wouldn't be out begging on the streets.

'Excellent. Very good. I am so glad. I know it will work out for the two of you.' Suddenly Helen brightened up. 'That way I can also keep track of what you are doing. We can keep in touch. Oh, that will be just fine.' For the first time in a long while Helen smiled.

Su Yin sniffed and then said, 'Thank you Mrs Makapeen. You are so good to me. Thank you.'

'One more thing, Amah.' Helen hesitated, her face clouded over.

'Yes?' said Su Yin.

Helen took a deep breath. A tear rolled down her cheek. 'Would you look after James for me? I promise we will be back. But while we are away would you keep an eye on James' grave?' She searched Su Yin's face as she waited.

Su Yin did not trust herself to speak. She could only nod.

Lightning Source UK Ltd.
Milton Keynes UK
UKHW01f2330290518
323433UK00001B/5/P